Praise for #1 *New York Times*
bestselling author

STEPHEN KING

"A master storyteller."

—*Los Angeles Times*

"The most wonderfully gruesome man on the planet."

—*USA Today*

"An undisputed master of suspense and terror."

—*The Washington Post*

"Stephen King knows exactly what scares you most. . . ."

—*Esquire*

"King probably knows more about scary goings-on in confined, isolated places than anybody since Edgar Allan Poe."

—*Entertainment Weekly*

"America's greatest living novelist."

—Lee Child

STEPHEN KING

WRITING AS **RICHARD BACHMAN**

A NOVEL

GALLERY BOOKS

New York   London   Toronto   Sydney   New Delhi

G

Gallery Books
An Imprint of Simon & Schuster, Inc.
1230 Avenue of the Americas
New York, NY 10020

This Gallery Books trade paperback edition August 2018

GALLERY BOOKS and colophon are registered trademarks
of Simon & Schuster, Inc.

For information about special discounts for bulk purchases,
please contact Simon & Schuster Special Sales at 1-866-506-1949
or business@simonandschuster.com.

The Simon & Schuster Speakers Bureau can bring authors
to your live event. For more information or to book an event,
contact the Simon & Schuster Speakers Bureau at 1-866-248-3049
or visit our website at www.simonspeakers.com.

Manufactured in the United States of America

20 19 18 17 16 15 14 13 12 11

ISBN 978-1-5011-9591-4
ISBN 978-1-4165-5991-7 (ebook)

For Tommy and Lori Spruce

And thinking of James T. Farrell

These are the slums of the heart.

JOHN D. MACDONALD

FULL DISCLOSURE

Dear Constant Reader,

This is a trunk novel, okay? I want you to know that while you've still got your sales slip and before you drip something like gravy or ice cream on it, and thus make it difficult or impossible to return.[1] It's a revised and updated trunk novel, but that doesn't change the basic fact. The Bachman name is on it because it's the last novel from 1966–1973, which was that gentleman's period of greatest productivity.

During those years I was actually two men. It was Stephen King who wrote (and sold) horror stories to raunchy skin-mags like *Cavalier* and *Adam*,[2] but it was Bachman who wrote a series of novels that didn't sell to anybody. These included *Rage*,[3] *The Long Walk, Roadwork,* and *The Running Man*.[4] All four were published as paperback originals.

Blaze was the last of those early novels . . . the fifth quarter,

1. In saying this, I assume you're like me and rarely sit down to a meal—or even a lowly snack—without your current book near at hand.

2. With this exception: Bachman, writing under the pseudonym of John Swithen, sold a single hard-crime story, "The Fifth Quarter."

3. Now out of print, and a good thing.

4. The Bachman novel following these was *Thinner,* and it was no wonder I got outed, since that one was actually written by Stephen King—the bogus author photo on the back flap fooled no one.

if you like. Or just another well-known writer's trunk novel, if you insist. It was written in late 1972 and early 1973. I thought it was great while I was writing it, and crap when I read it over. My recollection is that I never showed it to a single publisher—not even Doubleday, where I had made a friend named William G. Thompson. Bill was the guy who would later discover John Grisham, and it was Bill who contracted for the book following *Blaze,* a twisted but fairly entertaining tale of prom-night in central Maine.[5]

I forgot about *Blaze* for a few years. Then, after the other early Bachmans had been published, I took it out and looked it over. After reading the first twenty pages or so, I decided my first judgment had been correct, and returned it to purdah. I thought the writing was okay, but the story reminded me of something Oscar Wilde once said. He claimed it was impossible to read "The Old Curiosity Shop" without weeping copious tears of laughter.[6] So *Blaze* was forgotten, but never really lost. It was only stuffed in some corner of the Fogler Library at the University of Maine with the rest of their Stephen King/Richard Bachman stuff.

Blaze ended up spending the next thirty years in the dark.[7] And then I published a slim paperback original

5. I believe I am the only writer in the history of English story-telling whose career was based on sanitary napkins; that part of my literary legacy seems secure.

6. I have had the same reaction to *Everyman,* by Philip Roth, Thomas Hardy's *Jude the Obscure,* and *The Memory Keeper's Daughter,* by Kim Edwards—at some point while reading these books, I just start to laugh, wave my hands, and shout: "Bring on the cancer! Bring on the blindness! We haven't had those yet!"

7. Not in an actual trunk, though; in a cardboard carton.

called *The Colorado Kid* with an imprint called Hard Case Crime. This line of books, the brainchild of a very smart and very cool fellow named Charles Ardai, was dedicated to reviving old "noir" and hardboiled paperback crime novels, and publishing new ones. *The Kid* was decidedly softboiled, but Charles decided to publish it anyway, with one of those great old paperback covers.[8] The whole project was a blast . . . except for the slow royalty payments.[9]

About a year later, I thought maybe I'd like to go the Hard Case route again, possibly with something that had a harder edge. My thoughts turned to *Blaze* for the first time in years, but trailing along behind came that damned Oscar Wilde quote about "The Old Curiosity Shop." The *Blaze* I remembered wasn't hardboiled noir, but a three-handkerchief weepie. Still, I decided it wouldn't hurt to look. If, that was, the book could even be found. I remembered the carton, and I remembered the squarish type-face (my wife Tabitha's old college typewriter, an impossible-to-kill Olivetti portable), but I had no idea what had become of the manuscript that was supposedly inside the carton. For all I knew, it was gone, baby, gone.[10]

It wasn't. Marsha, one of my two valuable assistants,

8. A dame with trouble in her eyes. And ecstasy, presumably, in her pants.

9. Also a throwback to the bad old paperback days, now that I think of it.

10. In my career I have managed to lose not one but two pretty good novels-in-progress. *Under the Dome* was only 50 pages long at the time it disappeared, but *The Cannibals* was over 200 pages at the time it went MIA. No copies of either. That was before computers, and I never used carbons for first drafts—it felt *haughty,* somehow.

found it in the Fogler Library. She would not trust me with the original manuscript (I, uh, lose things), but she made a Xerox. I must have been using a next-door-to-dead typewriter ribbon when I composed *Blaze,* because the copy was barely legible, and the notes in the margins were little more than blurs. Still, I sat down with it and began to read, ready to suffer the pangs of embarrassment only one's younger, smart-assier self can provide.

But I thought it was pretty good—certainly better than *Roadwork,* which I had, at the time, considered mainstream American fiction. It just wasn't a noir novel. It was, rather, a stab at the sort of naturalism-with-crime that James M. Cain and Horace McCoy practiced in the thirties.[11] I thought the flashbacks were actually better than the front-story. They reminded me of James T. Farrell's *Young Lonigan* trilogy and the forgotten (but tasty) *Gas-House McGinty.* Sure, it was the three Ps in places,[12] but it had been written by a young man (I was twenty-five) who was convinced he was WRITING FOR THE AGES.

I thought *Blaze* could be re-written and published without too much embarrassment, but it was probably wrong for Hard Case Crime. It was, in a sense, not a crime novel at all. I thought it could be a minor tragedy of the underclass, if the re-writing was ruthless. To that end, I adopted the flat, dry tones which the best noir fiction seems to have, even using a type-font called American Typewriter to re-

11. And, of course, it's an homage to *Of Mice and Men*—kinda hard to miss that.
12. Purple, pulsing, and panting.

mind myself of what I was up to. I worked fast, never looking ahead or back, wanting also to capture the headlong
drive of those books (I'm thinking more of Jim Thompson
and Richard Stark here than I am of Cain, McCoy, or Farrell). I thought I would do my revisions at the end, with
a pencil, rather than editing in the computer, as is now
fashionable. If the book was going to be a throwback, I
wanted to play into that rather than shying away from it. I
also determined to strip all the sentiment I could from the
writing itself, wanted the finished book to be as stark as an
empty house without even a rug on the floor. My mother
would have said "I wanted its bare face hanging out." Only
the reader will be able to judge if I succeeded.

If it matters to you (it shouldn't—hopefully you came
for a good story, and hopefully you will get one), any royal-
ties or subsidiary income generated by *Blaze* will go to The
Haven Foundation, which was created to help freelance art-
ists who are down on their luck.[13]

One other thing, I guess, while I've got you by the lapel.
I tried to keep the *Blaze* time-frame as vague as possible,
so it wouldn't seem too dated.[14] It was impossible to take
out all the dated material, however; keeping some of it was
important to the plot.[15] If you think of this story's time-

13. To learn more about The Haven Foundation, you can go to my
website. That be www.stephenking.com.
14. I didn't like the idea of Clay Blaisdell growing up in post–World
War II America; all that has come to seem impossibly antique, although it
seemed (and probably was) okay in 1973, when I was pecking it out in the
trailer where my wife and I lived with our two children.
15. If I had written it today, certainly cell phones and Caller ID would
have needed to be taken into consideration.

frame as "America, Not All That Long Ago," I think you'll be okay.

May I close by circling back to where I started? This is an old novel, but I believe I was wrong in my initial assessment that it was a bad novel. You may disagree . . . but "The Little Match Girl" it ain't. As always, Constant Reader, I wish you well, I thank you for reading this story, and I hope you enjoy it. I won't say I hope you mist up a little, but—

Yeah. Yeah, I *will* say that. Just as long as they're not tears of laughter.

Stephen King (for Richard Bachman)
Sarasota, Florida
January 30th, 2007

CHAPTER 1

George was somewhere in the dark. Blaze couldn't see him, but the voice came in loud and clear, rough and a little hoarse. George always sounded as if he had a cold. He'd had an accident when he was a kid. He never said what, but there was a dilly of a scar on his adam's apple.

"Not that one, you dummy, it's got bumper stickers all over it. Get a Chevy or a Ford. Dark blue or green. Two years old. No more, no less. Nobody remembers them. And no stickers."

Blaze passed the little car with the bumper stickers and kept walking. The faint thump of the bass reached him even here, at the far end of the beer joint's parking lot. It was Saturday night and the place was crowded. The air was bitterly cold. He had hitched him a ride into town, but now he had been in the open air for forty minutes and his ears were numb. He had forgotten his hat. He always forgot something. He had started to take his hands out of his jacket pockets and put them over his ears, but George put the kibosh on that. George said his ears could freeze but not his hands. You didn't need your ears to hotwire a car. It was three above zero.

"There," George said. "On your right."

Blaze looked and saw a Saab. With a sticker. It didn't look like the right kind of car at all.

"That's your left," George said. "Your *right,* dummy. The hand you pick your nose with."

"I'm sorry, George."

Yes, he was being a dummy again. He could pick his nose with either hand, but he knew his right, the hand you write with. He thought of that hand and looked to that side. There was a dark green Ford there.

Blaze walked over to the Ford, elaborately casual. He looked over his shoulder. The beer joint was a college bar called The Bag. That was a stupid name, a bag was what you called your balls. It was a walk-down. There was a band on Friday and Saturday nights. It would be crowded and warm inside, lots of little girls in short skirts dancing up a storm. It would be nice to go inside, just look around—

"What are *you* supposed to be doing?" George asked. "Walking on Commonwealth Ave? You couldn't fool my old blind granny. Just do it, huh?"

"Okay, I was just—"

"Yeah, I know what you was just. Keep your mind on your business."

"Okay."

"What are you, Blaze?"

He hung his head, snorkled back snot. "I'm a dummy."

George always said there was no shame in this, but it was a fact and you had to recognize it. You couldn't fool anybody into thinking you were smart. They looked at you and saw the truth: the lights were on but nobody was home. If you were a dummy, you had to just do your business and get out. And if you were caught, you owned up to everything except the guys who were with you, because they'd get everything else out of you in the end, anyway. George said dummies couldn't lie worth shit.

Blaze took his hands out of his pockets and flexed them twice. The knuckles popped in the cold still air.

"You ready, big man?" George asked.

"Yes."

"Then I'm going to get a beer. Take care of it."

Blaze felt panic start. It came up his throat. "Hey, no, I ain't never done this before. I just watched you."

"Well this time you're going to do more than watch."

"But—"

He stopped. There was no sense going on, unless he wanted to shout. He could hear the hard crunch of packed snow as George headed toward the beer joint. Soon his footsteps were lost in the heartbeat of the bass.

"Jesus," Blaze said. "Oh Jesus Christ."

And his fingers were getting cold. At this temperature they'd only be good for five minutes. Maybe less. He went around to the driver's side door, thinking the door would be locked. If the door was locked, this car was no good because he didn't have the Slim Jim, George had the Slim Jim. Only the door was unlocked. He opened the door, reached in, found the hood release, and pulled it. Then he went around front, fiddled for the second catch, found that one, and lifted the hood.

There was a small penlight in his pocket. He took it out. He turned it on and trained the beam on the engine.

Find the ignition wire.

But there was so much spaghetti. Battery cables, hoses, spark-plug wires, the gas-line—

He stood there with sweat running down the sides of his face and freezing on his cheeks. This was no good. This wouldn't never be no good. And all at once he had an idea. It wasn't a very good idea, but he didn't have many and when he had one he had to chase it. He went back to the driver's side and opened the door again. The light came on, but he couldn't help that. If someone saw him fiddling around, they would just think he was having trouble getting started. Sure, cold night like this, that made sense, didn't it? Even George couldn't give him grief on that one. Not much, anyway.

He flipped down the visor over the steering wheel, hoping against hope that a spare key might flop down, sometimes folks kept one up there, but there was nothing except an old ice scraper. *That* flopped down. He tried the glove compartment next. It was full of papers. He raked them out onto the floor, kneeling on the seat to do it, his breath puffing. There were papers, and a box of Junior Mints, but no keys.

There, you goddam dummy, he heard George saying, *are you satisfied now? Ready to at least try hot-wiring it now?*

He supposed he was. He supposed he could at least tear some of the wires loose and touch them together like George did and see what happened. He closed the door and started toward the front of the Ford again with his head down. Then he stopped. A new idea had struck him. He went back, opened the door, bent down, flipped up the floormat, and there it was. The key didn't say FORD on it, it didn't say anything on it because it was a dupe, but it had the right square head and everything.

Blaze picked it up and kissed the cold metal.

Unlocked car, he thought. Then he thought: *Unlocked car and key under the floormat.* Then he thought: *I ain't the dumbest guy out tonight after all, George.*

He got in behind the wheel, slammed the door, slid the key in the ignition slot—it went in nice—then realized he couldn't see the parking lot because the hood was still up. He looked around quick, first one way and then the other, making sure that George hadn't decided to come back and help him out. George would never let him hear the end of it if he saw the hood still up like that. But George wasn't there. No one was there. The parking lot was tundra with cars.

Blaze got out and slammed the hood. Then he got back in and paused in the act of reaching for the door handle. What about George? Should he go in yonder beer-farm and get him? Blaze sat frowning, head down. The dome light cast yellow light on his big hands.

Guess what? he thought, raising his head again at last. *Screw him.*

"Screw you, George," he said. George had left him to hitchhike in, just meeting him here, then left him again. Left him to do the dirtywork, and it was only by the dumbest of dumb luck that Blaze had found a key, so screw George. Let *him* thumb a ride back in the three-degree cold.

Blaze closed the door, dropped the gear-shift into Drive, and pulled out of the parking space. Once in an actual lane of travel, he stomped down heavily and the Ford leaped, rear end fishtailing on the hard-packed snow. He slammed on the brakes, stiff with panic. What was he doing? What was he thinking of? Go without George? He'd get picked up before he went five miles. Probably get picked up at the first stop-n-go light. He couldn't go without George.

But George is dead.

That was bullshit. George was just there. He went inside for a beer.

He's dead.

"Oh, George," Blaze moaned. He was hunched over the wheel. "Oh, George, don't be dead."

He sat there awhile. The Ford's engine sounded okay. It wasn't knocking or anything, even though it was cold. The gas gauge said three-quarters. The exhaust rose in the rear-view, white and frozen.

George didn't come out of the beer joint. He couldn't come out cause he never went in. George was dead. Had been three months. Blaze started to shake.

After a little bit, he caught hold of himself. He began to drive. No one stopped him at the first traffic light, or the second. No one stopped him all the way out of town. By the time he got to the Apex town line, he was doing fifty. Sometimes the car slid a little on patches of ice, but this didn't bother him. He just turned with the skid. He had been driving on icy roads since he was a teenager.

Outside of town he pushed the Ford to sixty and let it ride. The high beams poked the road with bright fingers and rebounded brilliantly from the snowbanks on either side. Boy, there was going to be one surprised college kid when he took his college girl back to that empty slot. She'd look at him and say, *You are a dummy, I ain't going with you again, not here or nowhere.*

"Aren't," Blaze said. "If she's a college girl, she'll say aren't."

That made him smile. The smile changed his whole face. He turned on the radio. It was tuned to rock. Blaze turned the knob until he found country. By the time he reached the shack, he was singing along with the radio at the top of his voice and he had forgotten all about George.

CHAPTER 2

But he remembered the next morning.

That was the curse of being a dummy. You were always being surprised by grief, because you could never remember the important things. The only stuff that stuck was dumb stuff. Like that poem Mrs. Selig made them learn way back in the fifth grade: Under the spreading chestnut tree, the village smithy stands. What good was that? What good when you caught yourself peeling potatoes for two and got smacked all over again with knowing you didn't need to peel no two potatoes, because the other guy was never going to eat another spud?

Well, maybe it wasn't grief. Maybe that word wasn't the right word. Not if that meant crying and knocking your head against the wall. You didn't do that for the likes of George. But there was loneliness. And there was fear.

George would say: "Jesus, would you change your fuckin skivvies? Those things are ready to stand up on their own. They're disgusting."

George would say: "You only tied one, dimbulb."

George would say: "Aw, fuck, turn around and *I'll* tuck it in. Like havin a kid."

When he got up the morning after he stole the Ford, George was sitting in the other room. Blaze couldn't see him but knew he was sitting in the broke-down easy-chair like always, with his head down so his chin was almost on his chest. The first thing he said was, "You screwed up again, Kong. Congratcha-fuckin-lations."

Blaze hissed when his feet hit the cold floor. Then he fumbled his shoes on. Naked except for them, he ran and looked out the window. No car. He sighed with relief. It came out in a little puff he could see.

"No, I didn't. I put it in the shed, just like you told me."

"You didn't wipe the goddam tracks, though, did you? Why don't you put out a sign, Blaze? THIS WAY TO THE HOT CAR. You could charge admission. Why don't you just do that?"

"Aw, George—"

" 'Aw, George, aw, George.' Go out and sweep em up."

"Okay." He started for the door.

"Blaze?"

"What?"

"Put on your fucking pants first, why don't you?"

Blaze felt his face burn.

"Like a kid," George said, sounding resigned. "One who can shave."

George knew how to stick it in, all right. Only finally he'd gone and stuck it in the wrong guy, too often and too far. That was how you ended up dead, with nothing smart to say. Now George was just dead, and Blaze was making his voice up in his mind, giving him the good lines. George had been dead since that crap game in the warehouse.

I'm crazy for even trying to go through with this, Blaze thought. *A dum-dum like me.*

But he pulled on his underwear shorts (checking them carefully for stains first), then a thermal undershirt, then a flannel top shirt and a pair of heavy corduroy pants. His Sears workboots were under the bed. His Army surplus parka was hanging on the doorknob. He hunted for his mittens and finally found them on the shelf over the dilapidated woodstove in the combination kitchen–living room. He got his checkered cap with the earflaps and put it on, careful to give the visor a little good-luck twist to the left. Then he went out and got the broom leaning against the door.

The morning was bright and bitter. The moisture in his nose crackled immediately. A gust of wind drove snow as fine as powdered sugar into his face, making him wince. It was all right for George to give orders. George was inside drinking coffee by the stove. Like last night, taking off for a beer, leaving Blaze to figure out the car. And there he would still be if he hadn't had the dumb luck to find the keys somewhere, either under the floormat or in the glove compartment, he forgot which. Sometimes he didn't think George was a very good friend.

He swept the tracks away with the broom, pausing several minutes to admire them before he started. How the treads stood up and cast shadows, mostly, little perfect things. It was funny how little things could be so perfect and no one ever saw them. He looked at this until he was tired of looking (no George to tell him to hurry up) and then worked his way down the short driveway to the road, brushing the tracks away. The plow had gone by in the night, pushing back the snow-dunes the wind made across these country roads where there were open fields to one side and t'other, and any other tracks were gone.

Blaze tromped back to the shack. He went inside. Now it felt warm inside. Getting out of bed it had felt cold, but now it felt warm. That was funny, too—how your sense of things could change. He took off his coat and boots and flannel shirt and sat down to the table in his undershirt and cords. He turned on the radio and was surprised when it didn't play the rock George listened to but warmed right up to country. Loretta Lynn was singing that your good girl is gonna go bad. George would laugh and say something like, "That's right, honey—you can go bad all over my face." And Blaze would laugh too, but down deep that song always made him sad. Lots of country songs did.

When the coffee was hot he jumped up and poured two cups. He loaded one with cream and hollered, "George? Here's your coffee, hoss! Don't let it go cold!"

No answer.

He looked down at the white coffee. He didn't drink coffee-with, so what about it? Just what about it? Something came up in his throat then and he almost hucked George's goddam white coffee across the room, but then he didn't. He took it oversink and poured it down instead. That was controlling your temper. When you were a big guy, you had to do that or get in trouble.

Blaze hung around the shack until after lunch. Then he drove the stolen car out of the shed, stopping by the kitchen steps long enough to get out and throw snowballs at the license plates. That was pretty smart. It would make them hard to read.

"What in the name of God are you doing?" George asked from inside the shed.

"Never mind," Blaze said. "You're only in my head, anyway." He got in the Ford and drove out to the road.

"This isn't very bright," George said. Now he was in the back seat. "You're driving around in a stolen car. No fresh paintjob, no fresh plates, no nothing. Where you going?"

Blaze didn't say anything.

"You ain't going to Ocoma, are you?"

Blaze didn't say anything.

"Oh, fuck, you are," George said. "Fuck *me*. Isn't the once you *have* to go enough?"

Blaze didn't say anything. He was dummied up.

"Listen to me, Blaze. Turn around. You get picked up, it's out the window. Everything. The whole deal."

Blaze knew that was right, but wouldn't turn back. Why should George always get to order him around? Even dead, he wouldn't stop giving orders. Sure, it was George's plan, that one big score every small-timer dreams of. "Only we could really make it happen," he'd say, but usually when he was drunk or high and never like he really believed it.

They had spent most of their time running two-man short cons, and mostly George seemed satisfied with that no matter what he said when he was drunk or getting his smoke on. Maybe the Ocoma Heights score was just a game for George, or what he sometimes called mental masturbation when he saw guys in suits talking about politics on

TV. Blaze knew George was smart. It was his guts he had never been sure of.

But now that he was dead, what choice? Blaze was no good by himself. The one time he'd tried running the menswear con after George's death, he'd had to book like a bastard to keep from being picked up. He got the lady's name out of the obituary column just the way George did, had started in on George's spiel, had shown the credit slips (there was a whole bag of them at the shack, and from the best stores). He told her about how sad he was to have to come by at such a sad time, but business was business and he was sure she would understand that. She said she did. She invited him to stand in the foyer while she got her pockabook. He never suspected that she had called the police. If she hadn't come back and pointed a gun at him, he probably would have still been standing there waiting when the police ho'd up. His time sense had never been good.

But she came back with a gun and pointed it at him. It was a silver lady's gun with little swoops on the sides and pearl handles. "The police are on their way," she said, "but before they get here, I want you to explain yourself. I want you to tell me what kind of a lowlife preys on a woman whose husband isn't even cold in his grave yet."

Blaze didn't care what she wanted him to tell her. He turned and ran out the door and across the porch and down the steps to the walk. He could run pretty good once he got going, but he was slow getting going, and panic made him slower that day. If she had pulled the trigger, she might have put a bullet in the back of his big head or shot

off an ear or missed him entirely. With a little short-barrel
shooter like that, you couldn't tell. But she never fired.

When he got back to the shack, he was half-moaning
with fear and his stomach was tied in knots. He wasn't
afraid of jail or the penitentiary, not even of the police—although he knew they would confuse him with their questions, they always did—but he was afraid of how easy she
saw through him. Like it wasn't nothing to her. They had
hardly ever seen through George, and when they did, he
always knew it was happening and got them out.

And now this. He wasn't going to get away with it,
knew it, kept on anyway. Maybe he wanted to go back inside. Maybe that wouldn't be so bad, now that George was
wasted. Let someone else do the thinking and provide the
meals.

Maybe he was trying to get caught right now, driving
this hot car through the middle of Ocoma Heights. Right
past the Gerard house.

In the icebox of New England winter, it looked like a
frozen palace. Ocoma Heights was old money (that's what
George said), and the houses were really estates. They were
surrounded by big lawns in the summertime, but now the
lawns were glazed snowfields. It had been a hard winter.

The Gerard house was the best one of all. George called
it Early American Hot Shit, but Blaze thought it was
beautiful. George said the Gerards had made their money
in shipping, that World War I made them rich and World
War II made them holy. Snow and sun struck cold fire from
the many windows. George said there were over thirty
rooms. He had done the preliminary work as a meter-reader

from Central Valley Power. That had been in September. Blaze had driven the truck, which was borrowed rather than stolen, although he supposed the police would have called it stolen if they'd been caught. People were playing croquet on the side lawn. Some were girls, high school girls or maybe college girls, good-looking. Blaze watched them and started feeling horny. When George got back in and told him to wheel it, Blaze told him about the good-looking girls, who had gone around to the back by then.

"I saw em," George said. "Think they're better than anybody. Think their shit don't stink."

"Pretty, though."

"Who gives a rat's ass?" George asked moodily, and crossed his arms over his chest.

"Don't you ever get horny, George?"

"Over babies like that? You jest. Now shut up and drive."

Now, remembering that, Blaze smiled. George was like the fox who couldn't reach the grapes and told everyone they were sour. Miss Jolison read them that story in the second grade.

It was a big family. There was the old Mr. and Mrs. Gerard—he was eighty and still able to put away a pint of Jack a day, that's what George said. There was the middle Mr. and Mrs. Gerard. And then there was the young Mr. and Mrs. Gerard. The young Mr. Gerard was Joseph Gerard III, and he really was young, just twenty-five. His wife was a Narmenian. George said that made her a spic. Blaze had thought only Italians could be spics.

He turned around up the street and cruised past the house once more, wondering what it felt like to be married at twenty-two. He kept on going, heading home. Enough was enough.

The middle Gerards had other kids besides Joseph Gerard III, but they didn't matter. What mattered was the baby. Joseph Gerard IV. Big name for such a little baby. He was only two months old when Blaze and George did their meter-reading bit in September. That made him—um, there were one-two-three-four months between September and January—six months old. He was the original Joe's only great-grandson.

"If you're gonna pull a snatch, you got to snatch a baby," George said. "A baby can't ID you, so you can return it alive. It can't fuck you up by trying to escape or sending out notes or some shit. All a baby can do is lie there. It don't even know it's been snatched."

They had been in the shack, sitting in front of the TV and drinking beer.

"How much do you think they'd be good for?" Blaze asked.

"Enough so you'd never have to spend another winter day freezing your ass off selling fake magazine subscriptions or collecting for the Red Cross," George said. "How's that sound?"

"But how much would you ask?"

"Two million," George said. "One for you and one for me. Why be greedy?"

"Greedies get caught," Blaze said.

"Greedies get caught," George agreed. "That's what I taught you. But what's the workman worthy of, Blaze-a-rino? What'd I teach you about that?"

"His hire," Blaze said.

"That's right," George said, and hit his beer. "The workman's worthy of his fucking hire."

So here he was, driving back to the miserable shack where he and George had been living since drifting north from Boston, actually planning to go through with it. He thought he would be caught, but . . . two million dollars! You could go someplace and never be cold again. And if they caught you? The worst they could do would be put you in jail for life.

And if that happened, you'd still never be cold again.

When the stolen Ford was back in the shed, he remembered to brush the tracks away. That would make George happy.

He made himself a couple of hamburgers for his lunch.

"You really going through with it?" George asked from the other room.

"You lyin down, George?"

"No, standin on my head and jerkin off. I asked you a question."

"I'm gonna try. Will you help me?"

George sighed. "I guess I'll have to. I'm stuck with you now. But Blaze?"

"What, George?"

"Only ask for a million. Greedies get caught."

"Okay, only a million. You want a hamburger?"

No answer. George was dead again.

CHAPTER 3

He was getting ready to do the kidnapping that night, the sooner the better. George stopped him.

"What are you up to, dinkleballs?"

Blaze had been getting ready to go start the Ford. Now he stopped. "Gettin ready to do it, George."

"Do what?"

"Snatch the kid."

George laughed.

"What you laughin at, George?" *As if I don't know,* he thought.

"You."

"Why?"

"How are you gonna snatch him? Tell me that."

Blaze frowned. It turned his face, already ugly, into the face of a troll. "The way we planned it, I guess. Out'n his room."

"Which room?"

"Well—"

"How are you gonna get in?"

He remembered that part. "One of the upstairs windows. They got those simple catches on em. You saw that, George. When we was bein the lectric company. Remember?"

"Got a ladder?"

"Well—"

"When you get the kid, where you gonna put him?"

"In the car, George."

"Oh my fuckin word." George only said this when he had bottomed out and was at a loss for all other expression.

"George—"

"I *know* you're gonna put him in the fuckin car, I never thought you were gonna carry him home pigga-back. I meant when you get him back here. What are you gonna do then? Where you gonna put him?"

Blaze thought about the shack. He looked around. "Well—"

"What about didies? What about bottles? And baby food! Or did you think he was gonna have a hamburger and a bottle of beer for his fuckin dinner?"

"Well—"

"Shut up! You say that one more time and I'm gonna puke!"

Blaze sat down in a kitchen chair with his head down. His face was hot.

"And turn off the shit-kicking music! That woman sounds like she's about to fly up her own cunt!"

"Okay, George."

Blaze turned off the radio. The TV, an old Jap thing George picked up at a yard sale, was busted.

"George?"

No answer.

"George, come on, don't go away. I'm sorry." He could hear how scared he was. Almost blubbing.

"Okay," George said, just when Blaze was about to give up.

"Here's what you have to do. You have to pull a little score. Not a big one. Just a little one. That mom-n-pop where we used to stop for suds off Route 1 would probably be okay."

"Yeah?"

"You still got the Colt?"

"Under the bed, in a shoebox."

"Use that. And wear a stocking over your face. Otherwise the guy who works nights will recognize you."

"Yeah."

"Go in Saturday night, at closing. Say, ten minutes of one. They don't take checks, so you ought to get two, three hundred bucks."

"Sure! That's great!"

"Blaze, there's one more thing."

"What, George?"

"Take the bullets out of the gun, okay?"

"Sure, George, I know that, it's how we roll."

"It's how we roll, right. Hit the guy if you have to, but make sure it doesn't get to no more than page three in State and Local when it makes the paper."

"Right."

"You're an asshole, Blaze. You know that, right? You're never gonna bring this off. Maybe it'd be better if you got caught on the little one."

"I won't, George."

No answer.

"George?"

No answer. Blaze got up and turned on the radio. At supper he forgot and set two places.

CHAPTER 4

Clayton Blaisdell, Jr., was born in Freeport, Maine. His mother was hit by a truck three years later while crossing Main Street with a bag of groceries. She was killed instantly. The driver was drunk and driving without a license. In court he said he was sorry. He cried. He said he would go back to AA. The judge fined him and gave him sixty days. Little Clay got Life with Father, who knew plenty about drinking and nothing about AA. Clayton Senior worked for Superior Mills in Topsham, where he ran the picker and sorter. Co-workers claimed to have seen him do this job sober upon occasion.

Clay could already read when he started the first grade, and grasped the concept of two apples plus three apples with no trouble. He was big for his size even then, and although Freeport was a tough town, he had no trouble on the playground even though he was rarely seen there without a book in his hand or tucked under his arm. His father was bigger, however, and the other kids always found it interesting to see what would be bandaged and what would be bruised when Clay Blaisdell came to school on Mondays.

"It will be a miracle if he gets his size without being

badly hurt or killed," Sarah Jolison remarked one day in the teachers' room.

The miracle didn't happen. One hungover Saturday morning when not much was doing, Clayton Senior staggered out of the bedroom in the second-floor apartment he and his son shared while Clay was sitting crosslegged on the living room floor, watching cartoons and eating Apple Jacks. "How many times have I told you not to eat that shit in here?" Senior inquired of Junior, then picked him up and threw him downstairs. Clay landed on his head.

His father went down, got him, toted him upstairs, and threw him down again. The first time, Clay remained conscious. The second time, the lights went out. His father went down, got him, toted him upstairs, and looked him over. "Fakin sonofabitch," he said, and threw him down again.

"There," he told the limp huddle at the foot of the stairs that was his now comatose son. "Maybe you'll think twice before you tote that fucking shit into the living room again."

Unfortunately, Clay never thought twice about much of anything again. He lay unconscious in Portland General Hospital for three weeks. The doctor in charge of his case voiced the opinion that he would remain so until he died, a human carrot. But the boy woke up. He was, unfortunately, soft in the head. His days of carrying books under his arm were over.

The authorities did not believe Clay's father when he told them the boy had done all that damage falling downstairs once. Nor did they believe him when he said the four

half-healed cigarette burns on the boy's chest were the re-
sult of "some kind of peelin disease."

The boy never saw the second floor apartment again. He
was made a ward of the state, and went directly from the
hospital to a county home, where his parentless life began
by having his crutches kicked out from under him on
the playground by two boys who ran away chortling like
trolls. Clay picked himself up and re-set his crutches. He
did not cry.

His father did some protesting in the Freeport police station, and more in several Freeport bars. He threatened to go
to law in order to regain his son, but never did. He claimed
to love Clay, and perhaps he did, a little, but if so, his love
was the kind that bites and burns. The boy was better off
out of his reach.

But not much better. Hetton House in South Freeport was
little more than a poor farm for kids, and Clay's childhood
there was wretched, although a little better when his body
was mended. Then, at least, he could make the worst of the
bullies stand away from him in the play yard; him and the
few younger children who came to look to him for protec-
tion. The bullies called him Lunk and Troll and Kong, but
he minded none of those names, and he left them alone if
they left him alone. Mostly they did, after he licked the
worst of them. He wasn't mean, but when provoked he
could be dangerous.

The kids who weren't afraid of him called him Blaze, and
that was how he came to think of himself.

Once he had a letter from his father. *Dear Son,* it said.

Well, how are You doing. I am fine. Working these days up in Lincoln rolling Lumber. It would be good if the b*****ds didn't steal all the Overtime, HA! I am going to get a little place and will send for You once I do. Well, write me a little Letter and tell Your old Pa how it goes. Can you send a Foto. It was signed *With Love, Clayton Blaisdell.*

Blaze had no photo to send his father, but would have written—the music teacher who came on Tuesdays would have helped him, he was quite sure—but there was no return address on the envelope, which was dirty and simply addressed to *Clayton Blaisdell JR "The Orfan-Home" in FREEPORT MAINE.*

Blaze never heard from him again.

He was placed with several different families during his Hetton House tenure, every time in the fall. They kept him long enough to help pick the crops and help keep their roofs and dooryards shoveled. Then, when spring thaw came, they decided he wasn't quite right and sent him back. Sometimes it wasn't too bad. And sometimes— like with the Bowies and their horrible dog-farm—it was real bad.

When he and HH were quits, Blaze knocked around New England on his own. Sometimes he was happy, but not the way he wanted to be happy, not the way he saw people being happy. When he finally settled in Boston (more or less; he never put down roots), it was because in the country he was lonely. Sometimes when he was in the country he would sleep in a barn and wake in the night and go out and look at the stars and there were so many, and he knew they were there before him, and they would be there after him. That was sort of awful and sort of wonderful. Sometimes when he was hitchhiking and it was going on for November, the wind would blow around him and flap his pants and he would grieve for something that was lost, like that letter which had come with no address. Sometimes he would look at the sky in the spring and see a bird, and it might make him happy, but just as often it felt like something inside him was getting small and ready to break.

It's bad to feel like that, he would think, *and if I do, I shouldn't be watching no birds*. But sometimes he would look up at the sky anyway.

Boston was all right, but sometimes he still got scared. There were a million people in the city, maybe more, and not one gave a shake for Clay Blaisdell. If they looked at him, it was only because he was big and had a dent in his forehead. Sometimes he would have a little fun, and sometimes he would just get frightened. He was trying to have a little fun in Boston when he met George Rackley. After he met George, it was better.

CHAPTER 5

The Little Mom-N-Pop Store was Tim & Janet's Quik-Pik. Most of the rear shelves were overflowing with jug wine and beer stacked in cardboard cases. A giant cooler ran the length of the back wall. Two of the four aisles were dedicated to munchies. Beside the cash register stood a bottle of pickled eggs as large as a small child. Tim & Janet's also stocked such necessaries as cigarettes, sanitary napkins, hot dogs, and stroke-books.

The night man was a pimple-pocked dude who attended the Portland branch of the University of Maine during his days. His name was Harry Nason, and he was majoring in animal husbandry. When the big man with the dented forehead walked in at ten minutes of one, Nason was reading a book from the paperback rack. The book was called *Big and Hard*. The late-night rush had dried up to a trickle. Nason decided that after the big man had bought his jug or his six, he'd close up and go home. Maybe take the book along and beat off. He was thinking that the part about the traveling preacher and the two horny widows might be good for that when the big man put a pistol under his nose and said, "Everything in the register."

Nason dropped the book. Thoughts of beating off left his mind. He gaped at the gun. He opened his mouth to say something intelligent. The kind of thing a guy being stuck up on TV might say, if the guy being stuck up happened to be the hero of the show. What came out was "Aaaa."

"Everything in the register," the big man repeated. The dent in his forehead was frightening. It looked deep enough for a frog-pond.

Harry Nason recalled—in a frozen sort of way—what his boss had told him he should do in the event of a hold-up: give the robber everything with no argument. He was fully insured. Nason's body suddenly felt very tender and vulnerable, full of bags and waters. His bladder loosened. And all at once he seemed to have an absolute assful of shit.

"Did you hear me, man?"

"Aaaa," Harry Nason agreed, and punched NO SALE on the cash register.

"Put the money in a bag."

"Okay. Yes. Sure." He fumbled among the sacks under the counter and dumped most of them on the floor. At last he managed to hold onto one. He flipped up the bill-holders in the cash drawer and began to drop money into the bag.

The door opened and a guy and a girl, probably college kids, walked in. They saw the gun and stopped. "What's this?" the guy asked. He was smoking a cigarillo and wearing a button that said POT ROCKS.

"It's a hold-up," Nason said. "Please don't, uh, antagonize this gentleman."

"Too much," the guy with the POT ROCKS button said. He started to grin. He pointed at Nason. His fingernail was dirty. "Dude's ripping you off, man."

The hold-up man turned to POT ROCKS. "Wallet," he said.

"Dude," POT ROCKS said, not losing the grin, "I'm on *your* side. The prices this place charges . . . and everybody knows Tim and Janet Quarles are, like, the biggest right-wingers since Adolf—"

"Give me your wallet or I'll blow your head off."

POT ROCKS suddenly realized he might be in some trouble here; for sure he wasn't in a movie. The grin went bye-bye and he stopped talking. Several zits stood out brightly on his cheeks, which were suddenly pale. He dug a black Lord Buxton out of his jeans pocket.

"There's never a cop when you need one," his girlfriend said coldly. She was wearing a long brown coat and black leather boots. Her hair matched the boots, at least this week.

"Drop the wallet in the bag," the hold-up guy said. He held the bag out. Harry Nason always thought he could have become a hero at that point by braining the hold-up man with the giant bottle of pickled eggs. Only the hold-up man looked as if he might have a hard head. Very hard.

The wallet plopped into the bag.

The hold-up man skirted them and headed for the door. He moved well for a man his size.

"You pig," the girl said.

The hold-up man stopped dead. For a moment the girl was sure (so she later told police) that he was going to turn around, open fire, and lay them all out. Later, with the police, they would differ on the hold-up man's hair color (brown, reddish, or blond), his complexion (fair, ruddy, or pale), and his clothes (pea jacket, windbreaker, woolen lumberjack shirt), but they all agreed on his size—big—and his final words before leaving. These were apparently addressed to the blank, dark doorway, almost in a moan:

"Jeezus, George, I forgot the stocking!"

Then he was gone. There was a bare glimpse of him running in the cold white light of the big Schlitz sign that hung over the store's entrance, and then an engine roared across the street. A moment later he wheeled out. The car was a sedan, but none of them could ID the make or model. It was beginning to snow.

"So much for beer," POT ROCKS said.

"Go on back to the cooler and have one on the house," said Harry Nason.

"Yeah? You sure?"

"Sure I'm sure. Your girl, too. What the fuck, we're insured." He began to laugh.

When the police asked him, he said he had never seen the stickup guy before. It was only later that he had cause to wonder if he had not in fact seen the stickup guy the previous fall, in the company of a skinny little rat-faced man who was buying wine and mouthing off.

CHAPTER 6

When Blaze got up the next morning, snow had piled in drifts all the way to the eaves of the shack and the fire was out. His bladder contracted the second his feet hit the floor. He hurried to the bathroom on the balls of his feet, wincing and blowing out little puffs of white vapor. His urine arched in a high-pressure flow for perhaps thirty seconds, then slowly faded. He sighed, shook off, broke wind.

Much bigger wind was screaming and whooping around the house. The pines outside the kitchen window were dipping and swaying. To Blaze they looked like thin women at a funeral.

He dressed, opened the back door, and fought his way around to the woodpile under the south eaves. The driveway was completely gone. Visibility was down to five feet, maybe less. It exhilarated him. The grainy slap of the snow on his face exhilarated him.

The wood was solid chunks of oak. He gathered a huge armful, pausing only to stomp his feet before going back in. He made up the fire with his coat on. Then he filled the coffee pot. He carried two cups to the table.

He paused, frowning. He had forgotten something.

The money! He had never counted the money.

He started into the other room. George's voice froze him. George was in the bathroom.

"Asshole."

"George, I—"

"George, I'm an asshole. Can you say that?"

"I—"

"No. Say George, I'm the asshole who forgot to wear the stocking."

"I got the m—"

"*Say* it."

"George, I'm the asshole. I forgot."

"Forgot what?"

"Forgot to wear the stocking."

"Now say all of it."

"George, I'm the asshole who forgot to wear the stocking."

"Now say this. Say George, I'm the asshole who wants to get caught."

"No! That ain't true! That's a lie, George!"

"It's the truth is what it is. You want to get caught and go to Shawshank and work in the laundry. That's the truth, the whole truth, and nothing but the truth. That's the truth on a stick. You're bull-simple. *That's* the truth."

"No, George. It ain't. I promise."

"I'm going away."

"No!" Panic seemed to stop his breath. It was like the sleeve of the flannel shirt his old man had crammed down his throat once to stop him bawling. "Don't, I forgot, I'm a dummy, without you I'll never remember what to buy—"

"You have a nice time, Blazer," George said, and although his voice was still coming from the bathroom, now it seemed to be fading. "You have a good time getting caught. Have a good time doing time and ironing those sheets."

"I'll do everything you tell me. I won't fuck up again."

There was a long pause. Blaze thought George was gone. "Maybe I'll be back. But I don't think so."

"George! George?"

The coffee was boiling. He poured one cup and went into the bedroom. The brown sack with the money in it was under George's side of the mattress. He shook it out on the sheet, which he kept forgetting to change. It had been on for the whole three months George had been dead.

There was two hundred and sixty dollars from the little mom-n-pop. Another eighty from the college-boy's wallet. More than enough to buy . . .

What? What was he supposed to buy?

Diapers. That was the ticket. If you were going to snatch a baby, you had to have diapers. Other stuff, too. But he couldn't remember the other stuff.

"What was it besides diapers, George?" He said it with an air of off-hand casualness, hoping to surprise George into speech. But George didn't take the bait.

Maybe I'll be back. But I don't think so.

He put the money back in the brown bag and exchanged the college kid's wallet for his own, which was battered and scuffed and full of nicks. His own wallet held two greasy dollar bills, a faded Kodak of his old man and old lady with their arms around each other, and a photo-booth shot of him and his only real buddy from Hetton House, John Cheltzman. There was also his lucky Kennedy half-dollar, an old bill for a muffler (that had been when he and George had been running that big bad Pontiac Bonneville), and a folded-over Polaroid.

George was looking out of the Polaroid and smiling. Squinting a little, because the sun had been in his eyes. He was wearing jeans and workman's boots. His hat was twisted around to the left, like he always wore it. George said that was the good-luck side.

They worked a lot of gags, and most of them—the best of them—were easy to work. Some depended on misdirection, some on greed, and some on fear. They were what George called short cons. And he called the gags that depended on fear "short con heart-stoppers."

"I like the simple shit," George said. "Why do I like the simple shit, Blaze?"

"Not many moving parts," Blaze said.

"Correct-a-roonie! Not many moving parts."

In the best of the short con heart-stoppers, George dressed up in clothes he called "a little past sharp" and then toured some Boston bars he knew about. These weren't gay bars and they weren't straight bars. George called them "gray bars." And the mark always picked George up. George never had to make a move. Blaze had pondered this once or twice (in his ponderous way), but had never come to any conclusion about it.

George had a nose for the closet queers and AC/DC

swingers who went out once or twice a month with their wedding rings tucked away in their wallets. The wholesalers on their way up, the insurance men, the school administrators, the bright young bank executives. George said they had a smell. And he was kind to them. He helped them along when they were shy and couldn't find the right words. Then he'd say he was staying at a good hotel. Not a great hotel, but a good one. A safe one.

It was the Imperial, not far from Chinatown. George and Blaze had a deal going with the second shift desk-man and the bell-captain. The room they used might change, but it was always at the end of the hall, and never too close to another occupied room.

Blaze sat in the lobby from three to eleven, wearing clothes he wouldn't be caught dead in on the street. His hair always gleamed with oil. He read comic-books while waiting for George. He was never aware of passing time.

The true indicator of George's genius was that when he and the mark came in, the mark hardly ever looked nervous. Eager, but not nervous. Blaze gave them fifteen minutes, then went up.

"Never think about it as coming in the room," George said. "Think of it as going onstage. The only one who don't know it's showtime is the mark."

Blaze always used his key and walked onstage saying his first line: "Hank, darling, I'm so glad to be back." Then he got mad, which he did passably well, although probably not up to Hollywood standards: "Jesus, no! I'll kill him! Kill him!"

At that he would heave his three-hundred-pound bulk

at the bed, where the mark quivered in horror, by that time usually wearing only his socks. George would throw himself between the mark and his raging "boyfriend" at the last moment. A flimsy barrier at best, the mark would think. If he was capable of thinking. And the soap opera was on.

George: "Dana, listen to me—this isn't what it seems."

Blaze: "I'm gonna kill him! Get out of my way and let me kill him! I'm gonna throw him out the window!"

(Terrified squeals from the marks—there had been eight or ten in all.)

George: "Please, let me tell you."

Blaze: "I'm gonna rip his balls off!"

(The mark begins to plead for his life and his sexual equipment, not necessarily in that order.)

George: "No, you're not. You're going to go quietly down to the lobby and wait for me."

At this point, Blaze would make another lunge for the mark. George would restrain him—barely. Blaze would then tear the wallet from the mark's pants.

Blaze: "I got your name and address, bitch! I'm gonna call your wife!"

At this point, most marks forgot about their lives *and* their sexual equipment and began to concentrate on their sacred honor and neighborhood standing instead. Blaze found this strange, but it seemed always to be true. More truth was to be found in a mark's wallet. The mark would tell George he was Bill Smith, from New Rochelle. He was, of course, Dan Donahue, from Brookline.

The play, meanwhile, resumed; the show had to go on.

George: "Go downstairs, Dana—be a dear and go downstairs."

Blaze: "No!"

George: "Go downstairs or I will never speak to you again. I am sick of your tantrums and your possessiveness. I mean it!"

At this point Blaze would go, clutching the wallet to his breast, muttering threats, and making baleful eye-contact with the mark.

As soon as the door closed, the mark was all over George. He had to have his wallet back. He would do anything to get his wallet back. The money didn't matter, but the identification did. If Sally found out . . . and Junior! Oh God, think of little Junior . . .

George soothed the mark. He was good at this part. Perhaps, he would say, Dana could be reasoned with. In fact, Dana could almost certainly be reasoned with. He just needed a few minutes to cool down, and then for George to talk to him alone. To reason with him. And pet him a little, the big lunk.

Blaze, of course, was not in the lobby. Blaze was in a room on the second floor. When George went down there, they would count the take. Their worst score was forty-three dollars. Their best, taken from the executive of a large food-chain, was five hundred and fifty.

They gave the mark enough time to sweat and make bleak promises to himself. *George* gave the mark time enough. George always knew the right amount. It was amazing. It was like he had a clock in his head, and it was set different for each mark. At last he would return to the first room with the wallet and say that Dana finally listened to reason, but he won't give back the money. George had all he could do to make him give back the credit cards. Sorry.

The mark doesn't gave a tinker's damn about the money. He is thumbing through his wallet feverishly, making sure he still has his driver's license, Blue Cross card, Social Security, pictures. It's all there. Thank God, it's all there. Poorer but wiser, he dresses and creeps away, probably wishing his balls had never dropped in the first place.

During the four years before Blaze took his second fall, this con was the one they fell back on, and it never failed. They never had a bit of trouble from the heat, either. Although not bright, Blaze was a fine actor. George was only the second real friend he had ever had, and it was only necessary to pretend that the mark was trying to persuade George that Blaze was no good. That Blaze was a waste of George's time and talents. That Blaze, in addition to being a dummy, was a busher and a fuck-up. Once Blaze had convinced himself of these things, his rage became genuine. If George had stood aside, Blaze would have broken both of the mark's arms. Maybe killed him.

Now, turning the Polaroid snap over and over in his fingers, Blaze felt empty. He felt like when he looked up in the sky and saw the stars, or a bird on a telephone wire or chimbly with its feathers blowing. George was gone and he was still stupid. He was in a fix and there was no way out.

Unless maybe he could show George he was at least

smart enough to get this thing rolling. Unless he could show George he didn't mean to get caught. Which meant what?

Which meant diapers. Diapers and what else? Jesus, what else?

He fell into a doze of thought. He thought all that morning, which passed with snow whooping in its throat.

CHAPTER 7

He was as out of place in the Baby Shoppe of Hager's Mammoth Department Store as a boulder in a living room. He was wearing his jeans and his workboots with the rawhide laces, a flannel shirt, and a black leather belt with the buckle cinched on the left side—the good-luck side. He had remembered his hat this time, the one with the earflaps, and he carried it in one hand. He was standing in the middle of a mostly pink room that was filled with light. He looked left and there were changing-tables. He looked right and there were carriages. He felt like he'd landed on Planet Baby.

There were many women here. Some had big bellies and some had small babies. Many of the babies were crying and all of the women looked at Blaze cautiously, as if he might go berserk at any moment and begin laying waste to Planet Baby, sending torn cushions and ripped teddy bears flying. A saleslady approached. Blaze was thankful. He had been afraid to speak to anyone. He knew when people were afraid, and he knew where he didn't belong. He was dumb, but not that dumb.

The saleslady asked if he needed help. Blaze said he did. He had been unable to think of everything he needed no matter how hard he tried, and so resorted to the only form of subterfuge with which he was familiar: the con.

"I been out of state," he said, and bared his teeth at the saleslady in a grin that would have frightened a cougar. The saleslady smiled back bravely. The top of her head almost reached the midpoint of his ribcage. "I just found out my sister-in-law had a kid . . . a baby . . . while I was gone, see, and I want to outfit him. The whole works."

She lit up. "I see. How generous of you. How sweet. What would you like in particular?"

"I don't know. I don't know nothing . . . anything . . . about babies."

"How old is your nephew?"

"Huh?"

"Your sister-in-law's child?"

"Oh! Gotcha! Six months."

"Isn't that dear." She twinkled professionally. "What's his name?"

Blaze was stumped for a moment. Then he blurted, "George."

"Lovely name! From the Greek. It means, 'to work the earth.'"

"Yeah? That's pretty far out."

She kept smiling. "Isn't it. Well, what does she have for him now?"

Blaze was ready for this one. "None of the stuff they got now is too good, that's the thing. They're really strapped for cash."

"I see. So you want to . . . start from the ground up, as it were."

"Yeah, you catch."

"*Very* generous of you. Well, the place to begin would be at the end of Pooh Avenue, in the Crib Corner. We have some very nice hardwood cribs . . ."

Blaze was stunned at how much it took to keep one tiny scrap of human being up and running. He had considered his take from the beer-store to be quite respectable, but he left Planet Baby with a nearly flat wallet.

He purchased a Dreamland crib, a Seth Harney cradle, a Happy Hippo highchair, an E-Z Fold changing table, a plastic bath, eight nightshirts, eight pairs of Dri-Day rubber pants, eight Hager's infant undershirts with snaps he couldn't figure out, three fitted sheets that looked like table napkins, three blankets, a set of crib bumpers that were supposed to keep the kid from whamming his brains out if he got restless, a sweater, a hat, bootees, a pair of red shoes with bells on the tongues, two pairs of pants with matching shirts, four pairs of socks that were not big enough to fit over his fingers, a Playtex Nurser set (the plastic liners looked like the bags George used to buy his dope in), a case of stuff called Similac, a case of Junior Fruits, a case of Junior Dinners, a case of Junior Desserts, and one place-setting with the Smurfs on them.

The baby food tasted shitty. He tried it when he got home.

As the bundles piled up in the corner of the Baby Shoppe, the glances of the shy young matrons became longer and more speculative. It became an event, a landmark in memory—the huge, slouching man in woodsman's clothes following the tiny saleslady from place to place, listening, then buying what she told him to buy. The saleslady was Nancy Moldow. She was on commission, and as the afternoon progressed, her eyes took on an almost supernatural glow. Finally the total was rung up and when Blaze counted out the money, Nancy Moldow threw in four boxes of Pampers. "You made my day," she said. "In fact, you may have made my career in infant sales."

"Thank you, ma'am," Blaze said. He was very glad about the Pampers. He had forgotten the diapers after all.

And as he loaded up two shopping carts (a stockboy had the cartons containing the highchair and the crib), Nancy Moldow cried: "Be sure to bring the young man in to have his picture taken!"

"Yes, ma'am," Blaze mumbled. For some reason a memory of his first mug shot flashed into his mind, and a cop saying, *Now turn sideways and bend your knees again, Highpockets—Christ, who grew you so fuckin big?*

"The picture is compliments of Hager's!"

"Yes, ma'am."

"Lotta goodies, man," the stockboy said. He was perhaps twenty, and just getting over his adolescent acne. He wore a little red bowtie. "Where's your car parked?"

"The lot in back," Blaze said.

He followed the stockboy, who insisted on pushing one of the carts and then complained about how it steered on the packed snow. "They don't salt it down back here, see, and the wheels get packed up. Then the damn carts skid around. You can give your ankles a nasty bite if you don't watch out. Real nasty. I'm not complaining, but . . ."

Then what are you doing, Sporty? Blaze could hear George asking. *Eating cat-food out of the dog's bowl?*

"This is it," Blaze said. "This is mine."

"Yeah, okay. What do you want to put in the trunk? The highchair, the crib, or both?"

Blaze suddenly remembered he didn't have a trunk key.

"Let's put it all in the back."

The stockboy's eyes widened. "Ah, Jeez, man, I don't think it'll fit. In fact, I'm positive—"

"We can put some in front, too. We can stand that carton with the crib in it in the passenger footwell. I'll rack the seat back."

"Why not the trunk? Wouldn't that be, like, simpler?"

Blaze thought, vaguely, of starting some story about how the trunk was full of stuff, but the trouble with lies was one always led to another. Soon it was like you were traveling on roads you didn't know. You got lost. *I always tell the truth when I can,* George liked to say. *It's like driving close to home.*

So he held up the dupe. "I lost my car-keys," he said. "Until I find em, all I got is this."

"Oh," the stockboy said. He looked at Blaze as though he were dumb, but that was okay; he had been looked at that way before. "Bummer."

In the end, they got it all in. It took some artful packing, and it was a tight squeeze, but they made it. When Blaze looked into the rearview mirror, he could even see some of the world outside the back window. The carton holding the broken-down changing table cut off the rest of the view.

"Nice car," said the stockboy. "An oldie but a goodie."

"Right," Blaze said. And because it was something George sometimes said, he added: "Gone from the charts, but not from our hearts." He wondered if the stockboy was waiting for something. It seemed like he was.

"What's she got, a 302?"

"342," Blaze said automatically.

The stockboy nodded. He still stood there.

From inside the back seat of the Ford, where there was no room for him but where he was, anyway—somehow— George said: "If you don't want him to stand there for the rest of the century, tip the dipshit and get rid of him."

Tip. Yeah. Right.

Blaze dragged out his wallet, looked at the limited selection of bills, and reluctantly selected a five. He gave it to the stockboy. The stockboy made it disappear. "All right, man, increase the peace."

"Whatever," Blaze said. He got into the Ford and started it up. The stockboy was trundling the shopping carts back to the store. Halfway there, he stopped and looked back at Blaze. Blaze didn't like that look. It was a *remembering* look.

"I should've remembered to tip him quicker. Right, George?"

George didn't answer.

Back home, he parked the Ford in the shed again and carted all the baby crap into the house. He assembled the crib in the bedroom and set up the changing table next to it. There was no need to look at the directions; he only looked at the pictures on the boxes and his hands did the rest. The cradle went in the kitchen, near the woodstove . . .

but not *too* near. The rest of the stuff he piled in the bedroom closet, out of sight.

When it was done, a change had come over the bedroom that went deeper than the added furniture. Something else had been added. The atmosphere had changed. It was as if a ghost had been set free to walk. Not the ghost of someone who had left, someone who had gone down dead, but the ghost of someone yet to come.

It made Blaze feel strange.

CHAPTER 8

The next night, Blaze decided he ought to get cool plates for his hot Ford, so he stole a pair off a Volkswagen in the parking lot of Jolly Jim's Jiant Groceries in Portland. He replaced the plates from the VW with the Ford's plates. It could be weeks or months before the VW's owner realized he had the wrong set of plates, because the number on the little sticker was 7, meaning the guy didn't have to re-register until July. Always check the registration sticker. George had taught him that.

He drove to a discount store, feeling safe with his new plates, knowing he would feel safer still when the Ford was a different color. He bought four cans of Skylark Blue auto paint and a spray-gun. He went home broke but happy.

He ate supper sitting next to the stove, thumping his feet on the worn linoleum as Merle Haggard sang "Okie from Muskogee." Old Merle had really known how to dish it up to those fucking hippies.

After the dishes were washed, he ran the adhesive-patched extension cord out to the shed and hung a bulb over a beam. Blaze loved to paint. And Skylark Blue was one of his favorite colors. You had to like that name. It meant blue like a bird. Like a skylark.

He went back to the house and got a pile of old newspapers. George read a newspaper every day, and not just the funnies. Sometimes he read the editorials to Blaze and raged about the Redneck Republicans. He said the Republicans hated poor people. He referred to the President as That Goddam Wet in the White House. George was a Democrat, and two years ago they had put stickers for Democratic candidates on three different stolen cars.

All the newspapers were way old, and ordinarily that would have made Blaze feel sad, but tonight he was too excited about painting the car. He papered the windows and wheels. He Scotch-taped more pieces to the chrome trim.

By nine o'clock, the fragrant banana-smell of spray-paint filled the shed, and by eleven, the job was done. Blaze took off the newspapers and touched up a few places, then admired his work. He thought it was good work.

He went to bed, a little high from the paint, and woke up the next morning with a headache. "George?" he said hopefully.

No answer.

"I'm broke, George. I'm busted to my heels."

No answer.

Blaze moped around the house all day, wondering what to do.

The night man was reading a paperback epic called *Butch Ballerinas* when a Colt revolver was shoved in his face. Same Colt. Same voice saying gruffly, "Everything in the register."

"Oh no," Harry Nason said. "Oh Christ."

He looked up. Standing before him was a flat-nosed, Chinese horror in a woman's nylon stocking that trailed down his back like the tail of a ski-cap.

"Not you. Not again."

"Everything in the register. Put it in a bag."

No one came in this time, and because it was a week-night, there was less in the drawer.

The stick-up man paused on the way out and turned back. *Now,* Harry Nason thought, *I will be shot.* But instead of shooting him, the stick-up man said, "This time I re-membered the stocking."

Behind the nylon, he appeared to be grinning.

Then he was gone.

CHAPTER 9

When Clayton Blaisdell, Jr., came to Hetton House, there was a Headmistress. He didn't remember her name, only her gray hair, and her big gray eyes behind her spectacles, and that she read them the Bible, and ended every Morning Assembly by saying *Be good children and you shall prosper*. Then one day she wasn't in the office anymore, because she had a stroke. At first Blaze thought people were saying she had a stork, but finally he got it straight: *stroke*. It was a kind of headache that wouldn't go away. Her replacement was Martin Coslaw. Blaze never forgot *his* name, and not just because the kids called him The Law. Blaze never forgot him because The Law taught Arithmetic.

Arithmetic was held in Room 7 on the third floor, where it was cold enough to freeze the balls off a brass monkey in the winter. There were pictures of George Washington, Abraham Lincoln, and Sister Mary Hetton on the walls. Sister Hetton had pale skin and black hair scrooped back from her face and balled into a kind of doorknob on the back of her head. She had dark eyes that sometimes came back to accuse Blaze of things after lights-out. Mostly of being dumb. Probably too dumb for high school, just as The Law said.

Room 7 had old yellow floors and always smelled of floor-varnish, a smell that made Blaze sleepy even if he was wide awake when he walked in. There were nine fly-specked light globes that sent down thin, sad light on rainy days. There was an old blackboard at the front of the room, and over it were green placards upon which the alphabet marched in rolling Palmer Method letters—both the capital letters and the little fellows. After the alphabet came the numbers from 0 to 9, so beautiful and nice they made you feel stupid and clumsier than ever just looking at them. The desks were carved with overlapping slogans and initials, most worn to ghosts by repeated sandings and re-varnishings but never erased completely. They were bolted to the floor on iron discs. Each desk had an inkwell. The inkwells were filled with Carter's Ink. Spilled ink got you a stropping in the washroom. Black heel-marks on the yellow floor got you a stropping. Fooling in class got you a stropping, only class fooling was called Bad Deport-ment. There were other stropping offenses; Martin Coslaw believed in stropping and The Paddle. The Law's paddle was more feared in Hetton House than anything, even the bogeyman that hid under the beds of the little kids. The Paddle was a birch spatula, quite thin. The Law had drilled four holes in it to lessen air resistance. He was a bowler with a team called The Falmouth Rockers, and on Fridays he sometimes wore his bowling shirt to school. It was dark blue and had his name—Martin—in cursive gold over the breast pocket. To Blaze those letters looked almost (but not quite) like Palmer Method. The Law said that in bowling and in life, if a person made the spares, the strikes would take care of themselves. He had a strong right arm from making all those strikes and spares, and when he gave someone a stropping with The Paddle, it hurt a lot. He had been known to bite his tongue between his teeth while applying The Paddle to a boy with especially Bad Deportment. Sometimes he bit it hard enough to make it bleed, and for awhile there was a boy at Hetton House who called him Dracula as well as The Law, but then that boy made out, and they didn't see him anymore. Making out was what they called it when someone got placed with a family and stuck, maybe even adopted.

Martin Coslaw was hated and feared by all the boys at Hetton House, but no one hated him and feared him more than Blaze. Blaze was very bad at Arithmetic. He had been able to get back the hang of adding two apples plus three apples, but only with great effort, and a quarter of an apple plus a half an apple was always going to be beyond him. So far as he knew, apples only came in bites.

It was during Basic Arithmetic that Blaze pulled his first con, aided by his friend John Cheltzman. John was skinny, ugly, gangling, and filled with hate. The hate rarely showed. Mostly it was hidden behind his thick, adhesive-taped glasses and the idiotic, farmerish yuk-yuk-yuk that was his frequent laughter. He was a natural target of the older, stronger boys. They beat him around pretty good. His face was rubbed in the dirt (spring and fall) or washed in snow (winter). His shirts were often torn. He rarely emerged from the communal shower without getting ass-smacked by a few wet towels. He always wiped the dirt or snow off, tucked his ripped shirt-tail in, or went yuk-

yuk-yuk as he rubbed his reddening ass-cheeks, and the hate hardly ever showed. Or his brains. He was good in his classes—quite good, he couldn't help that—but anything above a B was rare. And not welcomed. At Hetton House, A stood for asshole. Not to mention ass-kicking.

Blaze was starting to get his size by then. He didn't have it, not at eleven or twelve, but he was starting to get it. He was as big as some of the big boys. And he didn't join in the playground beatings or the towel-snappings. One day John Cheltzman walked up to him while Blaze was standing beside the fence at the far end of the playground, not doing anything but watching crows light in the trees and take off again. He offered Blaze a deal.

"You'll have The Law again for math this half," John said. "Fractions continue."

"I hate fractions," Blaze said.

"I'll do your homework if you don't let those lugs tune up on me anymore. It won't be good enough to make him suspicious—not good enough to get you caught—but it'll be good enough to get you by. You won't get stood after." Being stood after wasn't as bad as being stropped, but it was bad. You had to stand in the corner of Room 7, face to the wall. You couldn't look at the clock.

Blaze considered John Cheltzman's idea, then shook his head. "He'll know. I'll get called on to recite, and then he'll know."

"You just look around the room like you're thinking," John said. "I'll take care of you."

And John did. He wrote down the homework answers and Blaze copied them in his own numbers that tried to look like the Palmer Method numbers over the blackboard but never did. Sometimes The Law called on him, and then Blaze would stand up and look around—anywhere but at Martin Coslaw, and that was all right, that was how just about everyone behaved when they were called on. During his looking-around, he'd look at Johnny Cheltzman, slumped in his seat by the door to the book closet with his hands on his desk. If the number The Law wanted was ten or under, the number of fingers showing would be the answer. If it was a fraction, John's hands would be in fists. Then they'd open. He was very quick about it. The left hand was the top half of the fraction. The right hand was the bottom. If the bottom number was over five, Johnny went back to fists and then used both hands. Blaze had no trouble at all with these signals, which many would have found more complex than the fractions they represented.

"Well, Clayton?" The Law would say. "We're waiting."

And Blaze would say, "One-sixth."

He didn't always have to be right. When he told George, George had nodded in approval. "A beautiful little con. When did it break down?"

It broke down three weeks into the half, and when Blaze thought about it—he *could* think, it just took him time and it was hard work—he realized that The Law must have been suspicious about Blaze's amazing mathematical turn-around all along. He just hadn't let on. Had been paying out the rope Blaze needed to hang himself with.

There was a surprise quiz. Blaze flunked with a grade of Zero. This was because the quiz was all fractions. The quiz had really been given for one purpose and one purpose only, and that was to catch Clayton Blaisdell, Jr. Below the Zero was a note scrawled in bright red letters. Blaze couldn't make it out, so he took it to John.

John read it. At first he didn't say anything. Then he told Blaze, "This note says, 'John Cheltzman is going to resume getting beat up.'"

"What? Huh?"

"It says 'Report to my office at four o'clock.'"

"What for?"

"Because we forgot about the tests," John said. Then he said, "No, *you* didn't forget. *I* forgot. Because all I could think about was getting those overgrown Blutos to stop hurting me. Now you're gonna beat me up and then The Law is gonna strop me and then the Blutos are gonna start in on me again. Jesus Christ, I wish I was dead." And he did look like he wished it.

"I'm not gonna beat you up."

"No?" John looked at him with the eyes of one who wants to believe but can't quite.

"You couldn't take the test for me, could you?"

Martin Coslaw's office was a fairly large room with HEAD-MASTER on the door. There was a small blackboard in it, across from the window. The window looked out on Hetton House's miserable schoolyard. The blackboard was dusted with chalk and—Blaze's downfall—fractions. Coslaw was seated behind his desk when Blaze came in. He was frowning at nothing. Blaze gave him something else to frown at. "Knock," he said.

"Huh?"

"Go back and knock," said The Law.

"Oh." Blaze turned, went out, knocked, and came back in.

"Thank you."

"Sure."

Coslaw frowned at Blaze. He picked up a pencil and began to tap it on his desk. It was a red grading pencil. "Clayton Blaisdell, Jr.," he said. He brooded. "Such a long name for such a short intellect."

"The other kids call me—"

"I don't care what the other kids call you, a kid is a baby goat, a kid is a piece of slang passed around by idiots, I don't care for it or those who use it. I am an instructor of Arithmetic, my task is to prepare young fellows such as yourself for high school—if they can be prepared—and also to teach them the difference between right and wrong. If my responsibilities ceased with the instruction of Arithmetic—and sometimes I wish they did, *often* I wish they did—that would not be the case, but I am also Headmaster, hence the instruction of right versus wrong, *quod erat demonstrandum*. Do you know what *quod erat demonstrandum* means, Mr. Blaisdell?"

"Nope," Blaze said. His heart was sinking and he could feel water rising in his eyes. He was big for his age but now he felt small. Small and getting smaller. Knowing that was how The Law wanted him to feel didn't change it.

"No, and never will, because even if you ever attain your sophomore year in high school—which I doubt—you will never get closer to Geometry than the drinking fountain at the end of the hall." The Law steepled his fingers and rocked back in his chair. His bowling shirt was hung over the back of his chair, and it rocked with him. "It means, 'that which was to be demonstrated,' Mr. Blaisdell, and what I demonstrated by my little quiz is that you are a cheater. A cheater is a person who does not know the difference between right and wrong. QED, *quod erat demonstrandum*. And thus, punishment."

Blaze cast his eyes down at the floor. He heard a drawer pulled open. Something was removed and the drawer was slid closed. He did not have to look up to know what The Law was now holding in his hand.

"I abhor a cheater," Coslaw said, "but I understand your mental shortcomings, Mr. Blaisdell, and thus I understand there is one worse than you in this little plot. That would be the one who first put the idea into your obviously thick head and then abetted you. Are you following me?"

"No," Blaze said.

Coslaw's tongue crept out a bit and his teeth engaged it firmly. He gripped The Paddle with equal or greater firmness.

"Who did your assignments?"

Blaze said nothing. You didn't tattle. All the comic-books, TV shows, and movies said the same thing. You didn't tattle. Especially not on your only friend. And there was something else. Something that struggled for expression.

"You hadn't ought to strop me," he said finally.

"Oh?" Coslaw looked amazed. "Do you say so? And why is that, Mr. Blaisdell? Elucidate. I am fascinated."

Blaze didn't know those big words, but he knew that look. He had been seeing it his whole life.

"You don't care nothing about teaching me. You just want to make me feel small, and hurt whoever stopped you doing it for a little while. That's wrong. You hadn't ought to strop me when you're the one who's wrong."

The Law no longer looked amazed. Now he only looked mad. So mad a vein was pulsing right in the middle of his forehead. "Who did your assignments?"

Blaze said nothing.

"How could you answer in class? How did that part work?"

Blaze said nothing.

"Was it Cheltzman? I think it was Cheltzman."

Blaze said nothing. His fists were clenched, trembling. Tears spilled out of his eyes, but he didn't think they were feeling-small tears now.

Coslaw swung The Paddle and struck Blaze high up on one arm. It made a crack like a small gun. It was the first time Blaze had ever been struck by a teacher anywhere except on the ass, although sometimes, when he was littler, his ear had been twisted (and once or twice, his nose). *"Answer me, you brainless moose!"*

"Fuck you!" Blaze cried, the nameless thing finally leaping all the way free. "Fuck you, fuck you!"

"Come here," The Law said. His eyes were huge, bugging out. The hand holding The Paddle had gone white. "Come here, you bag of God's trash."

And with the nameless thing that was rage now out of him, and because he was after all a child, Blaze went.

When he walked out of The Law's study twenty minutes later, his breath whistling raggedly in his throat and his nose bleeding—but still dry-eyed and close-mouthed—he became a Hetton House legend.

He was done with Arithmetic. During October and most of November, instead of going to Room 7, he went to Room 19 study hall. That was fine by Blaze. It was two weeks before he could lie on his back comfortably, and then that was fine, too.

One day in late November, he was once more summoned to Headmaster Coslaw's office. Sitting there in front of the blackboard were a man and a woman of middle age. To Blaze, they looked dry. Like they might have been blown in on the late autumn wind like leaves.

The Law was seated behind his desk. His bowling shirt was nowhere to be seen. The room was cold because the window had been opened to let in the bright, thin November sun. Besides being a bowling nut, The Law was a fresh air fiend. The visiting couple did not seem to mind. The dry man was wearing a gray suit-jacket with padded shoulders and a string tie. The dry woman was wearing a plaid coat and a white blouse under it. Both had blocky, vein-ridged hands. His were callused. Hers were cracked and red.

"Mr. and Mrs. Bowie, this is the boy of whom I spoke. Take off your hat, young Blaisdell."

Blaze took off his Red Sox cap.

Mr. Bowie looked at him critically. "He's a big 'un. Only eleven, you say?"

"Twelve next month. He'll be a good help around your place."

"He ain't got nothin, does he?" Mrs. Bowie asked. Her voice was high and reedy. It sounded strange coming from that mammoth breast, which rose under her plaid coat like a comber at Higgins Beach. "No TB nor nothin?"

"He's been tested," said Coslaw. "All our boys are tested regularly. State requirement."

"Can he chop wood, that's what I need to know," Mr. Bowie said. His face was thin and haggard, the face of an unsuccessful TV preacher.

"I'm sure he can," said Coslaw. "I'm sure he's capable of hard work. Hard *physical* work, I mean. He is poor at Arithmetic."

Mrs. Bowie smiled. It was all lip and no teeth. "I do the cipherin." She turned to her husband. "Hubert?"

Bowie considered, then nodded. "Ayuh."

"Step out, please, young Blaisdell," The Law said. "I'll speak to you later."

And so, without a word spoken by him, Blaze became a ward of the Bowies.

"I don't want you to go," John said. He was sitting on the cot next to Blaze's, watching as Blaze loaded a zipper bag with his few personal possessions. Most, like the zipper bag itself, had been provided by Hetton House.

"I'm sorry," Blaze said, but he wasn't, or not entirely—he only wished Johnny could come along.

"They'll start pounding on me as soon as you're down the road. Everybody will." John's eyes moved rapidly back and forth in their sockets, and he picked at a fresh pimple on the side of his nose.

"No they won't."

"They will, and you know it."

Blaze did know it. He also knew there was nothing he could do about it. "I got to go. I'm a minor." He smiled at John. "Miner, forty-niner, dreadful sorry, Clementine."

For Blaze, this was nearly Juvenalian wit, but John didn't even smile. He reached out and grasped Blaze's arm hard, as if to store its texture in his memory forever. "You won't ever come back."

But Blaze did.

The Bowies came for him in an old Ford pick-up that had been painted a grotesque and lap-marked white some years before. There was room for three in the cab, but Blaze rode in back. He didn't mind. The sight of HH shrinking in the distance, then disappearing, filled him with joy.

They lived in a huge, ramshackle farmhouse in Cumberland, which borders Falmouth on one side and Yarmouth on the other. The house was on an unpaved road and bore a thousand coats of road dust. It was unpainted. In front was a sign reading BOWIE'S COLLIES. To the left of the house was a huge dogpen in which twenty-eight Collies ran and barked and yapped constantly. Some had the mange. The hair fell out of them in big patches, revealing the tender pink hide beneath for the season's few remaining bugs to eat. To the right of the house was weedy pastureland. Behind it was a gigantic old barn where the Bowies kept cows. The house stood on forty acres. Most was given over to hay, but there was also seven acres of mixed soft and hardwoods.

When they arrived, Blaze jumped down from the truck with his zipper bag in his hand. Bowie took it. "I'll put that away for you. You want to get choppin."

Blaze blinked at him.

Bowie pointed to the barn. A series of sheds connected it to the house, zigzagging, forming something that was almost a dooryard. A pile of logs stood against one shed wall. Some were maple, some were plain pine, with the sap coagulating in blisters on the bark. In front of the pile stood an old scarred chopping block with an ax buried in it.

"You want to get choppin," Hubert Bowie said again.

"Oh," Blaze said. It was the first word he had said to either of them.

The Bowies watched him go over to the chopping block and free the ax. He looked at it, then stood it in the dust beside the block. Dogs ran and yapped ceaselessly. The smallest Collies were the shrillest.

"Well?" Bowie asked.

"Sir, I ain't never chopped wood."

Bowie dropped the zipper bag in the dust. He walked over and sat a maple chunk on the chopping block. He spat in one palm, clapped his hands together, and picked up the ax. Blaze watched closely. Bowie brought the blade down. The chunk fell in two pieces.

"There," he said. "Now they're stovelengths." He held out the ax. "You."

Blaze rested it between his legs, then spat in one palm and clapped his hands together. He went to pick up the ax, then remembered he hadn't put no chunk of wood on the block. He put one on, raised the ax, and brought it down. His piece fell in a pair of stovelengths almost identical to Bowie's. Blaze was delighted. The next moment he was sprawling in the dirt, his right ear ringing from the backhand blow Bowie had fetched him with one of his dry, work-hardened hands.

"What was that for?" Blaze asked, looking up.

"Not knowin how to chop wood," Bowie said. "And before you say it ain't your fault—boy, it ain't mine, neither. Now you want to get choppin."

His room was a tiny afterthought on the third floor of the rambling farmhouse. There was a bed and a bureau, nothing else. There was one window. Everything you saw through it looked wavy and distorted. It was cold in the room at night, colder in the morning. Blaze didn't mind the cold, but he minded the Bowies. Them he minded more and more. Minding became dislike and dislike finally became hate. The hate grew slowly. For him it was the only way. It grew at its own pace, and it grew completely, and it put forth red flowers. It was the sort of hate no intelligent person ever knows. It was its own thing. It was not adulterated by reflection.

He chopped a great deal of wood that fall and winter. Bowie tried to teach him how to hand-milk, but Blaze couldn't do it. He had what Bowie called hard hands. The cows grew skittish no matter how gently he tried to wrap his fingers around their teats. Then their nervousness came back to him, closing the circuit. The flow of milk slowed to a trickle, then stopped. Bowie never boxed his ears or slapped the back of his head for this. He would not have milking machines, he did not believe in milking machines, said those DeLavals used cows up in their prime, but would allow that hand-milking was a talent. And because it was, you could no more punish someone for not having it than you could punish someone for not being able to write what he called poitry.

"You can chop wood, though," he said, not smiling. "You got the talent for that."

Blaze chopped it and carried it, filling the kitchen wood-box four and five times a day. There was an oil furnace, but Hubert Bowie refused to run it until February, because the price of Number Two was so dear. Blaze also shoveled out the ninety-foot driveway once the snow got going, forked hay, cleaned the barn, and scrubbed Mrs. Bowie's floors.

On weekdays he was up at five to feed the cows (four on mornings when snow had fallen) and to get breakfast before the yellow SAD 106 bus came to take him to school. The Bowies might have done away with school if they had been able, but they were not.

At Hetton House, Blaze had heard both good stories and bad stories about "school out." Mostly bad ones from the big boys, who went to Freeport High. Blaze was still too young for that, however. He went to Cumberland District A during his time with the Bowies, and he liked it. He liked his teacher. He liked to memorize poems, to stand up in class and recite: "By the rude bridge that arched the flood . . ." He declaimed these poems in his red-and-black–checked hunting jacket (which he never took off, because he forgot it during fire drills), his green flannel pants, and his green gumrubber boots. He stood five-eleven, dwarfing every other sixth-grader in his class, and his height was overtopped by his grinning face and dented forehead. No one ever laughed at Blaze when he recited poems.

He had a great many friends even though he was a state kid, because he wasn't contentious or bullying. Nor was he sullen. In the schoolyard he was everyone's bear. He sometimes rode as many as three first-graders on his shoulders at once. He never took advantage of his size at keepaway. He would be tackled by five, six, seven players at once, swaying, swaying, usually grinning, his dented face turned up to the sky, finally toppling like a building, to the inevitable cheers of all. Mrs. Waslewski, who was a Catholic, saw him toting first-graders around on his shoulders one day when she had playground duty and started calling him St. Francis of the Little People.

Mrs. Cheney brought him along in reading, writing, and history. She understood early on that for Blaze, math (which he always called Arithmetic) was a lost cause. The one time she tried him on flash cards, he turned pale and she was convinced the boy actually came close to fainting.

He was slow but not retarded. By December he had moved from the first-grade adventures of Dick and Jane to the stories in *Roads to Everywhere,* the third-grade reader. She gave him a pile of Classics comic-books she kept bound in hardcovers to take back to the Bowies' with a note saying they were homework. His favorite, of course, was *Oliver Twist,* which he read over and over until he knew every word.

All this continued until January and might have continued until spring, except for two unfortunate events. He killed a dog and he fell in love.

He hated the Collies, but one of his chores was to feed them. They were purebreds, but poor diets and lives lived exclusively in the kennel and the pen made them ugly and neurotic. Most were cowardly and shied from the touch. They would lunge at you, yapping and snarling, only to sheer away and approach from a different angle. Sometimes they snuck in from behind. Then they might nip at your calves or buttocks before dashing off. The clamor at feeding time was hellish. They were out of Hubert Bowie's province. Mrs. Bowie was also the only one they would come to. She fawned over them in her buzzing voice. She always wore a red jacket when she was with the dogs, and it was covered with tawny hair.

The Bowies sold very few grown animals, but the pups fetched two hundred dollars each in the spring. Mrs. Bowie exhorted Blaze on the importance of feeding the dogs well—of feeding them what she called "a good mix." Yet *she* never fed them, and what Blaze put in their troughs was discount chow from a feed-store in Falmouth. This feed was called Dog's Worth. Hubert Bowie sometimes called it Cheap-Chow and sometimes Dog Farts. But never when his wife was around.

The dogs knew Blaze didn't like them, that he was afraid of them, and every day they grew more aggressive toward him. By the time the weather really began to turn cold, their dashes sometimes brought them close enough to nip him from the front. At night he sometimes woke from dreams in which they packed together, brought him down, and began to eat him alive. He would lie in his bed after these dreams, puffing cold vapor into the dark air and feeling himself over to make sure he was still whole. He knew he was, he knew the difference between what was dreams and what was real, but in the dark that difference seemed thinner.

Several times their bumping and dashing caused him to spill the food. Then he had to scrape it up as best he could from the packed, urine-spotted snow while they snarled and fought over it around him.

Gradually, one became the leader in their undeclared war against him. His name was Randy. He was eleven. He had one milky eye. He scared the shit out of Blaze. His teeth were like old yellow tusks. There was a white stripe down the center of his skull. He would approach Blaze from dead-on, from twelve o'clock high, haunches pumping under his ragged pelt. Randy's good eye seemed to burn while the bad one remained indifferent to it all, a dead lamp. His claws dug small clods of yellow-white impacted snow from the floor of the dogpen. He would accelerate until it seemed impossible he could do anything but launch himself into flight at Blaze's throat. The other dogs would be whipped into a frenzy by this, leaping and turning and snarling in the air. At the last instant, Randy's paws would come down stiff, spraying snow all over Blaze's green pants, and he would race away in a big loop, only to repeat the maneuver. But he was sheering off later and later, until he was close enough for Blaze to smell his heat and even his breath.

Then one evening toward the end of January, he knew the dog wasn't going to sheer off. He didn't know how this charge was different, or why, but it was. This time Randy meant it. He was going to leap. And when he did, the other dogs would come in quickly. Then it would be like in his dreams.

The dog came, speeding faster and faster, silent. This time there were no paws out. No skidding or turning. Its haunches tensed, then pushed down. A moment later Randy was in the air.

Blaze was carrying two steel buckets filled with Dog's Worth. When he saw Randy meant it this time, all his fear left him. He dropped his buckets at the same time Randy leaped. He was wearing rawhide gloves with holes in the fingers. He met the dog in midair with his right fist, under the long shovel-shelf of the jaw. The jolt ran all the way up to his shoulder. His hand went instantly and completely numb. There was a brief, bitter crack. Randy did a perfect one-eighty in the cold air and landed on his back with a thud.

Blaze realized all the other dogs had fallen silent only when they began to bark again. He picked up the buckets, went to the trough, and poured in the chow. Always before, the dogs had crowded in at once to begin snarking it up, growling and snapping for the best places, before he could even add water. He could do nothing about it; he was inef- fectual. Now, when one of the smaller Collies rushed for the trough with its stupid eyes gleaming and its stupid tongue hanging from the side of its stupid mouth, Blaze jerked at it with his gloved hands and it cut sidewards so fast its feet went out from under it and it landed on its side. The others shrank back.

Blaze added two buckets of water from the bib-faucet. "There," he said. "It's wet down. Go on and eat it."

He walked back to look at Randy while the other dogs ran to the feeding trough.

The fleas were already leaving Randy's cooling body to die in the piss-stained snow. The good eye was now almost as glazed-looking as the bad one. This awoke a feeling of pity and sadness in Blaze. Perhaps the dog had only been playing, after all. Just trying to scare him.

And he *was* scared. That, too. He would catch dickens for this.

He walked to the house with the empty buckets, head lowered. Mrs. Bowie was in the kitchen. She had a rubbing-board propped in the sink and was washing curtains on it. She was singing a hymn in her reedy voice as she worked.

"Aw, don't you track in on my floor, now!" she cried, seeing him. It was her floor, but he washed it. On his knees. Sullenness awoke in his breast.

"Randy's dead. He jumped me. I hit him. Killed him."

Her hands flew out of the soapy water and she screamed. "Randy? Randy! *Randy!*"

She ran around in a circle, grabbed her sweater from the peg near the woodstove, then ran for the door.

"Hubert!" she called to her husband. "Hubert, oh Hubert! Such a bad boy!" And then, as if still singing: "Ooooooo*OOOOOO*—"

She thrust Blaze out of her way and ran outside. Mr. Bowie appeared in one of the many shed doors, his scrawny face long with surprise. He strode to Blaze and grabbed him by one shoulder. "What happened?"

"Randy's dead," Blaze said stolidly. "He jumped me and I did him down."

"You wait," Hubert Bowie said, and went after his wife.

Blaze took off his red and black jacket and sat down on the stool in the corner. Snow melted off his boots and made a puddle. He didn't care. The heat from the woodstove made his face throb. He chopped the wood. He didn't care.

Bowie had to lead his wife back inside, because she had her apron over her face. She was sobbing loudly. The high pitch of her voice made her sound like a sewing machine.

"Go out into the shed," Bowie told him.

Blaze opened the door. Bowie helped him through it with the toe of his boot. Blaze fell down the two steps into the dooryard, got up, and went into the shed. There were tools in there—axes, hammers, a lathe, an emery wheel, a planer, a sander, other things he didn't know the names of. There were auto parts and boxes of old magazines. And a snow shovel with a wide aluminum scoop. His shovel. Blaze looked at it, and something about the shovel brought his hate of the Bowies to completion, finished it off. They received a hundred and sixty dollars a month for keeping him and he did their chores. He ate badly. He had eaten better at HH. It wasn't fair.

Hubert Bowie opened the door to the shed and stepped in. "I'm going to whip you now," he said.

"That dog jumped me. He was going for my throat."

"Don't say no more. You're only making it worse for yourself."

Every spring, Bowie bred one of his cows with Franklin Marstellar's bull, Freddy. On the wall of the shed was a walking-halter he called a "love-halter" and a nosepiece. Bowie took it from its peg and held it by the nosepiece, fingers curled through the lattices. The heavy leather straps held down.

"Bend over that work bench."

"Randy went for my throat. I'm telling you it was him or me."

"Bend over that work bench."

Blaze hesitated, but he did not think. Thinking was a long process for him. Instead he consulted the tickings of instinct.

It wasn't time yet.

He bent over the work bench. It was a long hard whipping, but he didn't cry. He did that later, in his room.

The girl he'd fallen in love with was a seventh-grader at Cumberland A School named Marjorie Thurlow. She had yellow hair and blue eyes and no breasts. She had a sweet smile that made the corners of her eyes turn up. On the playground, Blaze followed her with his own eyes. She made him feel empty in the pit of his stomach, but in a way that was good. He imagined himself carrying her books and protecting her from outlaws. These thoughts always made his face burn.

One day not long after the incident of Randy and the whipping, the District Nurse came to school to give immunization boosters. The children had been given release forms the week before; those parents who wanted their chil-

dren to have the shots had signed them. Now, the children
with signed forms queued up in a nervous line leading into
the cloakroom. Blaze was one of these. Bowie had called up
George Henderson, who was on the schoolboard, and asked
if the shots cost money. They didn't, so Bowie signed.

Margie Thurlow was also in line. She looked very pale.
Blaze felt bad for her. He wished he could go back and hold
her hand. The thought made his face burn. He bent his
head and shuffled his feet.

Blaze was first in line. When the nurse beckoned him
into the cloakroom, he took off his red-and-black–checked
jacket and unbuttoned the sleeve of his shirt. The nurse
took the needle out of a kind of cooker, looked at his slip,
then said: "Better unbutton the other sleeve too, big boy.
You're down for both."

"Will it hurt?" Blaze said, unbuttoning the other sleeve.

"Only for a second."

"Okay," Blaze said, and let her shoot the needle from the
cooker into his left arm.

"Right. Now the other arm and you're done."

Blaze turned the other way. She shot some more stuff
from another needle into his right arm. Then he left the
cloakroom, went back to his desk, and began to puzzle out
a story in his *Scholastic*.

When Margie came out, there were tears in her eyes
and more on her face, but she wasn't sobbing. Blaze felt
proud of her. When she passed his desk on her way to the
door (seventh-graders were in another room), he gave her a
smile. And she smiled back. Blaze folded that smile, put it
away, and kept it for years.

At recess, just as Blaze was coming out the door to the playground, Margie ran inside past him, sobbing. He turned to look after her, then walked slowly into the playground, brow creased, face unhappy. He came to Peter Lavoie, batting the tetherball on its post with one mittened hand, and asked if Peter knew what had happened to Margie.

"Glen hit her in the shot," Peter Lavoie said. He demonstrated on a passing boy, balling his fist and hitting the kid three times fast, *whap-whap-whap.* Blaze watched this, frowning. The nurse had lied. Both of his arms now hurt badly from the shots. The large muscles felt stiff and bruised. It was hard to even bend them without wincing. And Margie was a girl. He looked around for Glen.

Glen Hardy was a huge eighth-grader, the kind that will play football, then run to fat. He had red hair that he combed back from his forehead in big waves. His father was a farmer on the west end of town, and Glen's arms were slabs of muscle.

Somebody threw Blaze the keepaway ball. He dropped it on the ground without looking at it and started for Glen Hardy.

"Oh boy," Peter Lavoie said. "Blaze is goin after Glen!"

This news traveled quickly. Groups of boys began to move with studied casualness toward where Glen and some of the older boys were playing a clumsy, troll-like version of kickball. Glen was pitching. He rolled the ball quick and hard, making it bounce and skitter on the frozen ground.

Mrs. Foster, who had playground duty that day, was on the other side of the building, monitoring the little ones on the swings. She would not be a factor, at least not at first.

Glen looked up and saw Blaze coming. He dropped the kickball. He put his hands on his hips. Both teams collapsed to form a semicircle around him and behind him. They were all seventh- and eighth-graders. None were as big as Blaze. Only Glen was bigger.

The fourth-, fifth-, and sixth-graders were grouped loosely behind Blaze. They shuffled, adjusted their belts, pulled self-consciously at their mittens, and mumbled to each other. The boys on both sides wore expressions of absurd casualness. The fight had not been called yet.

"What do you want, fucknuts?" Glen Hardy asked. His voice was phlegmy. It was the voice of a young god with a winter cold.

"Why did you hit Margie Thurlow in the shot?" Blaze asked.

"I felt like it."

"Okay," Blaze said, and waded in.

Glen hit him twice in the face—*whap-whap*—before he even got close, and blood began to pour out of Blaze's nose. Then Glen backed away, wanting to keep the advantage of his reach. People were yelling.

Blaze shook his head. Drops of blood flew, splattering the snow on either side and in front of him.

Glen was grinning. "State kid," he said. "State kid, shit-for-brains state kid." He hit Blaze in the middle of Blaze's dented forehead and his grin faltered as pain exploded up his arm. Blaze's forehead was very hard, dented or not.

For a moment he forgot to back up and Blaze shot his fist out. He didn't use his body; he just used his arm like a piston. His knuckles connected with Glen's mouth. Glen screamed as his lips burst against his teeth and began to bleed. The yelling intensified.

Glen tasted his own blood and forgot about backing up. He forgot about taunting the ugly kid with the busted forehead. He just waded in, swinging roundhouse punches from port and starboard.

Blaze set his feet and met him. Faintly, from far away, he heard the shouts and exhortations of his classmates. They reminded him of the yapping Collies in the dogpen on the day he realized that Randy wasn't going to sheer off.

Glen got in at least three good blows, and Blaze's head rocked with them. He gasped, inhaling blood. He heard ringing in his ears. His own fist shot out again, and he felt the jolt all the way up to his shoulder. All at once the blood on Glen's mouth was spread on his chin and cheeks, too. Glen spat out a tooth. Blaze struck again, in the same place. Glen howled. He sounded like a little kid with his fingers caught in a door. He stopped swinging. His mouth was a ruin. Mrs. Foster was running toward them. Her skirt was flying, her knees were pumping, and she was blowing her little silver whistle.

Blaze's arm hurt real bad where the nurse had shot him, and his fist hurt, and his head hurt, but he struck out again, desperately hard, with a hand that felt numb and dead. It was the same hand he had used on Randy, and he struck as hard as he had that day in the pen. The blow caught Glen flush on the point of the chin. It made an audible *snap* sound that silenced the other children. Glen stood slackly, his eyes rolled up to whites. Then his knees unhinged and he collapsed in a heap.

I killed him, Blaze thought. Oh Jeez, I killed him like Randy.

But then Glen began to stir around and mutter in the back of his throat, like people do in their sleep. And Mrs. Foster was screaming at Blaze to go inside. As he went, Blaze heard her telling Peter Lavoie to go to the office and get the First Aid kit, to *run*.

He was sent from school. Suspended. They stopped the bleeding of his nose with an ice-pack, put a Band-Aid on his ear, and then sent him to walk the four miles back to the dog-farm. He got a little way down the road, then remembered his bag lunch. Mrs. Bowie always sent him with a slice of peanut-butter-bread folded over and an apple. It wasn't much, but it would be a long walk, and as John Cheltzman said, something beat nothing every day of the week.

They wouldn't let him in when he came back, but Margie Thurlow brought it out to him. Her eyes were still red from crying. She looked like she wanted to say something but didn't know how. Blaze knew how that felt and smiled at her to show it was all right. She smiled back. One of his eyes was swelled almost shut, so he looked at her with the other one.

When he got to the edge of the schoolyard, he looked back to see her some more, but she was gone.

"Go out t'shed," Bowie said.

"No."

Bowie's eyes widened. He shook his head a little, as if to clear it. "What did you say?"

"You shouldn't want to whip me."

"I'll be the judge of that. Get out in that shed."

"No."

Bowie advanced on him. Blaze backed up two feet and then balled up his swollen fist. He set his feet. Bowie stopped. He had seen Randy. Randy's neck had been broken like a cedar branch after a hard freeze.

"Go up to your room, you stupid sonofabitch," he said.

Blaze went. He sat on the side of his bed. From there he could hear Bowie hollering into the telephone. He figured he knew who Bowie was hollering at.

He didn't care. He didn't care. But when he thought of Margie Thurlow, he cared. When he thought of Margie he wanted to cry, the way he sometimes wanted to cry when he saw one bird sitting all by itself on a telephone wire. He didn't. He read *Oliver Twist* instead. He knew it by heart; he could even say the words he didn't know. Outside, the dogs yapped. They were hungry. It was their feeding time. No one called him to feed them, though he would have, if asked.

He read *Oliver Twist* until the station wagon from HH came for him. The Law was driving. His eyes were red with fury. His mouth was nothing but a stitch between his chin and his nose. The Bowies stood together in the long shadows of a January dusk and watched them drive off.

When they got to Hetton House, Blaze felt an awful sense of familiarity fall over him. It felt like a wet shirt. He had to bite his tongue to keep from crying out. Three months and nothing had changed. HH was the same pile of red and everlasting shit-brick. The same windows threw the same yellow light onto the ground outside, only now the ground was covered with snow. In the spring the snow would be gone but the light would be the same.

In his office, The Law produced The Paddle. Blaze could have taken it away from him, but he was tired of fighting. And he guessed there was always someone bigger, with a bigger paddle.

After The Law had finished exercising his arm, Blaze was sent to the common bedroom in Fuller Hall. John Cheltzman was standing by the door. One of his eyes was a slit of swelling purple flesh.

"Yo, Blaze," he said.

"Yo, Johnny. Where's your specs?"

"Busted," he said. Then cried: "Blaze, they broke my glasses! Now I can't read anything!"

Blaze thought about this. He was sad to be here, but it meant a lot to find Johnny waiting. "We'll fix em." An idea struck him. "Or we'll get shovel-chores in town after the next storm and save for new ones."

"Could we do that, do you think?"

"Sure. You got to see to help me with my homework, don't you?"

"Sure, Blaze, sure."

They went inside together.

CHAPTER 10

Apex Center was a wide place in the road boasting a barber shop, a VFW hall, a hardware store, The Apex Pentecostal Church of the Holy Spirit, a beer-store, and a yellow blinker-light. It was walking distance from the shack, and Blaze went down there the morning after he held up Tim & Janet's Quik-Pik for the second time. His goal was Apex Hardware, a scurgy little independent where he bought an aluminum extension ladder for thirty dollars, plus tax. It had a red tag on it saying PRICED 2 SELL.

He carried it back up the road, tromping stolidly along the plowed shoulder. He looked neither right nor left. It did not occur to him that his purchase might be remembered. George would have thought of it, but George was still away.

The ladder was too long for the trunk or the back seat of the stolen Ford, but it fit when he placed it with one end behind the driver's seat and the other jutting into the front passenger's seat. Once that was taken care of, he went into the house and turned the radio on to WJAB, which played until the sun went down.

"George?"

No answer. He made coffee, drank a cup, and lay down. He fell asleep with the radio on, playing "Phantom 409." When he woke up it was dark and the radio was just playing static. It was quarter past seven.

Blaze got up and fixed him some dinner—a bologna sandwich and a can of Dole pineapple chunks. He loved Dole pineapple chunks. He could eat them three times a day and never get his fill. He swallowed the syrup in three long gulps, then looked around. "George?"

No answer.

He prowled restlessly. He missed the TV. The radio wasn't company at night. If George was here, they could play cribbage. George always beat him because Blaze missed some of the runs and most of the fifteen-twos (they were Arithmetic), but it was fun charging up and down the board. Like being in a hoss-race. And if George didn't want to do that, they could always shuffle four decks of cards together and play War. George would play War half the night, drinking beer and talking about the Republicans and how they fucked the poor. (*"Why? I'll tell you why. For the same reason a dog licks his balls—because they can."*) But now there was nothing to do. George had showed him a solitaire game, but Blaze couldn't remember how it went. It was way too early to do the kidnapping. He hadn't thought to steal any comic-books or skin mags when he was in that store.

He finally settled down with an old issue of X-Men. George called the X-Men the Homo Core, as if they'd come from an apple, Blaze didn't know why.

He dozed off again at quarter to eight. When he woke up at eleven, he felt muzzy-headed and only halfway in the world. He could go now if he wanted—by the time he got to Ocoma Heights it would be past midnight—but all at once he didn't know if he wanted to. All at once it seemed very frightening. Very complicated. He had to think it over. Make plans. Maybe he could think of a way to get into the house on his own. Look it over. Make like he was from The Public Waterworks, or The Lectric Company. Draw out a map.

The empty cradle standing by the stove mocked him.

He fell asleep again and had an uneasy dream of running. He was chasing someone through deserted waterfront streets while seagulls whirled over the piers and warehouses in crying flocks. He didn't know if he was chasing George or John Cheltzman. And when he began to catch up a little and the figure looked back over one shoulder to grin mockingly at him, he saw it was neither one. It was Margie Thurlow.

When he woke, he was still sitting in the chair, still dressed, but the night was over. WJAB was on again. Henson Cargill was singing "Skip A Rope."

He got ready to go again the second night, but he didn't go. The day after that he went out and shoveled a long and senseless track toward the woods. He shoveled until he was winded and his mouth tasted like blood.

I'm going tonight, he thought, but the only place he went that night was to the local beer-store, to see if the new comic-books had come in. They had, and Blaze bought three. He fell asleep over the first one after supper, and when he woke it was midnight. He was getting up to go in the bathroom and take a leak—then he'd hit the rack—when George spoke.

"George?"

"Are you gutless, Blaze?"

"No! I ain't—"

"You been hanging around this place like a dog with its balls caught in a henhouse door."

"No! I ain't! I did lots of stuff. I got a good ladder—"

"Yeah, and some comic-books. You been havin a good time sittin around here, listenin to that shitkickin music and reading about superpower faggots, Blazer?"

Blaze muttered something.

"What did you say?"

"Nothing."

"I guess not, if you don't have the guts to say it out loud."

"All right—I said no one ast you to come back."

"Why you ungrateful lowlife sonofabitch."

"Listen, George, I—"

"I took care of you, Blaze. I admit it wasn't charity, you were good when you were used right, but it was me who knew how to do that. Did you forget? We didn't always have three squares a day, but we always had at least one. I saw that you changed your clothes and kept clean. Who told you to brush your fuckin teeth?"

"You did, George."

"Which you are now neglecting, by the way, and you're getting that Dead Mouse Mouth again."

Blaze smiled. He couldn't help it. George had a cute way of saying things.

"When you needed a whore, I got you one of those, too."

"Yeah, and one of em gave me the clap." For six weeks, peeing fit to kill him.

"Took you to the doctor, didn't I?"

"You did," Blaze admitted.

"You owe me this, Blaze."

"You didn't want me to do it!"

"Yeah, well I changed my mind. It was my plan, and you owe me."

Blaze considered this. As always, it took him a long and painful time. Then he burst out: "How can you owe a dead man? If people walked by, they'd hear me talkin to myself and answerin myself back and think I was crazy! I prob'ly *am* crazy!" Another idea occurred to him. "You can't do nothing with your cut! You're dead!"

"And you're alive? Sittin here, listenin to the radio playin those numbfuck cowboy songs? Readin comic-books and beatin your meat?"

Blaze blushed and looked at the floor.

"Forget and rob that same store every third or fourth week till they stake the place out and catch your ass? Sit here lookin at that numbfuck crib and sweetmother cradle in the sweet fuckin meanwhile?"

"I'm gonna chop the cradle up for kinnelin."

"Look at you," George said, and what was in his voice

sounded beyond sadness. It sounded like grief. "Same pants on every day for two weeks? Piss-stains in your underwear? You need a shave and you need a fuckin haircut in the worst way . . . sittin here in this shack in the middle of the mumblefuck woods. This ain't the way we roll. Don't you see that?"

"You went away," Blaze said.

"Because you were actin stupid. But this is stupider. You have to take your chance or you're gonna fall. You'll do five years here, six there, then they'll get you on three-strikes and you'll sit in The Shank for the rest of your life. Just a two-bit dummy who didn't know enough to brush his teeth or change his own socks. Just another crumb on the floor."

"Then tell me what to do, George."

"Go ahead with the plot, that's what you do."

"But if I get caught, it's the long bomb. Life." It had been preying on his mind more than he wanted to admit.

"That's gonna happen to you anyway, the way you're goin—ain't you been listenin to me? And hey! You'll be doin him a favor. Even if he don't remember it—which he won't—he'll have something he can blow off his bazoo about to his country club friends for the rest of his life. And the people you'll be rippin off, they stole the money them-selves, only like Woody Guthrie says, with a fountain pen instead of a gun."

"What if I get caught?"

"You won't. If you run into trouble with the money—if it's marked—you go on down to Boston and find Billy O'Shea. But the main thing is you just got to wake up."

"When should I do it, George? When?"

"When you wake up. When you wake up. Wake up. *Wake up!*"

Blaze woke up. He was in the chair. All the comic-books were on the floor and his shoes were on. *Oh George.*

He got up and looked at the cheap clock on top of the refrigerator. It was quarter past one. There was a soap-spotted mirror on one wall and he bent down so he could see himself. His face looked haunted.

He put on his coat and hat and a pair of mittens and went out to the shed. The ladder was still in the car but the car hadn't been running for three days and it cranked a long time before it started.

He got in behind the wheel. "Here I go, George. I'm gonna roll."

There was no answer. Blaze twisted his cap to the good-luck side and backed out of the shed. He made a three-point turn and then drove down to the road. He was on his way.

CHAPTER 11

There was no problem parking in Ocoma Heights, even though it was well patrolled by the fuzz. George had worked out this part of the plan months before he died. This part had been the seed.

There was a big condo tower opposite the Gerard estate and about a quarter of a mile up the road. Oakwood was nine stories high, its apartments inhabited by the working well-to-do—the *very* well-to-do—whose business interests lay in Portland, Portsmouth, and Boston. There was a gated visitors' parking lot on one side. When Blaze pulled up to the gate, a man stepped out of the little booth, zipping up a parka.

"Who are you calling on, sir?"

"Mr. Joseph Carlton," Blaze said.

"Yes, sir," the attendant said. He seemed unruffled by the fact that it was now nearly two in the morning. "Will you need a buzz-up?"

Blaze shook his head and showed the parking attendant a red plastic card. It had been George's. If the attendant said he would have to call upstairs—if he even looked suspicious—Blaze would know the card was no longer any good, that they had changed colors or something, and he would haul ass out of there.

The attendant, however, only nodded and went back into his booth. A moment later, the gate-arm swung up and Blaze drove into the lot.

There was no Joseph Carlton, at least Blaze didn't think there was. George said the apartment on the eighth floor was a playpen leased by some guys from Boston, guys he called Irish Smarties. Sometimes the Irish Smarties had meetings there. Sometimes they met girls who "did variations," according to George. Mostly they played cutthroat poker. George had been to half a dozen of those games. He got in because he had grown up with one of the Smarties, a prematurely gray mobster named Billy O'Shea with frog eyes and bluish lips. Billy O'Shea called George Raspy, because of his voice, or sometimes just Rasp. Sometimes George and Billy O'Shea talked about the nuns and the fadders.

Blaze had been to two of these high-stakes games with George, and could barely believe the amount of money on the table. At one, George had won five thousand dollars. At another he had lost two. It was Oakwood being near to the Gerard estate that had gotten George thinking seriously about the Gerard money and the small Gerard heir.

The visitors' parking lot was black and deserted. Plowed snow glittered under the single arc sodium light. The snow was heaped high against the Cyclone fence that divided the parking lot from the four acres of deserted parkland on the other side.

Blaze got out of the Ford, went around to the back door,

and pulled out his ladder. He was in action, and that was better. When he was moving, his doubts were forgotten.

He threw the ladder over the Cyclone fence. It landed silently, in a snowy dreampuff. He scrambled after, caught his pants on a jutting wire strand, and went tumbling head-first into snow that was three feet deep. It was stunning, exhilarating. He thrashed for a moment, and made an inadvertent snow-angel getting up.

He hooked an arm into his ladder and began to trudge toward the main road. He wanted to come out opposite the Gerard place, and he was concentrating on that. He wasn't thinking about the tracks he was leaving—the distinctive waffle tread of his Army boots. George might have thought of it, but George wasn't there.

He paused at the road and looked both ways. Nothing was coming. On the other side, a snow-hooded hedge stood between him and the darkened house.

He ran across the road, hunched over as if that would hide him, and heaved the ladder over the hedge. He was about to wade through himself, just bulling a path, when some light—the nearest streetlamp or perhaps only starglow—traced a silvery gleam running through the denuded branches. He peered closer and felt his heart bump.

It was a wire strung on slim metal stakes. Three-quarters of the way up each stake, the wire ran through a porcelain conductor. An electrified wire, then, just like in the Bowies' cow pasture. It would probably buzz anyone who came in contact with it hard enough to make them pee in their pants and set off an alarm at the same time. The chauffeur or the butler or whoever would call the cops, and that would be that. Over-done-with-gone.

"George?" he whispered.

Somewhere—up the road?—a voice whispered: "Jump the fucker."

He backed off—still nothing coming on the road in either direction—and ran at the hedge. A second before he got there his legs bunched and thrust him upward in an awkward, rolling broad-jump. He scraped through the top of the hedge and landed sprawling in the snow beside his ladder. His leg, lightly scratched coming over the Oakwood Cyclone fence, left droplets of type AB-negative blood on both the snow and several branches of the hedge.

Blaze picked himself up and took stock. The house was a hundred yards away. Behind it was a smaller building. Maybe a garage or a guest house. Maybe even servants' quarters. In between was a wide snowfield. He would be easily observed there, if anyone was awake. Blaze shrugged. If they were, they were. There was nothing he could do about it.

He grabbed the ladder and trotted toward the protect-ing shadows of the house. When he got there he crouched down, getting his breath back and looking for any signs of alarm. He saw none. The house slumbered.

There were dozens of windows upstairs. Which one? If he and George had figured this out—if he had known—he had forgotten. Blaze laid his hand against the brick as if expecting it to breathe. He peered into the nearest window and saw a large, gleaming kitchen. It looked like the con-

trol room of the Starship *Enterprise*. A nightlight over the
stove cast a soft glow across Formica and tile. Blaze wiped
his palm across his mouth. Indecision was trying to crowd
in, and he went back to get the ladder to forestall it. Any
action, even the most trivial. He was trembling.

This is life! a voice inside him screamed. *For this they give
you the long bomb! There's still time, you can still—*

"Blaze."

He almost cried out.

"Any window. If you don't remember, you'll have to
creep the joint."

"I can't, George. I'll knock something over . . . they'll
hear and come and shoot me . . . or . . ."

"Blaze, you got to. It's the only thing."

"I'm scared, George. I want to go home."

No answer. But in a way, that *was* the answer.

Breathing in harsh, muffled grunts that sent out clouds
of vapor, he unhooked the latches that held the ladder's
extension and pulled it to its greatest length. His fingers,
clumsy in the mittens, had to fumble twice to secure the
latches again. He had threshed about a great deal in the
snow now, and he was white from head to toe—a snowman,
a Yeti. There was even a little snowdrift on the bill of his
cap, still twisted to the good-luck side. Yet except for the
click-clunk of the latches and the soft plosives of his breathing, it was quiet. The snow muffled everything.

The ladder was aluminum, and light. He raised it easily.
The top rung reached to just below the window over the
kitchen. He would be able to reach the catch on that window from two or three rungs farther down.

He began to climb, shaking off snow as he went. The ladder settled once, making him freeze and hold his breath, but then it was solid. He started up again. He watched the bricks go down in front of him, then the windowsill. Then he was looking in a bedroom window.

There was a double bed. Two people slept in it. Their faces were nothing but white circles. Just blurs, really.

Blaze stared in at them, amazed. His fear was forgotten. For no reason he could understand—he wasn't feeling sexy, or at least he didn't think he was—he started getting a hardon. He had no doubt that he was looking at Joseph Gerard III and his wife. He was staring at them but they didn't know it. He was looking right into their world. He could see their bureaus, their nightstands, their big double bed. He could see a big full-length mirror with himself in it, looking in from out here where it was cold. He was looking in at them and they didn't know it. His body shook with excitement.

He tore his eyes away and looked at the window's inside catch. It was a simple little slip-lock, easy enough to open with the right tool, what George would have called a gimme. Of course Blaze didn't have the right tool, but he wouldn't need one. The lock wasn't engaged.

They're fat, Blaze thought. They're fat, stupid Republicans. I may be dumb, but they're stupid.

Blaze placed his feet as far apart on the ladder as they would go, to increase his leverage, then began to apply pressure to the window, increasing it gradually. The man in the bed shifted from one side to the other in his sleep and Blaze paused until Gerard had settled back into the rut of his dreams. Then he put the pressure back on.

He was beginning to think that maybe the window had been sealed shut somehow—that that was why the lock wasn't engaged—when it came open the tiniest crack. The wood groaned softly. Blaze let up immediately.

He considered.

It would have to be fast: open the window, climb through, close the window again. Otherwise the inrush of cold January air would wake them for sure. But if the sliding window really squalled against the frame, that would wake them up, too.

"Go on," George said from the base of the ladder. "Take your best shot."

Blaze wriggled his fingers into the crack between the bottom of the window and the jamb, then lifted. The window rose without a sound. He swung a leg inside, followed it with his body, turned, and closed the window. It *did* groan coming back down, and *thumped* into place. He froze in a crouch, afraid to turn and look at the bed, ears attuned to catch the slightest sound.

Nothing.

But oh yes there was. Yes, there were plenty. Breathing, for instance. Two people breathing nearly together, as if they were riding a bicycle built for two. Tiny mattress creaks. The tick of a clock. The low whoosh of air—that would be the furnace. And the house itself, exhaling. Running down as it had been for fifty or seventy-five years. Hell, maybe a hundred. Settling on its bones of brick and wood.

Blaze turned around and looked at them. The woman was uncovered to the waist. The top of her nightgown had pulled to the side and one breast was exposed. Blaze looked at it, fascinated by the rise and fall, by the way the nipple had peaked in the brief draft—

"Move, Blaze! Christ!"

He high-stepped across the room like a caricature lover who has hidden under the bed, his breath held and his chest puffed out like a cartoon colonel's.

Gold gleamed.

There was a small triptych on one of the bureaus, three photos bound in gold and shaped like a pyramid. On the bottom were Joe Gerard III and his olive-skinned Narmenian wife. Above them was IV, a hairless infant with a baby blanket pulled to his chin. His dark eyes were popped open to look at the world he had so lately entered.

Blaze reached the door, turned the knob, and paused to look back. She had flung one arm across her bared breast, hiding it. Her husband was sleeping on his back with his mouth open, and for a moment, before he snorted thickly and wrinkled his nose, he looked dead. This made Blaze think of Randy, and how Randy had lain on the frozen ground with the fleas and ticks leaving his body.

Beyond the bed, there was a splotched sugaring of snow on the inside window ledge and on the floor. Both were already melting.

Blaze eased the door open, ready to halt at the first hint of a squeak, but there was no squeak. He slipped through to the other side as soon as the gap was wide enough. Outside was a kind of combination hallway and gallery. There was a thick, lovely carpet under his feet. He closed the bedroom door behind him, approached the darker darkness of the railing that went around the gallery, and looked down.

He saw a staircase that rose in two graceful twists from a wide entrance hall that went out of sight. The polished floor threw up scant, glimmering light. Across the way was a statue of a young woman. Facing her, on this side of the balcony, was a statue of a young man.

"Never mind the statues, Blaze, find the kid. That ladder's standin right out there—"

One of the two staircases went down to the first floor on his right, so Blaze turned left and padded up the hall. Out here there was no sound but the faint whisper of his feet on the rug. He couldn't even hear the furnace. It was eerie.

He eased the next door open and looked into a room with a desk in the middle and books on the walls—shelves and shelves of books. There was a typewriter on the desk and a pile of papers held down by a chunk of black glassy-looking rock. There was a portrait on the wall. Blaze could make out a man with white hair and a frowning face that seemed to be saying *You thief*. He closed the door and went on.

The next door opened on an empty bedroom with a canopy bed. Its coverlet looked tight enough to bounce nickels on.

He moved up the line, feeling trickles of sweat start on his body. He was hardly ever conscious of time passing, but now he was. How long had he been in this rich and sleeping house? Fifteen minutes? Twenty?

The third room was occupied by another sleeping man and woman. She was moaning in her sleep, and Blaze closed that door quickly.

He went around the corner. What if he had to go up-stairs, to the third floor? The idea filled him with the kind of terror he felt in his infrequent nightmares (these were usually of Hetton House, or the Bowies). What would he say if the lights went on right now and he was caught? What could he say? That he came in to steal the silverware? There was no silverware on the second floor, even a dummy knew that.

There was one door on the short side of the hallway. He opened it and looked into the baby's room.

He stared for a long moment, hardly believing he had gotten so far. It wasn't a pipe dream. He could do it. The thought made him want to run.

The crib was almost exactly like the one he had bought himself. There were Walt Disney characters on the walls. There was a changing table, a rack crowded with creams and ointments, and a little baby dresser painted some bright color. Maybe red, maybe blue. Blaze couldn't tell in the dark. There was a baby in the crib.

It was his last chance to run and he knew it. As of now, he might still be able to melt away as unknown as he had come. They would never guess what had almost happened. But he would know. Perhaps he would go in and lay one of his big hands on the baby's small forehead, then leave. He had a sudden picture of himself twenty years from now, seeing Joseph Gerard IV's name on the society page of the paper, what George called news of rich bitches and whinny-ing horses. There would be a picture of a young man in a dinner jacket standing next to a young girl in a white dress. The young girl would be holding a bouquet of flowers. The story would tell where they had been married and where they were going on their honeymoon. He would look at that picture and he would think: *Oh buddy. Oh buddy, you never had no idea.*

But when he went in, he knew it was for keeps.

This is how we roll, George, he thought.

The baby was sleeping on his stomach, head turned to the side. One small hand was tucked under his cheek. His breathing moved the blankets over him up and down in small cycles. His skull was covered with a fuzz of hair, no more than that. A red teething ring lay beside him on the pillow.

Blaze reached for him, then pulled back.

What if he cried?

At the same instant he spotted something that brought his heart into his mouth. It was a small intercom set. The other end would be in the mother's room, or the babysitter's room. If the baby cried—

Gently, gently, Blaze reached out and pushed the power button. The red light over it died out. As it did, he wondered if there was a buzzer or something that went off when the power went off. As a warning.

Attention, mother. Attention, babysitter. The intercom is on the blink because a big stupid kidnapper just turned it off. There is a stupid kidnapper in the house. Come and see. Bring a gun.

Go on, Blaze. Take your best shot.

Blaze took a deep breath and let it out. Then he untucked the blankets and scooped them around the baby as he picked him up. He cradled him gently in his arms. The baby whined and stretched. His eyes flickered. He made a kitteny *neeyup* sound. Then his eyes closed again and his body relaxed.

Blaze exhaled.

He turned, went back to the door, and went back into the hall, realizing he was doing more than just leaving the kid's room, the nursery. He was crossing a line. He could no longer claim to be a simple burglar. His crime was in his arms.

Going down the ladder with a sleeping infant was impossible, and Blaze did not even consider it. He went to the stairs. The hallway was carpeted, but the stairs weren't. His first footfall on the first polished wood riser was loud, obvious, and unmuffled. He paused, listening, drawn straight to attention in his anxiety, but the house slept on.

Now, though, his nerves began to unravel. The baby seemed to gain weight in his arms. Panic nibbled at his will. He could almost glimpse movement in the corners of his eyes—first one side, then the other. At each step he expected the baby to stir and cry. And once it started, its wails would wake the house.

"George—" he muttered.

"Walk," George said from below him. "Just like in the old joke. Walk, don't run. Toward the sound of my voice, Blazer."

Blaze began to walk down the stairs. It was impossible to be soundless, but at least none of his steps was as loud as that horrible first one. The baby joggled. He couldn't hold him perfectly still, no matter how he tried. So far the kid was still sleeping, but any minute, any *second*—

He counted. Five steps. Six. Seven. Eighter from Decatur. It was a very long staircase. Made, he supposed, for colorful cunts to sweep up and down at big dances like in *Gone with the Wind*. Seventeen. Eighteen. Nine—

It was the last step and his unprepared foot came down hard again: *Clack!* The baby's head jerked. It gave a single cry. The sound was very loud in the stillness.

A light went on upstairs.

Blaze's eyes widened. Adrenaline shot into his chest and belly, making him stiffen and squeeze the baby to him. He made himself loosen up—a little—and stepped into the shadow of the staircase. There he stood still, his face twisted in fear and horror.

"Mike?" a sleepy voice called.

Slippers shuffled to the railing just overhead.

"Mikey-Mike, is that you? Is it you, you bad thing?" The voice was directly overhead, speaking in a stage-whispery, others-are-sleeping tone. It was an old voice, querulous. "Go in the kitchen and see the nice saucer of milk Mama left out." A pause. "If you knock over a vase, Mama will spank."

If the kid cried now—

The voice over Blaze's head muttered something too full of phlegm for him to make out, and then the slippers shuffled away. There was a pause—it felt like a hundred years long—and then a door clicked softly shut, closing away the light.

Blaze stood still, trying to control his need to tremble. Trembling might wake the kid. Probably *would* wake the kid. Which way was the kitchen? How was he going to take the ladder and the kid both? What about the electric wire? *What—how—where—*

He moved in order to stifle the questions, creeping up the hall, bent over the wrapped child like a hag with a bindle. He saw double glass doors standing ajar. Waxed tiles glimmered beyond. Blaze pushed through and was in a dining room.

It was a rich room, the mahogany table meant to hold twenty-pound turkeys at Thanksgiving and steaming roasts on Sunday afternoons. China glowed behind the glass doors of a tall, fancy dresser. Blaze passed on like a wraith, not pausing, but even so, the sight of the great table and the chairs with their soldierly high backs awoke a smoldering resentment in his breast. Once he had scrubbed kitchen floors on his knees, and George said there were lots more just like him. Not just in Africa, either. George said people like the Gerards pretended people like him weren't there. Well let them put a doll in that crib upstairs and pretend it was a real baby. Let them pretend that, if they were so good at pretending.

There was a swing door at the far end of the dining room. He went through it. Then he was in the kitchen. Looking out the frost-jeweled window next to the stove, he could see the legs of his ladder.

He looked around for a place to lay the baby while he opened the window. The counters were wide, but maybe not wide enough. And he didn't like the idea of putting a kid on the stove even if the stove was turned off.

His eye lit on an old-fashioned market basket hanging from a hook on the pantry door. It looked roomy enough, and it had a handle. It had high sides, too. He took it down and put it on a small wheeled serving cart standing against one wall. He tucked the baby into it. The baby stirred only slightly.

Now the window. Blaze lifted it, and was confronted with a storm window beyond that. There had been no storm windows upstairs, but this one was screwed right into the frame.

He began opening cupboards. In the one below the sink, he found a neat pile of dishwipers. He took one out. It had an American eagle on it. Blaze wrapped his mittened hand in it and punched out the storm window's lower pane. It shattered with relative quiet, leaving a large, jagged hole. Blaze began to poke out the pieces that pointed in toward the center like big glass arrows.

"Mike?" That same voice. Calling softly. Blaze stiffened. That wasn't coming from upstairs. That was—

"Mikey, what did you-ums knock over?"

—from down the hall and coming closer—

"You'll wake the whole house, you bad boy."

—and closer—

"I'm going to put you down cellar before you spoil it for yourself."

The door swung open, and a silhouette woman entered behind a battery-powered nightlight in the shape of a candle. Blaze got a blurred impression of an elderly woman, walking slowly, trying to preserve the silence like juggled eggs. She was in rollers; her head, in silhouette, looked like something out of a science fiction movie. Then she saw him.

"Who—" That one word. Then the part of her brain that dealt with emergencies, old but not dead, decided talking wasn't the right thing in this situation. She drew in breath to scream.

Blaze hit her. He hit her as hard as he had hit Randy, as hard as he had hit Glen Hardy. He didn't think about it; he was startled into it. The old lady folded to the floor with her nightlight beneath her. There was a muffled tinkle as the bulb shattered. Her body lay twisted half-in and half-out of the swing door.

There was a low and plaintive *miaow*. Blaze grunted and looked up. Green eyes peered down at him from the top of the refrigerator.

Blaze turned back to the window and batted out the rest of the glass shards. When they were gone, he stepped out through the hole he'd made in the lower half of the storm window and listened.

Nothing.

Yet.

Shattered glass glittered on the snow like a felon's dream.

Blaze pulled the ladder away from the building, freed the latches, lowered it. It gave out a terrifying ratcheting sound that made him feel like screaming. Once the latches were hooked again, he picked the ladder up and began to run. He came out of the house's shadow and was halfway across the lawn when he realized he had forgotten the baby. It was still on the serving cart. All sensation left the arm holding the ladder and it plopped into the snow. He turned and looked back.

There was a light on upstairs.

For a moment Blaze was two people. One of them was just sprinting for the road—*balls to the wall,* George would have said—and the other was going back to the house. For a moment he couldn't make up his mind. Then he went back, moving fast, his boots kicking up little puffs of snow.

He slit his mitten and cut the flesh of his palm on a shard of glass that was still sticking out of the window-frame. He barely felt it. Then he was inside again, grabbing the basket, swinging it dangerously, almost spilling the baby out.

Upstairs, a toilet flushed like thunder.

He lowered the basket to the snow and went after it without a backward glance at the inert form on the floor behind him. He picked the basket up and just *booked*.

He stopped long enough to get the ladder under one arm. Then he ran to the hedge. There he stopped to look at the baby. The baby was still sleeping peacefully. Joe IV was unaware he had been uprooted. Blaze looked back at the house. The upstairs light had gone out again.

He sat the basket down on the snow and tossed the ladder over the hedge. A moment later, lights bloomed on the highway.

What if it was a cop? Jesus, what if?

He lay down in the shadow of the hedge, very aware of how clearly his footprints back and forth across the lawn must show. They were the only ones there.

The headlights swelled, held bright for a moment, then faded without slowing down.

Blaze got up, picked up his basket—it was his basket now—and walked to the hedge. By parting the top with his arm he was able to lift the basket over and put it down on the far side. He just couldn't lower it all the way. He had to drop it the last couple of feet. It thudded softly into the snow. The baby found his thumb and began to suck it. Blaze could see his mouth pursing and relaxing in the glow of the nearest streetlight. Pursing and relaxing. Almost like a fish-mouth. The night's deep cold had not touched it yet. Nothing peeked out of its blankets but its head and that one tiny hand.

Blaze jumped the hedge, got his ladder, and picked up the basket again. He crossed the road in a hurried crouch. Then he moved across the field on his earlier diagonal path. At the Cyclone fence surrounding the Oakwood parking lot, he put the ladder up again (it wasn't necessary to extend it this time), and carried his basket to the top.

He straddled the fence with the basket balanced across his straining legs, aware that if his scissors-lock slipped, his balls were going to get the surprise of their life. He jerked the ladder up in one smooth pull, gasping at the added strain on his legs. It teetered for a moment, overbalanced, then fell back down on the parking lot side. He wondered if anyone was watching him up here, but that was a stupid thing to wonder about. There was nothing he could do about it if someone was. He could feel the cut on his hand now. It throbbed.

He straightened the ladder, then balanced the basket on the top rung, steadying it with one hand while he swung carefully onto a lower rung. The ladder shifted a little, and he paused. Then it held still.

He went down the ladder with the basket. At the bottom, he crooked the ladder under one arm again and crossed to where the Ford was parked.

He put the baby on the passenger seat, opened the back door, and worked the ladder inside. Then he got in behind the wheel.

But he couldn't find the key. It wasn't in either of his pants pockets. Not in his coat pockets, either. He was afraid he had lost it falling down and would have to go back over the fence to look for it when he saw it poking out of the ignition. He had forgotten to take it along. He hoped George hadn't seen that part. If George hadn't, Blaze wouldn't tell him. Never in a million years.

He started the car and put the basket in the passenger footwell. Then he drove back to the little booth. The guard came out. "Leaving early, sir?"

"Bad cards," Blaze said.

"It happens to the best of us. Good night, sir. Better luck next time."

"Thanks," Blaze said.

He stopped at the road, looked both ways, then turned toward Apex. He carefully observed all the speed limits, but he never saw a police car.

Just as he was pulling into his own driveway, baby Joe woke up and started to cry.

CHAPTER 12

Once back at Hetton House, Blaze caused no trouble. He kept his head down and his mouth shut. The boys who had been big 'uns when he and John had been little 'uns either made out, went out to work, went away to vocational schools, or joined the Army. Blaze grew another three inches. Hair sprouted on his chest and grew lushly on his crotch. This made him the envy of the other boys. He went to Freeport High School. It was all right, because they didn't make him do Arithmetic.

Martin Coslaw's contract was renewed, and he watched Blaze come and go unsmilingly, watchfully. He did not call Blaze into his office again, although Blaze knew he could. And if The Law told him to bend over and take the paddle, Blaze knew he would do it. The alternative was North Windham Training Center, which was a formatory. He had heard that in the formatory boys were actually whipped— like on ships—and sometimes put in a little metal box called The Tin. Blaze didn't know if these things were true, and had no wish to find out. What he knew was he was afraid of the formatory.

But The Law never called him in to be paddled, and Blaze never gave him cause. He went to school five days a week, and his chief contact with the Head became The Law's voice, bellowing over the intercoms first thing in the morning and before lights-out at night. At Hetton House the day always began with what Martin Coslaw called a homily (*homily grits,* John sometimes said when he was feeling funny) and ended with a Bible verse.

Life moved along. He could have become the King of the Boys if he had wished, but he did not wish. He wasn't a leader. He was the farthest thing from a leader. He tried to be nice to people, though. He tried to be nice to them even when he was warning them he would crack their skulls open if they didn't lay off his friend Johnny. Pretty soon after Blaze came back, they did lay off him.

Then, on a summer night when Blaze was fourteen (and looking six years older in the right light), something happened.

The boys were hauled to town on an ancient yellow bus every Friday, assuming that as a group they didn't have too many DDs—discipline demerits. Some would just wander aimlessly up and down Main Street, or sit in the town square, or go up an alley to smoke cigarettes. There was a pool hall, but it was off-limits to them. There was also a second-run movie theater, the Nordica, and those boys who had enough money to buy a ticket could go in and see how Jack Nicholson, Warren Beatty, or Clint Eastwood looked when those gentlemen were younger. Some of the boys earned their money delivering papers. Some mowed lawns in the summer and shoveled snow in the winter. Some had jobs at HH itself.

Blaze had become one of those. He was the size of a

man—a big one—and the chief custodian hired him to do chores and odd jobs. Martin Coslaw might have objected, but Frank Therriault didn't answer to that priss. He liked Blaze's broad shoulders. A quiet man himself, Therriault also liked Blaze's way of saying yes and no and not much more. The boy didn't mind heavy work, either. He'd lug packs of Bird shingles up a ladder or hundred-pound sacks of cement all afternoon. He'd move classroom furniture and filing cabinets up and down stairs, not saying boo to a goose. And there was no quit in him. Best thing? He seemed perfectly happy with a dollar-sixty an hour, which allowed Therriault to pocket an extra sixty bucks a week. Eventually he bought his wife a swanky cashmere sweater. It had a boat neck. She was delighted.

Blaze was delighted, too. He was making a cool thirty bucks a week, which was more than enough to pay for the movies, plus all the popcorn, candy, and soda he could put away. He bought John's ticket, too, cheerfully, as a matter of course. He would have been happy to throw in all the usual snacks, as well, but for John the movie was usually enough. He watched greedily, his mouth agape.

Back at Hetton, John was beginning to write stories. They were stumbling things, cribbed from the movies he watched with Blaze, but they began to earn him a certain popularity with his peers. The other boys didn't like you to be smart, but they admired a certain kind of cleverness. And they liked stories. They were hungry for stories.

On one of their trips they saw a vampire movie called *Second Coming*. John Cheltzman's version of this classic ended with Count Igor Yorga ripping the head from a half-clad young lovely with "quakeing breasts the size of watermelons" and jumping into the River Yorba with the head under his arm. The strangely patriotic name of this underground classic was *The Eyes of Yorga Are Upon You*.

But this night John didn't want to go, even though another horror movie was playing. He had the runs. He'd been five times that morning and afternoon despite half a bottle of Pepto from the infirmary (a glorified closet on the second floor). He thought he wasn't done, either.

"Come on," Blaze urged. "The Nordica's got a terrific crapper downstairs. I took a shit there once myself. We'll stick real close to it."

Thus persuaded, despite the dire rumblings in his vitals, John went with Blaze and got on the bus. They sat up front, behind the driver. They were almost the big 'uns now, after all.

John was okay during the previews, but just as the Warner Bros logo was coming on, he stood up, slid past Blaze, and started up the aisle in a crabwise walk. Blaze was sympathetic, but that was life. He turned his attention back to the screen where a dust storm was blowing around in what looked like the Desert of Maine, only with pyramids. Soon he was deeply involved in the story, frowning with concentration.

When John sat back down beside him, he was hardly aware of him until John started yanking his sleeve and whispering, "Blaze! *Blaze!* F'God sakes, Blaze!"

Blaze came out of the movie like a sound sleeper waking from a nap. "Whats'sa matter? You sick? You shit yourself?"

"No . . . no. Look at this!"

Blaze peered at what John was holding just below seat-level. It was a wallet.

"Hey! Where'd you—"

"Shh!" Somebody in front of them hissed.

"—get *that*?" Blaze finished in a whisper.

"In the men's!" John whispered back. He was trembling with excitement. "It musta fallen out of some guy's pants when he sat down to take a dump! There's money in it! Lots of money!"

Blaze took the wallet, holding it well out of sight. He opened the bill compartment. He felt his stomach drop. Then it seemed to bounce, and cram itself halfway up his throat. The bill compartment was full of dough. One, two, three fifty-dollar bills. Four twenties. Couple of fives. Some ones.

"I can't count it all up," he whispered. "How much?"

John's voice rose in slightly awed triumph, but it went unnoticed. The monster was after a girl in brown shorts and the audience was happily screaming. "Two hundred and forty-eight bucks!"

"Jesus," Blaze said. "You still got that rip in the linin of your coat?"

"Sure."

"Put it in there. They may frisk us goin out."

But no one did. And John's runs were cured. Finding that much money seemed to have scared the shit out of him.

John bought a Portland *Press Herald* from Stevie Ross, who had a paper route, on Monday morning. He and Blaze went out behind the toolshed and opened it to the classified ads.

John said that was the place to look. The lost and founds were on page 38. And there, between a LOST French Poodle and a FOUND pair of women's gloves, was the following item:

LOST A man's black leather wallet
with the initials RKF stamped beside
the photo compartment. If found, call
555-0928 or write Box 595 care of this
newspaper. REWARD OFFERED.

"Reward!" Blaze exclaimed, and punched John on the shoulder.

"Yeah," John said. He rubbed where Blaze had punched. "So we call the guy and he gives us ten bucks plus a pat on the head. BFD." This stood for big fucking deal.

"Oh." The word REWARD had been standing in letters of gold two feet high in Blaze's mind. Now they collapsed to a pile of leaden rubble. "Then what should we do with it?"

It was the first time he had really looked to Johnny for leadership. The two hundred and forty-eight bucks was a mystifying problem. If you had two bits, you bought a Coke. Two bucks got you into the movies. Going further now, struggling, Blaze supposed you could ride the bus all the way to Portland and go to the show there. But for a sum of this size, his imagination was no good. All he could think of was clothes. Blaze cared nothing for clothes.

"Let's run away," John said. His narrow face was bright with excitement.

Blaze considered. "You mean, like . . . forever?"

"Naw, just till the wad's gone. We'll go to Boston . . .
eat in big restaurants instead of Mickey D's . . . get a hotel
room . . . see the Red Sox play . . . and . . . and . . ."

But he could go no further. Joy overcame him. He leaped
on Blaze, laughing and pounding his back. His body was
lean under his clothes, light and hard. His face burned
against Blaze's cheek like the side of a furnace.

"Okay," Blaze said. "That'd be fun." He thought about
it. "Jesus, Johnny, Boston? Boston!"

"Ain't it a royal pisser!"

They began to laugh. Blaze carried John all the way
around the toolshed, both of them laughing and pounding
each other on the back. John finally made him stop.

"Someone'll hear, Blaze. Or see. Put me down."

Blaze recaptured the newspaper, which had begun to
flutter all over the yard. He folded it up and rammed it
down in his hip pocket. "We goin now, Johnny?"

"Not for awhile. Maybe not for three days. We gotta
make a plan and we gotta be careful. If we aren't, they'll
catch us before we get twenty miles. Bring us back. Do you
know what I'm saying?"

"Yeah, but I'm not very good at makin plans, Johnny."

"That's okay, I got most of it figured out already. The
important thing is that they'll think we just buzzed off,
because that's what kids do when they make out from this
shitfarm, right?"

"Right."

"Only we got money, right?"

"Right!"

Blaze was overcome with the deliciousness of it again, and pounded Johnny on the back until he almost knocked him over.

They waited until the following Wednesday night. In the meantime, John called the Greyhound terminal in Portland and found out there was a bus for Boston every morning at seven AM. They left Hetton House at a little past midnight, John figuring it would be safest to walk the fifteen miles into the city rather than attract attention by hitchhiking. Two kids on the road after midnight were runaways. Period.

They went down the fire escape, hearts thumping at each rusty rattle, and jumped from the lowest platform. They ran across the playground where Blaze had taken his first beatings as a newcomer many years before. Blaze helped John climb over the chainlink fence on the far side. They crossed the road under a hot August moon and started to walk, diving into the ditch whenever an infrequent car showed headlights on the horizon ahead or behind them.

They were on Congress Street by six o'clock, Blaze still fresh and excited, John with circles under his eyes. Blaze was carrying the wad in his jeans. The wallet they had thrown into the woods.

When they reached the bus depot, John collapsed onto a bench and Blaze sat down beside him. John's cheeks were flushed again, but not with excitement. He seemed to be having trouble with his breath.

"Go over and get two round-trippers on the seven

o'clock," he told Blaze. "Give her a fifty. I don't think it'll be more, but have a twenty ready, just in case. Have it in your hand. Don't let her see the roll."

A policeman walked over, tapping his nightstick. Blaze felt his bowels turn to water. This was where it ended, before it had even gotten started. Their money would be taken away. The cop might turn it in, or he might keep it for himself. As for them, they would be driven back to HH, maybe in handcuffs. Black visions of North Windham Training Center rose before his eyes. And The Tin.

"Mornin, boys. Here kinda early, ain'tcha?" The clock on the depot wall read 6:22.

"Sure are," John said. He nodded toward the ticket-cage. "Is that where a fella goes to get his ticket?"

"You bet," the cop said, smiling a little. "Where you headed?"

"Boston," John said.

"Oh? Where's you boys' folks?"

"Oh, him and me aren't related," John said. "This fella's retarded. His name's Martin Griffin. Deaf n dumb, too."

"Is that so?" The cop sat down and studied Blaze. He didn't look suspicious; he just looked like someone who had never seen a person before who'd scored the trifecta—deaf, dumb, and retarded.

"His mumma died last week," John said. "He stays with us. My folks work, but since it's summer vacation, they said to me, would you take 'im, and I said I would."

"Big job for a kid," the cop said.

"I'm a little scared," John said, and Blaze bet he was telling the truth there. He was scared, too. Scared plenty.

The cop nodded to Blaze and said, "Does he under-stand . . . ?"

"What happened to her? Not too good."

The cop looked sad.

"I'm takin him to his auntie's house. That's where he's gonna stay for a few days." John brightened. "Me, I might get to go to a Red Sox game. As sort of a reward for . . . you know . . ."

"Well, I hope you do, son. It's an ill wind that don't blow somebody a little good."

They were both silent, considering this. Blaze, newly mute, was silent, too.

Then the cop said, "He's a big one. Think you can handle him?"

"He's big, but he minds. Want to see?"

"Well—"

"Here, I'll make 'im stand up. Watch." John made a number of meaningless finger-gestures in front of Blaze's eyes. When he stopped, Blaze stood up.

"Say, that's pretty good!" the cop said. "He always mind you? Because, a big boy like this on a bus full a people—"

"Naw, he always minds. No more harm in 'im than a paper sack."

"Okay. I take your word for it." The cop got to his feet. He hitched up his gunbelt and pushed on Blaze's shoul-ders. Blaze sat back down again on the bench. "You take care, young fella. You know his auntie's phone number if you get in trouble?"

"Yes sir, I sure do," John said.

"Okay, keep em flyin, sarge." He flipped John a little salute and went strolling out of the bus station.

When he was gone, they looked at each other and almost broke into giggles. But the ticket agent was now watching and they looked down at the floor instead, Blaze biting the insides of his lips.

"You got a bathroom in here?" John called to the ticket agent.

"Over there." She pointed.

"C'mon, Marty," John said, and Blaze just about had to howl at that. When they got into the john, they finally collapsed into each other's arms.

"That was really good," Blaze said when he could talk again without laughing. "Where'd you get that name?"

"When I saw him, all I could think of was how The Law was going to get us again. And Griffin, that's the name of a mythical bird—you know, I helped you with that story in your English book—"

"Yeah," Blaze said delightedly, not remembering the griffin at all. "Yeah, sure, right."

"But they'll know it was us when they find out we're gone from Hell House," John said. He had turned serious. "That cop'll remember for sure. He'll be mad, too. Christ, won't he!"

"We're gonna get caught, aren't we?"

"Naw." John still looked tired, but the exchange with the cop had put the sparkle back in his eyes. "Once we get to Boston, we'll drop right out of sight. They aren't gonna look too hard for a couple of kids."

"Oh. Good."

"But I better buy the tickets. You keep on bein a mutie until we get to Boston. It's safer that way."

"Sure."

So Johnny bought the tickets and they got on the bus, which seemed mostly filled with guys in uniform and young women traveling with little kids. The driver had a pot belly and a satchel ass, but his gray uniform had creases in the pants and Blaze thought it was really sharp. He thought he would like to be a Greyhound Bus driver when he grew up.

The doors hissed shut. The heavy engine rumbled up to a roar. The bus backed out of its dock and turned onto Congress Street. They were moving. They were going somewhere. Blaze couldn't fill his eyes up enough.

They went over a bridge and got on Route 1. Then they began to roll faster. They went past oiltanks and billboards advertising motels and PROUTY'S, MAINE'S BEST LOBSTER RESTAURANT. They went past houses and Blaze saw a man out watering his lawn. The man was wearing Bermuda shorts and wasn't going nowhere. Blaze felt sorry for him. They went past tidal flats with seagulls flying over them. What John called Hell House was behind them. It was summer and the day was brightening.

Finally he turned to John. If he didn't tell someone how good he felt, he thought he would split wide open. But John had fallen asleep with his head on one shoulder. In his sleep he looked old and tired.

Blaze considered this for a moment—uneasily—then turned back to the Scenicruiser window. It pulled him like a magnet. He sightsaw and forgot about John for awhile as he watched the tawdry Seacoast Strip between Portland and Kittery slide by. In New Hampshire they got on the turnpike and then they were in Massachusetts. Not long after that they were crossing a big bridge, and then he guessed they were in Boston.

There were miles of neon, thousands of cars and buses, and buildings in every direction. Yet still the bus kept going. They passed an orange dinosaur guarding a car lot. They passed a huge sailing ship. They passed a herd of plastic cows in front of some restaurant. He saw people everywhere. They frightened him. He also loved them because they were strange to him. John slept on, snoring a little in the back of his throat.

Then they breasted a hill and there was an even *bigger* bridge with even bigger buildings beyond it, skyscrapers shooting into the blue like silver and gold arrows. Blaze tore his eyes away, as if it had been an atomic bomb blast.

"Johnny," he said, almost moaning it. "Johnny, wake up. You gotta see this."

"Huh? Wha?" John woke slowly, knuckling his eyes. Then he saw what Blaze had been seeing through the big Scenicruiser window, and his eyes popped wide. "Mother of God."

"Do you know where we should go?" Blaze whispered.

"Yeah, I think so. My God, are we goin over that bridge? We got to, don't we?"

It was the Mystic, and they went over it. It first took them up to the sky and then below the ground, like a giant version of the Wild Mouse at Topsham Fair. And when they finally came out into the sun again, it was shining between buildings so tall you couldn't see the tops of them through the Big Dog's windows.

When Blaze and Johnny finally got off at the Tremont Street terminal, the first thing they did was look for cops. They need not have bothered. The terminal was huge. Announcements blared from overhead like the voice of God. Travelers schooled like fish. Blaze and Johnny huddled close together, shoulder to shoulder, as if afraid opposing currents of travelers might sweep them apart, never to see each other again.

"Over there," Johnny said. "Come on."

They walked over to a bank of phones. They were all in use. They waited by the one on the end until the black man using it finished his call and walked away.

"What was that thing around his head?" Blaze asked, staring after the black man with fascination.

"Aw, that's to keep his hair straight. Like a turban. I think they call em doo-rags. Don't stare, you look like a hick. Squeeze up next to me."

Blaze did.

"Now gimme a di—holy shit, this thing takes a *quarter*." John shook his head. "I don't know how people live here. Gimme a quarter, Blaze."

Blaze did.

There was a phone book bound in stiff plastic covers on the shelf of the kiosk. John consulted it, dropped his quarter, and dialed. When he spoke, he deepened his voice. When he hung up, he was smiling.

"We got two nights at the Hunington Avenue YMCA.

Twenty bucks for two nights! Call me a Christian!" He raised his hand.

Blaze slapped it, then said, "But we can't spend almost two hundred bucks in two days, can we?"

"In a town where a phone-call costs a quarter? You shittin me?" John looked around with glowing eyes. It was as though he owned the bus terminal and everything in it. Blaze would not see anyone with that exact same look in his eyes for a long time—not until he met George.

"Listen, Blaze, let's go to the ballgame now. What do you say?"

Blaze scratched his head. It was all going too fast for him. "How? We don't even know how to get there."

"Every cab in Boston knows how to get to Fenway."

"Cabs cost money. We ain't—"

He saw Johnny smiling, and he began to smile, too. Sweet truth dawned in a burst. They *did*. They *did* have money. And this was what money was for: to cut through the bullshit.

"But . . . what if there's no day game?"

"Blaze, why do you think I picked today to go?"

Blaze began to laugh. Then they were in each other's arms again, just like in Portland. They pounded each other on the back and laughed into each other's faces. Blaze never forgot it. He picked John up and twirled him around twice in the air. People turned to look, most of them smiling at the big galoot and his skinny pal.

They went out and got their cab, and when the hackie dropped them on Lansdowne Street, John tipped him a buck. It was quarter to one and the scant daytime crowd was just starting to trickle in. The game was a thriller. Boston beat the Birds in ten, 3–2. Boston fielded a bad team that year, but on that August afternoon they played like champs.

After the game, the boys wandered the downtown area, rubbernecking and trying to avoid cops. The shadows were growing long by then, and Blaze's belly was rumbling. John had gobbled a couple of dogs at the game, but Blaze had been too enthralled by the spectacle of the ballplayers on the field—real people with sweat on their necks—to eat. He had also been awed by the size of the crowd, thousands of people all in the same place. But now he was hungry.

They went into a dim narrow place called Lindy's Steak House that smelled of beer and charring beef. A number of couples sat in high booths padded with red leather. To the left was a long bar, scratched and pitted but still glowing like there was light in the wood. There were bowls of salted nuts and pretzels spotted along it every three feet or so. Behind the bar were photos of ballplayers, some signed, and a painting of a barenaked woman. The man presiding over the bar was very large. He bent toward them.

"What's yours, boys?"

"Uh," John said. For the first time that day he appeared stymied.

"Steak!" Blaze said. "Two big steaks, n milk to go with."

The big man grinned, showing formidable teeth. He looked like he could have chewed a phone book to ribbons. "Got money?"

Blaze slapped a twenty on the counter.

The big man picked it up and checked Andy Jackson by the light. He snapped the bill between his fingers. Then he made it disappear. "Okay," he said.

"No change?" John asked.

The big man said, "No, and you won't be sorry."

He turned, opened a freezer, and took out two of the biggest, reddest steaks Blaze had ever seen in his life. There was a deep grill at the end of the bar, and when the big man tossed the steaks on, almost contemptuously, flames leaped up.

"Hicks' special, comin right up," he said.

He drew a few beers, put out new dishes of nuts, then made salads and put them on ice. When the salads were taken care of, he flipped the steaks and walked back to John and Blaze. He placed his dishwater-reddened mitts on the bar and said, "You fellas see that gent at the far end of the bar, sittin all by his lonesome?"

Blaze and John looked. The gent at the end of the bar was dressed in a natty blue suit and was morosely sipping a beer.

"That's Daniel J. Monahan. *Detective* Daniel J. Monahan, of Boston's Finest. I don't suppose you'd like to talk to him about how a couple of hicks such as your fine selves have twenty to put down on prime beef?"

John Cheltzman looked suddenly sick. He reeled a little on his stool. Blaze put a hand out to steady him. Mentally he set his feet. "We got that money fair and square," he said.

"That right? Who'd you stick up fair and square? Or was it a fair and square muggin?"

"We got that money fair and square. We found it. And if you spoil it for Johnny and me, I'll bust you one."

The man behind the bar looked at Blaze with a mixture of surprise, admiration, and contempt. "You're big, but you're a fool, boy. Close either fist and I'll put you on the moon."

"If you spoil our holiday, I'll bust you one, mister."

"Where you from? New Hampshire Correctional? North Windham? Not from Boston, that's for sure. You boys got hay in your hair."

"We're from Hetton House," Blaze said. "We ain't crooks."

The Boston detective at the end of the bar had finished his beer. He gestured with the empty glass for another. The big man saw it and cracked a smile. "Sit tight, the both of you. No need to put on your skates."

The big man brought Monahan another beer and said something that made Monahan laugh. It was a hard sound, not much humor in it.

The bartender-cook came back. "Where's this Hetton House place?" Now it was John he was speaking to.

"In Cumberland, Maine," John said. "They let us go to the movies in Freeport on Friday night. I found a wallet in the men's bathroom. There was money inside. So we ran away to have a holiday, just like Blaze said."

"Just happened to find a wallet, huh?"

"Yes, sir."

"And how much was in this fabled wallet?"

"About two hundred and fifty dollars."

"Baldheaded Jaysus, and I bet you got it all in your pockets, too."

"Where else?" John looked mystified.

"Baldheaded *Jaysus,*" the big man said again. He looked up at the scalloped tin ceiling. He rolled his eyes. "And you tell a stranger. Just as easy as kiss your hand."

The big man leaned forward with his fingers splayed on the bar. His face had been cruelly handled by the years, but it wasn't cruel.

"I believe you," he said. "You got too much hay in your hair to be liars. But that cop down there . . . boys, I could sic him on you like a dog on a rat. You'd be cellbound while him and me was splittin that money."

"I'd bust you one," Blaze said. "That's our money. Me and Johnny found it. Look. We been in that place, and it's a bad place to be in. A guy like you, maybe you think you know stuff, but . . . aw, never mind. We *earned* it!"

"You're gonna be a bruiser when you get your full growth," the big man said, almost to himself. Then he looked at John. "Your friend here, he's a few tools short of a full box. You know that, right?"

John had recovered himself. He didn't say anything, only returned the big man's gaze steadily.

"You take care of him," the big man said, and he smiled suddenly. "Bring him back here when he gets his full growth. I want to see what he looks like then."

John didn't smile back—looked more solemn than ever, in fact—but Blaze did. He understood it was all right.

The big man produced the twenty-dollar bill—it seemed to come from nowhere—and shoved it at John. "These steaks are on the house, boys. You take that and go to the baseball tomorrow. If you ain't had your pockets picked by then."

"We went today," John said.

"Was it good?" the big man asked.

And now John did smile. "It was the greatest thing I ever saw."

"Yeah," the big man said. "Sure it was. Watch out for your buddy."

"I will."

"Because buddies stick together."

"I know it."

The big man brought the steaks, and Caesar salads, and new peas, and huge mounds of string-fries, and huge glasses of milk. For dessert he brought them wedges of cherry pie with scoops of vanilla ice cream melting on top. At first they ate slowly. Then Detective Monahan of Boston's Finest left (without paying nothing, so far as Blaze could see) and they both pitched to. Blaze had two pieces of pie and three glasses of milk and the third time the big guy refilled Blaze's glass, he laughed out loud.

When they left, the neon signs in the street were coming on.

"You go to the Y," the big man said before they did. "Do it right away. City's no place for a couple of kids to be wandering around at night."

"Yes, sir," John said. "I already called and fixed it."

The big man smiled. "You're all right, kid. You're pretty good. Keep the bear close, and walk behind him if anyone comes up and tries to brace you. Especially kids wearing colors. You know, gang jackets."

"Yes sir."

"Take care of each other."

That was his final word on it.

The next day they rode the subways until the novelty wore off and then they went to the movies and then they went to the ballgame again. It was late when they got out, almost eleven, and someone picked Blaze's pocket, but Blaze had put his share of their money in his underwear the way Johnny told him to and the pickpocket got a big handful of nothing. Blaze never saw what he looked like, just a narrow back weaving its way into the crowd exiting through Gate A.

They stayed two more days and saw more movies and one play that Blaze didn't understand, although Johnny liked it. They sat in something called the lodge that was five times as high as the balcony at the Nordica. They went into a department store photo booth and had their pictures made: some of Blaze, some of Johnny, some of them both together. In the ones together, they were laughing. They rode the subways some more until Johnny got train-sick and threw up on his sneakers. Then a Negro man came over and shouted at them about the end of the world. He seemed to be saying it was their fault, but Blaze couldn't tell for sure. Johnny said the guy was crazy. Johnny said there were a lot of crazy people in the city. "They breed here like fleas," Johnny said.

They still had some money left, and it was Johnny who suggested the final touch. They took a Greyhound back to Portland, then spent the rest of their dividend on a taxi.

John fanned the remaining bills in front of the startled driver—almost fifty dollars' worth of crumpled fives and ones, some smelling fragrantly of Clayton Blaisdell, Jr.'s underpants—and told him they wanted to go to Hetton House, in Cumberland.

The cabbie dropped his flag. And at five minutes past two on a sunny late summer afternoon, they pulled up at the gate. John Cheltzman took half a dozen steps up the drive toward the brooding brick pile and fainted dead away. He had rheumatic fever. He was dead two years later.

CHAPTER 13

By the time Blaze got the baby into the shack, Joe was screaming his head off. Blaze stared at him in wonder. He was furious! The face was flushed across the forehead and the cheeks, even the bridge of the tiny nose. His eyes were squinched shut. His fists made tiny circles of rage in the air.

Blaze felt sudden panic. What if the kid was sick? What if he had the flu or something? Kids caught the flu every day. Sometimes they died of it. And he couldn't very well take him to a doctor's office. What did he know about kids, anyway? He was just a dummy. He could barely take care of himself.

He had a sudden wild urge to take the baby back out to the car. To drive him to Portland and leave him on somebody's doorstep.

"George!" he cried. "George, what should I do?"

He was afraid George had gone away again, but George answered up from the bathroom. "Feed him. Give him something out of one of those jars."

Blaze ran into the bedroom. He clawed one of the cartons out from under the bed, opened it, and selected a jar at random. He took it back to the kitchen and found a spoon.

He put the jar on the table beside the wicker basket and opened the lid. What was inside looked awful, like puke. Maybe it was spoiled. He smelled it anxiously. It smelled all right. It smelled like peas. That was all right, then.

He hesitated, just the same. The idea of actually putting food in that open, screaming mouth seemed somehow . . . irreversible. What if the little motherfucker choked on it? What if he just didn't want it? What if it was somehow the wrong stuff for him and . . . and . . .

His mind tried to put up the word POISON, and Blaze wouldn't look at it. He stuffed half a spoonful of cold peas in the baby's mouth.

The cries stopped at once. The baby's eyes popped open, and Blaze saw they were blue. Joe spit some of the peas back and Blaze tucked the goop back in with the end of the spoon, not thinking about it, just doing it. The baby sucked contentedly.

Blaze fed him another spoonful. It was accepted. And another. In seven minutes, the entire jar of Gerber Peas was gone. Blaze had a crick in his back from bending over the wicker basket. Joe belched a runnel of green foam. Blaze mopped it off the small cheek with the tail of his own shirt.

"Bring it up again and we'll vote on it," he said. This was one of George's witticisms.

Joe blinked at the sound of his voice. Blaze stared back, fascinated. The baby's skin was clear and unblemished. His head was capped with a surprising thatch of blond hair. But his eyes were what got Blaze. He thought they were old eyes somehow, wise eyes. They were the washed-out blue of desert skies in a Western movie. The corners turned up a little, like the eyes of Chinese people. They gave him a fierce look. Almost a warrior look.

"You a fighter?" Blaze asked. "You a fighter, little man?"

One of Joe's thumbs crept into his mouth and he began to suck it. At first Blaze thought he might want a bottle (and he hadn't figured out the Playtex Nurser gadget yet), but for the time being the kid seemed content with his thumb. His cheeks were still flushed, not with crying now but from his trip through the night.

His lids began to droop, and the corners of his eyes lost that fierce upward tilt. But still he peered at this man, this six-foot-seven stubbled giant with the crazed and scare-crowed brown hair who stood over him. Then the eyes closed. His thumb dropped out of his mouth. He slept.

Blaze straightened up and his back popped. He turned away from the basket and started for the bedroom.

"Hey dinkleballs," George said from the bathroom. "Where do you think you're going?"

"To bed."

"The hell you are. You're going to figure out that bottle gadget and fix the kid four or five, for when he wakes up."

"The milk might go sour."

"Not if you put it in the fridge. You warm it up when you need it."

"Oh."

Blaze got the Playtex Nurser kit and read the instructions. He read them twice. It took him half an hour. He didn't understand hardly anything the first time and even less the second.

"I can't, George," he said at last.

"Sure you can. Throw those instructions away and just *roll*."

So Blaze threw the instructions into the stove and then just fooled with the gadget, the way you did with a carb that wasn't set quite right. Eventually, he figured out that you fitted the plastic liner over the gadget's nozzle and then plunged it into the bottle shell. Bingo. Pretty slick. He prepared four bottles, filled them with canned milk, and put them away in the fridge.

"Can I go to bed now, George?" he asked.

No answer.

Blaze went to bed.

Joe woke him in the first gray light of morning. Blaze stumbled out of bed and went into the kitchen. He had left the baby in the basket, and now the basket was rocking back and forth on the table with the force of Joe's anger.

Blaze picked him up and laid him against his shoulder. He saw part of the problem right away. The kid was soaked through.

Blaze took him into the bedroom and laid him on his bed. He looked amazingly small, lying there in the indentation of Blaze's body. He was wearing blue pj's, and he kicked his feet indignantly.

Blaze took off his pajamas and the rubber pants beneath. He put a hand on Joe's belly to hold him still. Then he bent close to observe the way the diapers were pinned together. He took them off and threw them in the corner.

He observed Joe's penis and felt instant delight. Not much longer than his thumbnail, but standing straight up. Pretty cute.

"That's quite a rod you got there, skinner," he said.

Joe left off crying to stare up at Blaze with wide, surprised eyes.

"I said that's quite a rod you got on you."

Joe smiled.

"Goo-goo," Blaze said. He felt an unwilling idiot grin tug the corners of his mouth.

Joe gurgled.

"Goo-goo-baby," Blaze said.

Joe laughed aloud.

"Goo-goo-bayyy-beee," Blaze said, delighted.

Joe pissed in his face.

The Pampers were another struggle. At least they didn't have pins, just tapes, and they seemed to have their own built-in rubber pants—plastic, actually—but he wrecked two before he finally got one on like the picture on the box. When the job was done, Joe was wide awake and chewing on the ends of his fingers. Blaze supposed he wanted something to eat, and thought a bottle might be best.

He was heating it under the hot water faucet in the kitchen, turning it around and around, when George said: "Did you dilute it the way the broad in the store said to?"

Blaze looked at the bottle. "Huh?"

"That's straight canned milk, isn't it?"

"Sure, right out of the can. Is it spoiled, George?"

"No, it isn't spoiled. But if you don't take off the cap and put in some water, he'll puke."

"Oh."

Blaze used his fingernails to pull the top off the Playtex Nurser and poured about a quarter of the bottle down the sink. He added enough water to fill it back up, stirred it with a spoon, and put the nipple back on.

"Blaze." George didn't sound mad, but he sounded awful tired.

"What?"

"You gotta get a baby book. Somethin that tells you how to take care of him. Like the manual to a car. Because you keep forgetting things."

"Okay, George."

"You better get a newspaper, too. Only don't buy them too close to here. Buy them someplace bigger."

"George?"

"What?"

"Who's gonna take care of the kid while I'm gone?"

There was a long pause, one so long Blaze thought George had gone away again. Then he said: "I will."

Blaze frowned. "You can't, George. You're—"

"I said I will. Now get your ass in there and feed 'im!"

"But . . . if the kid gets in trouble . . . chokes, or some-thin and I'm gone—"

"*Feed him, goddammit!*"

"Okay, George, sure."

He went into the other room. Joe was fussing and kick-ing on the bed, still chewing his fingers. Blaze burped the bottle the way the lady showed him, pushing a finger up inside the plastic bag until a drop of milk formed on the nipple. He sat down by the baby and carefully removed Joe's fingers from his mouth. Joe started to cry, but when Blaze put the rubber nipple where his fingers had been, the lips closed over it and he began to suck. The small cheeks went in and out.

"That's right," Blaze said. "That's right, you little bagger."

Joe drank all of it. When Blaze picked him up to burp him, he spit a little back, getting some on the shirt of Blaze's thermal underwear. Blaze didn't mind. He wanted to change the baby into one of his new outfits, anyway. He told himself he only wanted to see if it fit.

It did. When Blaze was done with that, he took off his own top and smelled the baby's burp-up. It smelled vaguely cheesy. Maybe, he thought, the milk was still a little too thick. Or maybe he should have stopped and burped the kid halfway through the bottle. George was right. He needed a book.

He looked down at Joe. The baby had bunched a small piece of blanket in his hands and was examining it. He was a cute little shit. They were going to be worried about him, Joe Gerard III and his wife. Probably thinking the kid had been tucked away in a bureau drawer, screaming and hungry, with crappy diapers. Or worse still, lying in a shallow hole chipped out of frozen earth, a tiny scrap of manchild gasping away its last few breaths in frozen vapor. Then into a green plastic Hefty Bag . . .

Where had he gotten that idea?

George. George had said that. He had been talking about the Lindbergh snatch. The kidnapper's name had been Hopeman, Hoppman, something like that.

"George? George, don't you hurt 'im while I'm gone."

No answer.

He heard the first item on the news, while he was making his breakfast. Joe was on the floor, on a blanket Blaze had spread for him. He was playing with one of George's newspapers. He had pulled a tent of it over his head and was kicking with excitement.

The announcer had just finished telling about a Republican Senator who had taken a bribe. Blaze was hoping George heard it. George liked stuff like that.

"Topping area news is an apparent kidnapping in Ocoma Heights," the announcer said. Blaze stopped stirring his potatoes around in the frying pan and listened carefully. "Joseph Gerard IV, infant heir to the Gerard shipping fortune, was taken from the Gerards' Ocoma Heights estate either late last night or early this morning. A sister of Joseph Gerard, the boy's great-grandfather—once known as 'the boy wonder of American shipping'—was found unconscious on the kitchen floor by the family cook early this morning. Norma Gerard, said to be in her mid-seventies, was taken to the Maine Medical Center, where her condition is listed as critical. When asked if he had called for FBI assistance, Castle County Sheriff John D. Kellahar said he could not comment at this time. He would also not comment on the possibility of a ransom note—"

Oh yeah, Blaze thought. I got to send one of those.

"—but he did say police have a number of leads which are being actively investigated."

Like what? Blaze wondered, and smiled a little. They always said stuff like that. What leads could they have, if the old lady was *el zonko*? He had even taken the ladder with him. They said stuff like that, that was all.

He ate his breakfast on the floor and played with the baby.

When he got ready to go out that afternoon, the kid had been fed and freshly changed and lay sleeping in the cradle. Blaze had tinkered with the formula a little more, and this time had burped him halfway through. It worked real good. It worked like a charm. He'd also changed the kid's diapers. At first all that green shit had scared him, but then he remembered. Peas.

"George? I'm going now."

"Okay," George said from the bedroom.

"You better come out here and watch him. In case he wakes up."

"I will, don't worry."

"Yeah," Blaze said, without conviction. George was dead. He was talking to a dead man. He was asking a dead man to babysit. "Hey, George. Maybe I oughta—"

"Oughtta-shmotta, coulda-woulda. Go on, get out of here."

"George—"

"Go on, I said! Roll!"

Blaze went.

•   •   •

The day was bright and sparkling and a little warmer. After a week of single-number temperatures, twenty degrees felt like a heatwave. But there was no pleasure in the sunshine, no pleasure to be had in driving the back roads to Portland. He didn't trust George with the baby. He didn't know why, but he sure didn't. Because, see, now George was a part of himself, and he most likely took all the parts with him when he went somewhere, even the George part. Didn't that make sense?

Blaze thought it did.

And then he started wondering about the woodstove. What if the house burned down?

This morbid picture entered his head and wouldn't leave. A chimney fire from the stove he'd stoked special so Joe wouldn't be cold if he kicked off his blanket. Sparks sputtering from the chimney onto the roof. Most dying, but one spark finding a dry shingle and catching hot, reaching out to the explosively dry clapboards beneath. The flames then racing across the beams. The baby beginning to cry as the first tendrils of smoke grew thicker and thicker . . .

He suddenly realized he had pushed the stolen Ford up to seventy. He eased off the accelerator. That was worse and more of it.

He parked in the Casco Street lot, gave the attendant a couple of bucks, and went around to Walgreens. He picked up an *Evening Express,* then went to the rack of paperbacks by the soda fountain. A lot of Westerns. Gothics. Mysteries. Science fiction. And then, on the bottom shelf, a thick book with a smiling, hairless baby on the cover. He worked out the title quickly; there were no hard words in it. *Child and Baby Care*. There was a picture of an old dude surrounded by kids on the back cover. Probably the guy who wrote it.

He paid for his stuff and shook open the newspaper going out the door. He stopped suddenly on the sidewalk, mouth open.

There was a picture of him on the front page.

Not a photo, he saw with relief, but a police drawing, one of those they made with Identi-Kits. It wasn't even that good. They didn't have the bashed-in place in his forehead. His eyes were the wrong shape. His lips were nowhere near that thick. But somehow it was still recognizably him.

The old lady must have woken up, then. Only the subheading did away with that idea, and in a hurry.

FBI ENTERS SEARCH FOR BABYNAPPERS
Norma Gerard Succumbs to Head Injury

Special to the *Evening Express*

By James T. Mears

THE MAN WHO DROVE the getaway car in the Gerard baby kidnapping—and possibly the only kidnapper—is pictured on this page, in an *Evening Express* exclusive. The drawing was made by Portland P.D. sketch artist John Black from a description given by Morton Walsh, a night attendant at Oakwood, a new high-rise condominium tower a quarter of a mile from the Gerard family compound.

Walsh told Portland police and Castle County Sheriff's deputies earlier today that the suspect said he was visiting Joseph Carlton, a name that is apparently fictitious. The suspected babynapper was driving a blue Ford sedan, and Walsh said there was a ladder in the back. Walsh is being held as a material witness, and there is speculation about his failure to question the driver more closely on his intentions, given the lateness of the hour (approximately 2 AM).

A source close to the investigation has suggested that the Joseph Carlton "mystery apartment" may have ties to organized crime, raising the possibility that the infant kidnapping could have been a well-organized criminal "caper." Neither FBI agents (now on scene) nor local police would comment on this possibility.

There are other leads at the present time, although no ransom letter or call has been announced. One of the kidnappers may have left blood at the crime scene, possibly from a cut received in his scramble over the Oakwood parking lot fence, which is of the chain-link type. Sheriff John D. Kellahar called it "one more strand in the rope that will eventually hang this man or gang of men."

In other developments, Norma Gerard, the kidnapped boy's great-great-aunt, succumbed during an operation at Maine Medical Center to relieve pressure on her (go to Page 2, Col 5)

Blaze turned to page two, but there wasn't much there. If the cops had other stuff, they were holding it back.

There was a picture of "The Kidnap House," and another of "Where the Babynappers Entered." There was a small box that said *Appeal to Kidnappers from Father, Page 6.* Blaze didn't turn to page 6. The time always got away from him when he was reading, and he couldn't afford that now. He'd been away too long already, it would take him at least another forty-five minutes to get home, and also—

Also, the car was hot.

Walsh, that miserable bastard. Blaze almost hoped the organization whacked the miserable bastard for blowing their apartment. Meantime, though—

Meantime, he would just have to take his chances. Maybe he could get back okay. Things would be a lot worse if he just left the car. It had his fingerprints all over it—what George called "dabs." Maybe they had the license plate number, though; maybe Walsh had written it down. He turned this over slowly and carefully and decided Walsh wouldn't have written it down. Probably. Still, they knew it was a Ford, and blue . . . but of course it had been green originally. Before he painted it. Maybe that would make a difference. Maybe it would still be okay. Maybe not. It was hard to know.

He approached the parking lot carefully, lurking his way up to it, but he saw no cops and the attendant was reading a magazine. That was good. Blaze got in, started the Ford up, and waited for cops to descend from a hundred hiding places. None did. When he drove out, the attendant took the yellow ticket from under his windshield wiper with hardly a glance.

Getting clear of Portland, and then Westbrook, seemed

to take forever. It was a little bit like driving with an open jug of wine between your legs, only worse. He was sure that every car that pulled up close behind him was an unmarked police car. He actually saw only one copmobile on his trip out of the city, crossing the intersection of Routes 1 and 25, breaking trail for an ambulance with its siren howling and its lights flashing. Seeing that actually comforted him. A police car like that, you knew what it was.

After Westbrook dropped behind, he swung off onto a secondary road, then onto two-lane blacktop that turned to frozen dirt and wound cross-country through the woods to Apex. He did not feel entirely safe even there, and when he turned into the long driveway leading to the shack, he felt as if great weights were dropping off his body.

He drove the Ford into the shed and told himself it could stay there until hell was a skating rink. He had known that kidnapping was big, and that things would be hot, but this was scorching. The picture, the blood he'd left behind, the quick and painless way that glorified doorman had given up the organization's private playpen . . .

But all those thoughts faded as soon as he got out of the car. Joe was screaming. Blaze could hear him even outside. He ran across the dooryard and burst into the house. George had done something, George had—

But George hadn't done anything. George wasn't anywhere around. George was dead and he, Blaze, had left the baby all alone.

The cradle was rocking with the force of the baby's anger, and when Blaze got to Joe, he saw why. The kid had thrown up most of his ten o'clock bottle, and rancid, reeking milk, half-dry, was lathered on his face and soaking into his pajama top. His face was an awful plum color. Sweat stood out on it in beads.

In a kind of shutter-frame, Blaze saw his own father, a hulking giant with red eyes and big hurting hands. The picture left him agonized with guilt and horror; he had not thought of his father in years.

He snatched the baby out of the cradle with such suddenness that Joe's head rolled on his neck. He stopped crying out of surprise as much as anything.

"There," Blaze crooned, beginning to walk around the room with the baby on his shoulder. "There, there. I'm back. Yes I am. There, there. Don't cry no more. I'm right here. Right here."

The baby fell asleep before Blaze had made three full turns around the room. Blaze changed him, doing the diapers faster than before, buttoned him up, and popped him back in the cradle.

Then he sat down to think. To really think, this time. What came next? A ransom note, right?

"Right," he said.

Make it out of letters from magazines; that was how they did it in the movies. He got a stack of newspapers, girly magazines, and comic-books. Then he began to cut out letters.

I HAVE THE BABY.

There. That was a good start. He went over to the window and turned on the radio and got Ferlin Husky singing "Wings of a Dove." That was a good one. An oldie but a goodie. He rummaged around until he found a tablet of

Hytone paper George had bought in Renny's and then mixed up some flour-and-water paste. He hummed along with the music as he worked. It was a rusted, grating sound like an old gate swinging on bad hinges.

He went back to the table and pasted on the letters he had so far. A thought struck him: did paper take fingerprints? He didn't know, but it didn't seem very possible. Better not to take chances, though. He crumpled up the paper with the letters pasted on it and found George's leather gloves. They were too small for him, but he stretched them on. Then he hunted out the same letters all over again and pasted them up:

I HAVE THE BABY.

The news came on. He listened carefully and heard that somebody had called the Gerard home demanding two thousand dollars in ransom. This made Blaze frown. Then the newscaster said a teenage boy had made the call from a phone booth in Wyndham. The police had traced the call. When they caught him, he said he had been playing a prank.

Tell em it's a prank all night, they'll still put you away, kiddo, Blaze thought. Kidnapping is hot.

He frowned, thought, cut out more letters. The weather forecast came on. Fair and a little colder. Snow on the way soon.

I HAVE THE BABY. IF YOU WANT TO SEE HIM ALIVE AGAIN

If you want to see him alive again, what? *What?* Confusion rose in Blaze's mind. Call collect, operators are standing by? Stand on your head and whistle Dixie? Send two

boxtops and fifty cents in coin? How did you go about getting the dough without getting caught?

"George? I can't remember this part."

No answer.

He put his chin in one hand and really put on his thinking cap. He had to be very cool. Cool like George. Cool like
John Cheltzman had been that day in the bus station when
they had been running away to Boston. You had to use your
nut. You had to use your old bean, old bean.

He would have to pretend he was part of a gang, that
was for sure. Then they couldn't grab him when he picked
up the swag. If they did, he'd tell them they had to let him
go or his partners would kill the kid. Run a bluff. Hell,
run a *con*.

"That's how we roll," he whispered. "Right, George?"

He crumpled up his second try and searched out more
letters, scissoring them into neat blocks.

**OUR GANG HAS THE BABY. IF YOU WANT TO
SEE HIM ALIVE AGAIN**

That was good. That was right on the jack. Blaze admired it for awhile, then went to check the baby. The
baby was asleep. His head was turned, and one small fist
was tucked under his cheek. His lashes were very long,
and darker than his hair. Blaze liked him. He never would
have said a rug-monkey could be good-looking, but this
one was.

"You're a stud, Joey," he said, and then ruffled the baby's
hair. His hand was bigger than the baby's whole head.

Blaze went back to the scattered magazines and newspapers and scraps on the table. He deliberated awhile, nib-

bling a little of his flour-water paste as he did. Then he got back to work.

OUR GANG HAS THE BABY. IF YOU WANT TO SEE HIM ALIVE AGAIN GET $$ 1 MILLION $$ IN UNMARKED BILLS. PUT MONEY IN BRIFCASE. BE READY TO GO ON A MOMENTS NOTISE. SINCIRELY YOURS,

THE KIDNAPERS OF JOE GERARD 4.

There. It told them some stuff, but not too much. And it would give him some time to think out a plan.

He found a dirty old envelope and put his letter in it, then cut out letters on the front to say:

THE GERARDS
OCOMA
IMPORTANT!

He didn't know exactly how he was going to mail it. He didn't want to leave the baby with George again, and he didn't dare use the hot Ford, but he didn't want to mail it in Apex, either. Everything would have been so much easier with George. He could have just stayed home and baby-sat while George took care of the brain stuff. He wouldn't mind feeding Joe and changing him and all that stuff. He wouldn't mind a bit. He sort of liked it.

Well, it didn't matter. The mail wouldn't go until tomorrow morning anyway, so he had time to make a plan. Or remember George's.

He got up and checked the baby again, wishing the TV wasn't bust. You got good ideas from the TV sometimes.

Joe was still sleeping. Blaze wished he would wake up so that he could play with him. Make him grin. The kid looked like a real boy when he grinned. And he was dressed now, so Blaze could goof with him and not worry about getting pissed on.

Still, he was asleep and there was no help for that. Blaze turned off the radio and went into the bedroom to make plans, but fell asleep himself.

Before drifting off, it occurred to him that he felt sort of good. For the first time since George died, he felt sort of good.

CHAPTER 14

He was at a carnival—maybe the Topsham Fair, where the boys from Hetton House were allowed to go once each year on the rickety old blue bus—and Joe was on his shoulder. He felt foglike terror as he walked down the midway, because pretty soon *they* would spot him and it would be all over. Joe was awake. When they passed one of the funny mirrors that stretched you thin, Blaze saw the kid goggling at everything. Blaze kept walking, shifting Joe from one shoulder to the other when he got heavy, keeping an eye out for the cops at the same time.

All around him, the carnival rolled in unhealthy neon majesty. From the right came the amplified beat of a pitchman's voice: *"C'mon over here, got it all over here, six beautiful girls, half a dozen honeys, they all come straight from Club Diablo in Boston, these girls will tease you please you make you think you're in Gay Paree!"*

This ain't no place for a kid, Blaze thought. This is the last place in the world for a little kid.

On the left was the House of Fun with its mechanical clown out front, rocking back and forth in clockspring gales of hilarity. Its mouth was turned upward in an expression of humor so large it was like a grimace of pain. Its lunatic laugh played over and over again from a tape-loop buried deep in its guts. A huge man with a blue anchor tattooed on one bicep threw hard rubber balls at wooden milk bottles stacked in a pyramid; his slicked-back hair gleamed under the colored lights like an otter's hide. The Wild Mouse rose and then went into a clatter-ing dive, trailing the shrieks of country girls packed into tube tops and short skirts. The Moon Rocket rolled up, down, and all around, the faces of the riders stretched into goblin masks by the speed of the thing. A Babel of odors rose: French fries, vinegar, tacos, popcorn, choco-late, fried clams, pizza, peppers, beer. The midway was a flat brown tongue, littered with a thousand shucked wrappers and a million stamped cigarette butts. Under the glare of the lights, all faces were flat and grotesque. An old man with a runner of green snot hanging from his nose walked past, eating a candy apple. Then a boy with a plum-colored birthmark swarming up one cheek. An old black woman beneath a blonde beehive wig. A fat man in Bermuda shorts with varicose veins, wearing a tee-shirt saying PROPERTY OF THE BRUNSWICK DRAGONS.

"Joe," someone was calling. "Joe . . . *Joe!*"

Blaze turned and tried to pinpoint the voice from the crowd. And then he saw her, wearing that same nightgown with her cakes practically falling out of the lace top. Joe's pretty young mother.

Terror seized him. She was going to see him. She

couldn't help but see him. And when she did, she would take his baby away. He held Joe tighter, as if embrace could insure possession. The little body was warm and re-assuring. He could feel the flutter of the child's life against his chest.

"There!" Mrs. Gerard screamed. "There he is, the man who stole my baby! Get him! Catch him! Give me back my baby!"

People turned to look. Blaze was near the merry-go-round now, and the calliope music was huge. It bounded and echoed.

"Stop him! Stop that man! Stop the baby-thief!"

The man with the tattoo and the slicked-back hair began to walk toward him and now, at last, Blaze could run. But the midway had grown longer. It stretched away for miles, an endless Highway of Fun. And they were all behind him: the boy with the swarming birthmark, the black woman in her blonde wig, the fat man in the Bermuda shorts. The mechanical clown laughed and laughed.

Blaze ran past another pitchman, who was standing beside a huge guy wearing what looked like an animal skin. The sign over his head billed him as Leopard Man. The pitchman raised his microphone and began to speak. His amplified voice rolled down the midway like thunder.

"Hurry, hurry, hurry! You're just in time to see Clayton Blais-dell, Jr., the noted babynapper! Lay that kid down, fella! He's right over here, folks, direct from Apex where he lives on the Parker Road, and the hot car is stashed in the shed out back! Hurry, hurry, hurry, see the live babynapper, right here—"

He ran faster, breath sobbing in and out, but they were gaining. He looked back and saw that Joe's mother was leading the posse. Her face was changing. It was growing paler, except for her lips. They were getting redder. Her teeth were growing down over them. Her fingers were hooking into red-tipped claws. She was becoming the Bride of Yorga.

"Get him! Catch him! Kill him! *The babynapper!*"

Then George was hissing at him from the shadows. "In here, Blaze! Quick! *Move,* goddammit!"

He veered in the direction of the voice and found himself in the Mirror Maze. The midway was suddenly broken up into a thousand distorted pieces. He bumped and thrust his way down the narrow corridor, panting like a dog. Then George was in front of him (and behind him, and to either side of him) and George was saying: "You have to make them drop it from a plane, Blaze. From a plane. Make them drop it from a plane."

"I can't get out," Blaze moaned. "George, help me to get out."

"That's what I'm trying to do, asshole! *Make them drop it from a plane!*"

They were all outside now, and peering in, but the mirrors made it seem as if they were all around him. *"Get the babynapper!"* Gerard's wife shrieked. Her teeth were now huge.

"Help me, George."

Then George smiled, and Blaze saw that his teeth were long, too. Too long. "I'll help you," he said. "Give me the baby."

But Blaze didn't. Blaze backed away. A million Georges advanced on him, holding out their hands to take the baby. Blaze turned and plunged down another glittering aisle, bouncing from side to side like a pinball, trying to hold Joe protectively. This was no place for a kid.

CHAPTER 15

Blaze came awake in the first thin light of dawn, at first not sure where he was. Then everything came back and he collapsed on his side, breathing hard. His bed was drenched in sweat. Christ, what an awful dream.

He got up and padded into the kitchen to check on the baby. Joe was deeply asleep, lips pursed as if he was having big serious thoughts. Blaze looked at him until his eyes picked up the slow, steady rise of the kid's chest. His lips moved, and Blaze wondered if Joe was dreaming about the bottle, or his mother's titty.

Then he put on the coffee and sat down at the table in his long underwear. The paper he had bought yesterday was still there, amid the scraps of his kidnap note. He began to read the story about the kidnapping again, and his eye once more fell on the box at the bottom of page 2: *Appeal to Kidnappers from Father, Page 6*. Blaze turned over to page six, where he found a half-page broadside, outlined in black. He read:

TO THE PEOPLE WHO HAVE OUR CHILD!

WE WILL MEET ANY DEMANDS, ON CONDI-
TION THAT YOU CAN PROVIDE US WITH EVI-

DENCE THAT JOE IS STILL ALIVE. WE HAVE THE GUARANTEE OF THE FEDERAL BUREAU OF INVESTIGATION (FBI) THAT THERE WILL BE NO INTERFERENCE WITH YOUR COLLECTION OF THE RANSOM, BUT *WE MUST HAVE PROOF THAT JOE IS ALIVE*!

HE IS EATING THREE TIMES A DAY, CANNED BABY DINNERS AND VEG FOLLOWED BY 1/2 A BOTTLE. THE FORMULA HE'S USED TO IS CANNED MILK AND BOILED, STERILIZED WATER IN A RATIO OF 1:1.

PLEASE DO NOT HURT HIM, BECAUSE WE LOVE HIM SO VERY MUCH.

JOSEPH GERARD III

Blaze closed the paper. Reading that made him feel unhappy, like hearing Loretta Lynn sing "Your Good Girl's Gonna Go Bad."

"Oh Jeez, boo-hoo," George said so suddenly from the bedroom that Blaze jumped.

"Shh, you'll wake 'im up."

"Fuck that," George said. "He can't hear me."

"Oh," Blaze said. He guessed that was true. "What's a ratty-o, George? It says make him his bottles in a ratty-o of one-something-one."

"Never mind," George said. "Really worried about him, aren't they? 'He is eating three times a day, followed by a half a bottle . . . don't hurt him, cuz we wuv him-wuv him-wuv him.' Man, this piles the pink horseshit to a new high."

"Listen—" Blaze began.

"No, I won't *listen*! Don't tell me to *listen*! He's all they have, right? That and about forty million smackareenies! Ought to get the money and then send the kid back in pieces. First a finger, then a toe, then his little—"

"George, *you shut up*!"

He clapped a hand over his mouth, shocked. He had just told George to shut up. What was he thinking about? What was wrong with him?

"George?"

No answer.

"George, I'm sorry. It's just that you shouldn't say things, you know, like that." He tried to smile. "We have to give the kid back alive, right? That's the plan. Right?"

No answer, and now Blaze started to feel really miserable.

"George? George, what's wrong?"

No answer for a long time. Then, so softly he might not have heard it, so softly it might have only been a thought in his own head:

"You'll have to leave him with me, Blaze. Sooner or later."

Blaze wiped his mouth with the palm of his hand. "You better not do anything to 'im, George. You just better not. I'm warning you."

No answer.

By nine o'clock, Joe was up, changed, fed, and playing on the kitchen floor. Blaze was sitting at the table and listening to the radio. He had cleared off the scraps of paper and thrown out the hardened flour paste, and the only thing on the table was his letter to the Gerards. He was trying to figure out how to mail it.

He had heard the news three times. The police had picked up a man named Charles Victor Pritchett, a big drifter from Aroostook County who had been laid off some sawmill job a month earlier. Then he had been released. Probably that scrawny little door-opener Walsh couldn't make him for it, Blaze reasoned. Too bad. A good suspect would have taken the heat off for awhile.

He shifted restlessly in his chair. He had to get this kidnapping off the ground. He had to make a plan about mailing the letter. They had a drawing of him, and they knew about the car. They even knew about the color—that bastard Walsh again.

His mind moved slowly and heavily. He got up, made more coffee, then got out the newspaper again. He frowned at the police sketch of himself. Big, square-jawed face. Broad, flat nose. Thick shock of hair, hadn't been cut in quite awhile (George had done it last time, snipping away indifferently with a pair of kitchen shears). Deepset eyes. Only a suggestion of his big ole neck, and they probably wouldn't have any idea of how big he really was. People never did when he was sitting down, because his legs were the longest part of him.

Joe began to cry, and Blaze heated a bottle. The baby pushed it away, so Blaze dandled him absently on his lap. Joe quieted at once and began to stare around at things from his new elevation: the three pin-ups on the far side of the room, the greasy asbestos shield screwed into the wall behind the stove, the windows, dirty on the inside and frosty on the outside.

"Not much like where you came from, huh?" Blaze asked.

Joe smiled, then tried his strange, unpracticed laugh that made Blaze grin. The little guy had two teeth, their tops just peeking through the gums. Blaze wondered if some of the others struggling to come through were giving him trouble; Joe chewed his hands a lot, and sometimes whined in his sleep. Now he began to drool, and Blaze wiped his mouth with an old Kleenex that was wadded up in his pocket.

He couldn't leave the baby with George again. It was like George was jealous, or something. Almost like George wanted to—

He might have stiffened, because Joe looked around at him with a funny questioning expression, like *What's up with you, buddy?* Blaze hardly noticed. Because the thing was . . . now *he* was George. And that meant that part of him wanted to—

Again he shied away from it, and when he did, his troubled mind found something else to seize on.

If *he* went somewhere, *George* went somewhere, too. If he was George now, that only made sense. A leads to B, simple as can be, Johnny Cheltzman would have said.

If *he* went, *George* went.

Which meant that George was powerless to hurt Joe no matter how much he might want to.

Something inside him loosened. He still didn't like the idea of leaving the baby, but better to leave him alone than with somebody who might hurt him . . . and besides, he had to do it. There was no one else.

But he could sure use a disguise, with them having that drawing of him and all. Something like a nylon stocking, only natural. What?

An idea came to him. It didn't come in a flash, but slowly. It rose in his mind like a bubble rising to the surface of water so thick it's nearly mud.

He put Joe back on the floor, then went into the bathroom. He laid out scissors and a towel. Then he got George's Norelco shaver out of the medicine cabinet, where it had been sleeping all these months with the cord wrapped around it.

He cut his hair in big unlovely bunches, cut until what was left stuck up in bristly patches. Then he plugged in the Norelco and shaved those off, too. He went back and forth until the electric razor was hot in his hand and his newly nude scalp was pink with irritation.

He regarded his image in the mirror curiously. The dent in his brow showed more clearly than ever, all of it uncovered for the first time in years, and it *was* sort of horrible to look at—it looked almost deep enough to hold a cup of coffee, if he was lying on his back—but otherwise Blaze didn't think he looked much like the crazed babynapper in the police sketch. He looked like some foreign guy from Germany or Berlin or someplace. But his eyes, they were still the same. What if his eyes gave him away?

"George has shades," he said. "That's the ticket . . . isn't it?"

He vaguely realized he was actually making himself more conspicuous rather than less, but maybe that was all right. What else could he do, anyway? He couldn't help being six-foot-whatever. All he could do was try and make his looks work for him rather than against him.

He certainly didn't realize that he had done a better job of disguise than George ever could have, no more than he realized that George was now the creation of a mind working at a feverish, half-crazed pitch below the burnt-out surface of stupidity. For years he had identified himself as a dummy, coming to accept it as just one more part of his life, like the dent in his forehead. Yet something continued to work away beneath the burnt-out surface. It worked with the deadly instinct of living things—moles, worms, microbes—beneath the surface of a burnt-over meadow. This was the part that remembered everything. Every hurt, every cruelty, every bad turn the world had done him.

He was hiking at a good pace along an Apex back road when an old pulp truck with an oversized load wheezed up beside him. The man inside was grizzled and wearing a thermal undershirt under a checkered wool coat.

"Climb up!" he bawled.

Blaze swung onto the running board and then climbed into the cab. Said thank you. The driver nodded and said, "Goin to Westbrook." Blaze nodded back and gave the guy a thumbs-up. The driver clashed the gears and the truck began to roll again. Not as if it particularly wanted to.

"Seen you before, ain't I?" the trucker shouted over the

flailing motor. His window was broken and blasts of cold January air whirled in, fighting with the baking air from the heater. "Live on Palmer Road?"

"Yeah!" Blaze shouted back.

"Jimmy Cullum used to live out there," the trucker said, and offered Blaze an incredibly battered package of Luckies. Blaze took one.

"Some guy," Blaze said. His newly bald head did not show; he was wearing a red knitted cap.

"Went down south, Jimmy did. Say, your buddy still around?"

Blaze realized he must mean George. "Naw," he said. "He found work in New Hampshire."

"Yeah?" the trucker said. "Wish he'd find me some."

They had reached the top of the hill and now the truck began down the other side, picking up speed along the rutted washboard, banging and clobbering. Blaze could almost feel the illegal load pushing them. He had driven overweight pulp trucks himself; had once taken a load of Christmas trees to Massachusetts that had to've been half a ton over the limit. It had never worried him before, but it did now. It dawned on him that only he stood between Joe and death.

After they'd gotten on the main road, the driver mentioned the kidnapping. Blaze tensed a little, but he wasn't particularly surprised.

"They find the guy grabbed that kid, they ought to string him up by his balls," the pulper offered. He shifted up to third with a hellish grinding of gears.

"I guess so," Blaze said.

"It's gettin as bad as those plane hijacks. Remember those?"

"Yep." He didn't.

The driver tossed the stub of his cigarette out the window and immediately lit another one. "It's got to stop. They ought to have mandatory death penalties for guys like that. A firing squad, maybe."

"You think they'll get the guy?" Blaze asked. He was starting to feel like a spy in a movie.

"Does the Pope wear a tall hat?" the driver asked, turning onto Route 1.

"I guess so."

"What I mean is, it goes without saying. Of course they'll get 'im. They always do. But the kid'll be dead, and you can quote me on that."

"Oh, I dunno," Blaze said.

"Yeah? Well, *I* know. Whole idea is crazy. Kidnappin in this day and age? The FBI'll mark the bills or copy the serial numbers or put invisible marks on em, the kind you can only see with an ultraviolet light."

"I guess so," Blaze said, feeling troubled. He hadn't thought about those sorts of things. Still, if he was going to sell the money in Boston, to that guy George knew, what did it matter? He started to feel better again. "You think those Gerards will really fork over a million bucks?"

The driver whistled. "Is that how much they're askin?"

Blaze felt in that moment as if he could gladly have bitten off his own tongue and swallowed it. "Yeah," he said. And thought *Oh, George.*

"That's somethin new," the driver said. "Wasn't in the morning paper. Did you hear about it on the radio?"

George said, quite clearly: "Kill him, Blaze."

The driver cupped his hand to his ear. "What? Didn't quite get that."

"I said yeah, on the radio." He looked down at his hands, folded in his lap. They were big hands, powerful. One of them had broken a Collie's neck with a single blow, and back then he hadn't even had his growth.

"They might get that ransom," the driver said, flipping out his second cigarette butt and lighting a third, "but they'll never get to spend it. Nossir. Not *never.*"

They were headed up Route 1 now, past frozen marshes and clam-shacks shuttered for the winter. The trucker was avoiding the turnpike and the weighing stations there. Blaze didn't blame him.

If I hit 'im right in the throat, where his adam's apple is, he'd wake up in heaven before he even knew he was dead, Blaze thought. Then I could grab the wheel and pull 'im over. Prop 'im up on the passenger side. Anyone who sees him'll think he's just catching him a little catnap. Poor fella, they'll think, he was probably drivin all n—

". . . goin?"

"Huh?" Blaze asked.

"I said, where you goin? I forgot."

"Oh. Westbrook."

"Well, I gotta swing off on Marah Road a mile up. Meetin a buddy, you know."

"Oh," Blaze said. "Yeah."

And George said: "You got to do it now, Blazer. Right time, right place. It's how we roll."

So Blaze turned toward the driver.

"How about another cigarette?" the driver asked. "You in'trested?" He cocked his head a little as he spoke. Offering a perfect target.

Blaze stiffened a little. His hands twitched in his lap. Then he said, "No. Tryin to quit."

"Yeah? Good for you. Cold as a witch's tit in here, ain't it?" The driver downshifted in anticipation of his turn, and from below them came a series of barking explosions as the engine backfired down its rotting tailpipe. "Window's broke. Radio, too."

"Too bad," Blaze said. His throat felt as if as if someone had just fed him a spoonful of dust.

"Yeah, yeah, life sucks and then y'die." He applied the brakes. They screamed like souls in pain. "You have to hit the ground runnin; sorry, but she stalls out in first."

"Sure," Blaze said. Now that the moment had come and gone, he felt sick to his stomach. And afraid. He wished he had never seen the driver.

"Say hi to your buddy when you see 'im," the driver said, and downshifted another gear as the overloaded truck swerved onto what Blaze assumed was Marah Road.

Blaze opened the door and jumped out onto the frozen shoulder, slamming the door behind him. The driver honked his horn once, and then the truck roared over the hill in a cloud of stinking exhaust. Soon it was just a sound, dwindling away.

Blaze started up Route 1 with his hands jammed in his pockets. He was in the exurban sprawl south of Portland, and in a mile or two he came to a big shopping center with stores and a cinema complex. There was a laundrymat there called The Giant Kleen Kloze U-Wash-It. There was a mailbox in front of the laundrymat, and there he mailed his ransom note.

There was a newspaper dispenser inside. He went in to get one.

"Look, Ma," a little kid said to his mother, who was unloading kleen kloze from a coin-op dryer. "That guy's got a hole in his head."

"Hush," the kid's mother said.

Blaze smiled at the boy, who immediately hid behind his mother's leg. From this place of safety he peered out and up.

Blaze got his paper and went out with it. A hotel fire had pushed the kidnap story to the bottom of page one, but the sketch of him was still there. SEARCH FOR KIDNAPPERS GOES ON, the headline said. He stuffed the newspaper in his back pocket. It was a bummer. While cutting across the parking lot to the road, he spotted an old Mustang with the keys in it. Without giving it much thought, Blaze got in and drove it away.

CHAPTER 16

Clayton Blaisdell, Jr., became the prime suspect in the kidnapping at 4:30 PM on that same gray January afternoon,
about an hour and a half after he dropped his letter into
the mailbox in front of the Giant Kleen Kloze U-Wash-It.
There was "a break in the case," as law enforcement officials
like to say. But even before the phone call that came to the
FBI number listed in that day's story about the snatch, ID
had become only a matter of time.

The police had a wealth of information. There was the
description given by Morton Walsh (whose ass would be
canned by his Boston employers as soon as the furor died
down). There were a number of blue threads plucked from
the top of the chainlink fence surrounding the Oakwood
visitors' parking lot, identified as being from D-Boy jeans,
a discount brand. There were photos and casts of boot-
treads with distinctive wear-patterns. There was a blood
sample, type AB, Rh-negative. There were photos and
casts of the feet of an extendable ladder, now identified
as a Craftwork Lightweight Supreme. There were pho-
tographs of boot-prints inside the house, featuring those
same distinctive wear-patterns. And there was a dying
declaration by Norma Gerard, identifying the police art-

ist's sketch as a reasonable likeness of the man who had assaulted her.

Before lapsing into a coma, she had added one detail that Walsh had left out: the man had a massive dent in his forehead, as if he had once been hit there with a brick or a length of pipe.

Very little of this information had been given to the press.

Other than the dent in the forehead, investigators were particularly interested in two facts. First, D-Boy jeans were sold at only a few dozen outlets in northern New England. Second, and even better, Craftwork Ladders was a small Vermont company that wholesaled only to independent hardware stores. No Ames, no Mammoth Mart, no Kmart. A small army of officers began visiting these independent dealers. They had not reached Apex Hardware ("The Helpful Place!") on the day Blaze mailed his letter, but it was now only a matter of hours before they did.

At the Gerard home, traceback equipment had been installed. Joseph Gerard IV's father had been carefully coached on how to handle the inevitable call when it came. Joe's mother was upstairs, stuffed with tranks.

None of the law enforcement officials were under any orders to take the kidnapper or kidnappers alive. Forensic experts estimated that one of the men they were after (maybe the only man) stood at least six feet, four inches tall and weighed in the two-fifty range. The fractured skull of Norma Gerard offered testimony, if any were needed, of his strength and brutality.

Then, at 4:30 PM on that gray day, SAC Albert Sterling got a call from Nancy Moldow.

As soon as Sterling and his partner, Bruce Granger, stepped into the Baby Shoppe, Nancy Moldow said: "There's something wrong with your picture. The man you want has a big hole in the middle of his forehead."

"Yes, ma'am," Sterling said. "We're holding that back."

Her eyes got round. "So *he* won't know that *you* know."

"That's correct."

She gestured to the young fellow standing next to her. He was wearing a blue nylon duster, a red bowtie, and a thrilled look. "This is Brant. He helped that . . . that . . . *him* out with the things he bought."

"Full name?" Agent Granger asked the kid in the blue duster. He opened his notebook.

The stockboy's adam's apple went up and down like a monkey on a stick. "Brant Romano. Sir. That guy was driving a Ford." He named the year with what Sterling deemed to be a high degree of confidence. "Only it wasn't blue, like it says in the paper. It was green."

Sterling turned to Moldow. "What did this man buy, ma'am?"

She actually laughed a little. "My laws, what *didn't* he. All baby things, of course, that's what we sell here. A crib, a cradle, a changing table, clothes . . . the works. He even bought a single place serving."

"Do you have a complete list?" Granger asked.

"Of course. I never suspected he was up to something

awful. He actually seemed like a nice enough man, although that dented place in his forehead . . . that *hole* . . ."

Granger nodded sympathetically.

"And he didn't seem terribly bright. But bright enough to fool me, I guess. He said he was buying things for a little nephew, and silly Nan believed him."

"And he was big."

"My laws, a *giant!* It was like being with a . . . a . . ." She trilled nervous laughter. "A bull in a baby shop!"

"How big?"

She shrugged. "I'm five-feet-four, and I only came up to his *ribs*. That would make him——"

"You probably won't believe this," said Brant the stockboy, "but I thought he had to be, like, six-seven. Maybe even six-eight."

Sterling prepared to ask a final question. He had saved it for last because he was almost sure it would lead to a dead end.

"Mrs. Moldow, how did this man pay for his purchases?"

"Cash," she said promptly.

"I see." He looked at Granger. It was the answer they had expected.

"You should have *seen* all the cash he had in his wallet!"

"Spent most of it," Brant said. "He tipped me five, but by then the cupboard was mostly, like, bare."

Sterling ignored this. "And since it was a cash purchase, you don't have any record of the man's name."

"No. No record. Hager's will get around to putting in security cameras in a few years, I suppose——"

"Centuries," said Brant. "This place is, like, cheap to the max."

"Well, then," Sterling said, flipping his notebook closed, "we'll be going. But I want to give you my card in case you think of anyth—"

"I *do* happen to know his name," Nancy Moldow said.

They both turned back to her.

"When he opened his wallet to take out that big stack of money, I saw his driver's license. I remember the name partly because that kind of sale is a once-in-a-lifetime thing, but mostly because it was such a . . . a *stately* name. It didn't seem to fit him. I remember thinking that a man like him should be named Barney or Fred. You know, like on *The Flintstones*."

"What was the name?" Sterling asked.

"Clayton Blaisdell. In fact, I think it was Clayton Blaisdell, *Jr.*"

By five-thirty that evening, they had their man tabbed. Clayton Blaisdell, Jr., aka Blaze, had been popped twice, once for assault and battery against the headmaster of the state home where the kid was living—a place called Hetton House—and once more, years later, for bunco and fraud. A suspected accomplice, George Thomas Rackley, aka Rasp, had gotten off because Blaze wouldn't testify against him.

According to police files, Blaisdell and Rackley had been a team for at least eight years before Blaisdell's fall on the bunco rap, which had been a religious con just a little too complex for the big boy's limited mental talents. At South Portland Correctional, he had taken an IQ test and scored low enough to be placed in a category called "borderline restricted." In the margin, someone had written, in big red letters: RETARDED.

Sterling found the details of the con itself quite amusing. In the gag, there was a big man in a wheelchair (Blaisdell) and a little guy pushing him who introduced himself to marks as the Rev. Gary Crowell (almost certainly Rackley). The Rev. Gary (as he styled himself) claimed to be raising money for a revivalist swing through Japan. If the marks—mostly old ladies with a little stashed in the bank—proved hard to convince, the Rev. Gary performed a miracle. He caused the big guy in the wheelchair to walk again, through the power of Jesus.

The circumstances of the arrest were even more amusing. An octogenarian named Arlene Merrill got suspicious and called the police while the Rev. Gary and his "assistant" were in the living room. Then she walked back to the living room to talk to them until the police arrived.

The Rev. Gary smelled it and took off. Blaisdell stayed. In his report, the arresting officer wrote, *"Suspect said he did not flee because he had not been healed yet."*

Sterling considered all this and decided that there were two kidnappers, after all. At least two. Rackley had to be in on it with him, a guy as dumb as Blaisdell sure hadn't pulled this thing off alone.

He picked up the phone, made a call. A few minutes later he got a callback that surprised him. George Thomas "Rasp" Rackley had died the previous year. He had been found knifed in the area of a known crap-game on the Portland docks.

Shit. Someone else, then?

Someone running the big lug the way Rackley no doubt once had?

Just about had to be, didn't there?

By seven that night, a statewide all-points—what would become known as a BOLO a few years later—was out on Clayton Blaisdell, Jr.

By that time Jerry Green of Gorham had discovered his Mustang had been stolen. The car was on State Police hot-sheets forty minutes or so later.

Around that same time, Westbrook PD gave Sterling the number of a woman named Georgia Kingsbury. Ms. Kingsbury had been reading the evening paper when her son looked over her shoulder, pointed to the police sketch, and asked, "Why is that man from the laundry-mat in the paper? And how come that doesn't show the hole in his head?"

Mrs. Kingsbury told Sterling: "I took one look and said oh my God."

At 7:40, Sterling and Granger arrived at the Kingsbury home. They showed mother and son a copy of Clayton Blaisdell, Jr.'s mug shot. The copy was blurry, but the Kingsburys' identification was still immediate and posi-tive. Sterling guessed that once you saw Blaisdell, you re-membered him. That this hulk was the last person Norma Gerard had seen in her lifelong home made Sterling sick with anger.

"He smiled at me," the Kingsbury boy said.

"That's nice, son," Sterling said, and ruffled his hair.

The boy flinched away. "Your hand is cold," he said.

In the car Granger said, "You think it's odd that the big boss would send a guy like that shopping for the kid? A guy so easy to remember?"

When Sterling considered, he did think it a little odd, but Blaisdell's shopping spree suggested something else, as well. It was optimistic, and so he preferred to concentrate on that. All that baby stuff suggested they meant to keep the kid alive, at least for awhile.

Granger was still looking at him, waiting for an answer.

So Sterling said, "Who knows why these mopes do anything? Come on, let's go."

The all-but-positive ID of Blaisdell as one of the kidnappers went out to state and local law enforcement agencies at 8:05 PM. At 8:20, Sterling received a call from State Trooper Paul Hanscom, at the Portland barracks. Hanscom reported that a 1970 Mustang had been stolen from the same mall where Georgia Kingsbury had seen Blaisdell, and at approximately the same time. He wanted to know if the FBI would like that added to the APB. Sterling said the FBI would like that very much.

Now Sterling decided that he knew the answer to Agent Granger's question. It was really simple. The brains of the operation was brighter than Blaisdell—bright enough to hang back, especially with the added excuse of a baby to take care of—but not *that* bright.

And now it was really just a matter of waiting for the net to tighten. And hoping—

But Albert Sterling decided he could do more than just hope. At 10:15 that evening, he went down the hall to the men's and checked the stalls and urinals. The place was empty. That didn't surprise him. This was just a small office, really just a provincial bump on the FBI's ass. Also, it was getting late.

He went into one of the stalls, dropped to his knees, and folded his hands just as he had as a child. "God, this is Albert. If that baby is still alive, watch over him, would you? And if I get near the man who murdered Norma Gerard, please let him do something that will give me cause to kill the sonofabitch. Thank you. I pray in the name of Your Son, Jesus Christ."

And because the men's room was still empty, he threw in a Hail Mary for good measure.

CHAPTER 17

The baby woke him up at quarter to four in the morning, and a bottle didn't comfort him. When the crying continued, Blaze began to be a little scared. He put a hand on Joe's forehead. The skin felt cool, but the screams he was producing were frightening in their intensity. Blaze was afraid he'd bust a blood vessel, or something.

He put Joe on the changing table. He took off his diapers and didn't see how they could be the problem, either. They were dewy but not pooey. Blaze powdered the kid's bottom and put on fresh didies. The screams continued. Blaze began to feel desperate as well as frightened.

Blaze hoisted the shrieking infant onto his shoulder. He began to walk him in large circles around the kitchen. "Hushabye," he said. "You're all right. You're okay. You're *rockin'*. Go to sleep. Hushabye-hushaboo, zippity-doo. Shhh, baby, shhh. You'll wake up a bear sleepin in the snow and he'll want to eat us. Shhhhhhh."

Maybe it was the walking. Maybe it was the sound of Blaze's voice. In any case, Joe's screams shortened, then stopped. A few more turns around the shack's kitchen and the baby's head fell against the side of Blaze's neck.

His breathing lengthened into the long slow strokes of
sleep.

Blaze put him carefully down in the cradle and began
to rock it. Joe stirred but did not wake. One small hand
found its way into his mouth, and he began to chew furiously. Blaze started feeling better. Maybe there was nothing
wrong, after all. The book said they chewed their hands
that way when they were teething or hungry, and he was
pretty sure Joe wasn't hungry.

He looked down at the baby and thought, more con-
sciously this time, that Joe was sort of nice. Cute, too.
Anybody could see that. It would be interesting to see
him grow through all the stages the doctor talked about in
Child and Baby Care. Joe was about ready to start crawling
right now. Several times since Blaze had brought him to
the shack, the little fucker had been right up on his hands
and knees. Then he'd walk . . . and words would start coming out of all that babble . . . and then . . . then . . .

Then he'd *have* somebody.

The thought was unsettling. Blaze couldn't sleep anymore. He got up and turned on the radio, keeping the vol-
ume low. He searched through the before-sunrise chatter
of a thousand competing stations until he found the strong
signal of WLOB.

The 4:00 AM news had nothing fresh about the kidnapping. That seemed all right; the Gerards wouldn't be
getting his letter until later today. Maybe not even until
tomorrow, depending on when the mail got picked up
from the mall. Besides, he couldn't see why they should
have any leads. He'd been careful, and except for that guy

at Oakwood (Blaze had already forgotten his name), he thought this was what George would have called "a real clean gag."

Sometimes, after they pulled a good con, he and George would buy a bottle of Four Roses. Then they would go to a movie and chase the Roses with Coke they bought from the theater's refreshment stand. If the movie was a long one, George would sometimes be almost too drunk to walk by the time the final credits rolled. He was smaller, and the booze got to him quicker. They had been good times. They made Blaze think about the times when him and old Johnny Cheltzman had palled around, snickering at those old movies the Nordica showed.

Music came back on the radio. Joe was sleeping easily. Blaze thought he should go back to bed himself. There was a lot to do tomorrow. Or maybe even today. He wanted to send the Gerards another ransom note. He'd had a good idea for collecting the swag. It had come to him in a dream—a crazy one—he'd had the night before. He hadn't been able to make head or tail of it then, but the sweet, heavy, dreamless sleep from which the baby's crying had just roused him seemed to have clarified it. He'd tell them to drop the ransom from a plane. A small one that didn't fly very high. In the letter he would say that the plane should fly south along Route 1 from Portland to the Massachusetts border, looking for a red signal light.

Blaze knew just how to do it: road-flares. He would buy half a dozen from the hardware store in town, and set them out in a little bunch at the place he picked. They would make a good hard light. He knew just the place, too: a logging road south of Ogunquit. There was a clearing on that road where the truckers sometimes pulled over to eat their lunches or catch a snooze in the sleepers they had behind their cabs. The clearing was close to Route 1, and a pilot flying down the highway couldn't miss road-flares there, bunched close and shooting up like a big red flashlight. Blaze knew he still wouldn't have much time, but he thought he'd have enough. That first logging road led to a network of unmarked rambles with names like Boggy Stream Road and Bumpnose Road. Blaze knew them all. One of them led to Route 41 and from there he could turn back north. Find a place to hide out until the heat cooled down. He had even considered Hetton House. It was empty and boarded up now, with a FOR SALE sign in front of it. Blaze had been by there several times in the last few years, drawn back like a little kid who's had a scare in the neighborhood's supposedly haunted house.

Only for him, HH really *was* haunted. He should know; he was one of the ghosts.

Anyway, it was going to be all right, that was the main thing. It had been scary for awhile, and he was sorry about the old lady (whose first name he had also forgotten), but now it was turned into a real clean g—

"Blaze."

He glanced toward the bathroom. It was George, all right. The bathroom door was ajar, the way George always left it when he wanted to talk while he took a dump. "Crap coming out at both ends," he'd said once when he was doing that, and both of them laughed. He could be funny when he wanted to, but he didn't sound like he was in a funny mood this morning. Also, Blaze thought he had closed that door when he came out of the bathroom himself the last time. He supposed a draft could have blown it open again, but he didn't feel any dra—

"They've almost got you, Blaze," George said. Then, in a kind of despairing growl: "Dumb shit."

"Who does?" Blaze asked.

"The cops. Who did you think I meant, the Republican National Committee? The FBI. The State Police. Even the local humps in blue."

"No they ain't. I been doin real good, George. Honest. It's a clean gag. I'll tell you what I did, how careful I w—"

"If you don't blow this shack, they'll have you by noon tomorrow."

"How . . . what . . ."

"You're so stupid you can't even get out of your own way. I don't even know why I bother. You've made a dozen mistakes. If you're lucky, the cops have only found six or eight so far."

Blaze hung his head. He could feel his face heating up. "What should I do?"

"Roll outta this pop-stand. Right now."

"Where—"

"And get rid of the kid," George said. Almost as an afterthought.

"*What?*"

"Did I stutter? Get rid of him. He's dead fuckin weight. You can collect the ransom without him."

"But if I take him back, how will I—"

"I'm not talking about taking him back!" George stormed. "What do you think he is, a fuckin returnable bottle? I'm talking about killing him! Do it now!"

Blaze shifted his feet. His heart was beating fast and he hoped George would get out of the bathroom soon because he had to pee and he couldn't pee around no fuckin ghost. "Wait . . . I got to think. Maybe, George, if you went for a little walk . . . when you came back, we could work this out."

"You *can't* think!" George's voice rose until it was almost a howl. It was as if he were in pain. "Do the cops have to come and put a bullet in that stone you carry around on top of your neck before you realize that? You *can't* think, Blaze! But *I can*!"

His voice dropped. Became reasonable. Almost silky.

"He's asleep now, so he'll never feel a thing. Get your pillow—it even smells like you, he'll like that—and put it over his face. Hold it down real tight. I bet the parents are sure it's happened already. They probably got to work making a little replacement Republican the next fuckin night. Then you can take your shot at collecting the swag. And go someplace warm. We always wanted that. Right? Right?"

It *was* right. Someplace like Acapulco or the Bahamas.

"What do you say, Blaze-a-roonie? Am I right or am I right with Eversharp?"

"You're right, George. I guess."

"You know I am. It's how we roll."

Suddenly nothing was simple anymore. If George said

the police were close and getting closer, on that he was probably right. George had always had a sharp nose for blue. And the kid *would* slow him down if he left here in a hurry—George was right about that, too. His job now was to collect that fuckin ransom and then hide out someplace. But killing the kid? Killing *Joe?*

It suddenly occurred to Blaze that if he *did* kill him—and very, very gently—Joe would go right to heaven and be a baby angel there. So maybe George was right about that, too. Blaze himself was pretty sure he himself was going to hell, as were most other people. It was a dirty world, and the longer you lived, the dirtier you got.

He grabbed his pillow and carried it back to the main room, where Joe slept by the stove. His hand had fallen out of his mouth, but the fingers still bore the marks of his frantic chewing. It was a painful world, too. Not just dirty but painful. Teething was only the first and least of it.

Blaze stood over the cradle, holding the pillow, its case still dark with layers of hair-tonic he'd left on it. Back when he still had hair to put it on.

George was always right . . . except when he wasn't. To Blaze this still felt wrong.

"Jeez," he said, and the word had a watery sound.

"Do it quick," George said from the bathroom. "Don't make him suffer."

Blaze knelt down and put the pillow over the baby's face. His elbows were in the cradle, placed on either side of that small ribcage, and he could feel Joe's breath pull in twice . . . stop . . . pull in once more . . . stop again. Joe stirred and arched his back. He twisted his head at the same time, and began to breathe again. Blaze pressed the pillow tighter.

He didn't cry. Blaze thought it might be better if the kid would cry. For the baby to die silently, like an insect, seemed worse than pitiful. It was horrible. Blaze took the pillow away.

Joe turned his head, opened his eyes, closed them, smiled, and put his thumb in his mouth. Then he was just sleeping again.

Blaze was breathing in ragged gasps. Sweat stood out in beads on his dented forehead. He looked at the pillow, still in his fisted hands, and dropped it as if it were hot. He began to tremble, and he grasped his belly to stop it. It wouldn't stop. Soon he was shaking all over. His muscles hummed like telegraph wires.

"Finish it, Blaze."

"No."

"If you don't, I'm in the breeze."

"Go, then."

"You think you're going to keep him, don't you?" In the bathroom, George laughed. It sounded like a chuckling drainpipe. "You poor sap. You let him live and he'll grow up hating your guts. They'll see to it. Those good people. Those good rich asshole Republican millionaires. Didn't I never teach you nothing, Blaze? Let me say it in words even a sap can understand: if you were on fire, they wouldn't piss on you to put you out."

Blaze looked down at the floor, where the terrible pillow

lay. He was still shaking, but now his face was burning, too. He knew George was right. Still he said, "I don't plan to catch on fire, George."

"You don't plan *nothing*! Blazer, when that happy little goo-goo doll of yours grows up to be a man, he'll go ten miles out of his way just to spit on your fuckin grave. Now for the last time, *kill that kid*!"

"No."

Suddenly George was gone. And maybe he really had been there all along, because Blaze was sure he felt something— some presence—leave the shack. No windows opened and no doors slammed, but yes: the shack was emptier than it had been.

Blaze walked over to the bathroom door and booted it open. Nothing there but the sink. A rusty shower. And the crapper.

He tried to go back to sleep and couldn't. What he'd almost done hung inside his head like a curtain. And what George had said. *They've almost got you.* And *If you don't blow this shack, they'll have you by noon tomorrow.*

And worst of all: *When he grows up to be a man, he'll go ten miles out of his way just to spit on your fuckin grave.*

For the first time Blaze felt really hunted. In a way he felt already caught . . . like a bug struggling in a web from which there is no escape. Lines from old movies started occurring to him. *Take him dead or alive. If you don't come out now, we're comin in, and we're comin in shootin. Put up your hands, scumbucket—it's all over.*

He sat up, sweating. It was going on five, about an hour

since the baby's cries had awakened him. Dawn was on the way, but so far it was just a faint orange line on the horizon. Overhead, the stars turned on their old axle, indifferent to it all.

If you don't blow this shack, they'll have you by noon.

But where would he go?

He actually knew the answer to that question. Had known for days.

He got up and dressed in rapid, jerky gestures: thermal underwear, woolen shirt, two pairs of socks, Levi's, boots. The baby was still sleeping, and Blaze had time only to spare him a glance. He got paper bags from under the sink and began filling them with diapers, Playtex Nurser bottles, cans of milk.

When the bags were full, he carried them out to the Mustang, which was parked beside the stolen Ford. At least he had a key for the Mustang's trunk, and he put the bags in there. He ran both ways. Now that he had decided to go, panic nipped his heels.

He got another bag and filled it with Joe's clothes. He collapsed the changing table and took that, too, thinking incoherently that Joe would like it in a new place because he was used to it. The Mustang's trunk was small, but by transferring some of the bags to the back seat, he managed to cram the changing table in. The cradle could also go in the back seat, he reckoned. The baby dinners could go in the passenger seat footwell, with some baby blankets on top of them. Joe was really getting into the baby dinners, chowing down bigtime.

He made one more trip, then started the Mustang and turned on the heater to make the car nice and toasty-warm. It was five-thirty. Daylight was advancing. The stars had paled; now only Venus glowed brightly.

Back in the house, Blaze lifted Joe out of his cradle and put him on his bed. The baby muttered but didn't wake. Blaze took the cradle out to the car.

He went back in and looked around rather wildly. He took the radio from its place on the windowsill, unplugged it, wrapped the cord around it, and set it on the table. In the bedroom he hauled his old brown suitcase—battered and scuffed white at the corners—from under the bed. He piled the remainder of his clothes in, helter-skelter. On top of these he put a couple of girly magazines and a few comic-books. He took the suitcase and his radio out to the car, which was starting to get full. Then he went back to the house for the last time.

He spread a blanket, put Joe on it, wrapped him up, and put the entire bundle inside his jacket. Then he zipped the jacket up. Joe was awake now. He peered out of his cocoon like a gerbil.

Blaze carried him out to the car, got in behind the wheel, and put Joe down on the passenger seat.

"Now, don't go rolling around there, Skinner," he said.

Joe smiled and promptly pulled the blanket over his head. Blaze snorted a little chuckle, and in the same instant he saw himself putting the pillow over Joe's face. He shuddered.

He backed out of the shed, turned the car around, and

trundled down the driveway . . . and although he didn't know it, he was beating an area-wide necklace of road-blocks by less than two hours.

He used back roads and secondary roads to skirt Port-land and its suburbs. The steady sound of the motor and the heater's output sent Joe back to dreamland almost immediately. Blaze tuned to his favorite country music station, which came on at sunrise. He heard the morning scripture reading, then a farm report, then a right-wing editorial from Freedom Line in Houston that would have sent George into paroxysms of profanity. Finally came the news.

"The search for the kidnappers of Joseph Gerard IV con-tinues," the announcer said gravely, "and there may be at least one new development."

Blaze pricked up his ears.

"A source close to the investigation claims that the Port-land Postal Authority received a possible ransom demand in the mail last night, and sent the letter by car directly to the Gerard home. Neither local authorities nor Federal Bureau of Investigation lead agent Albert Sterling would offer any comment."

Blaze paid no attention to that part. The Gerards had gotten his letter, and that was good. Next time he would have to call them. He hadn't remembered to bring any newspapers or envelopes or anything to make paste with, anyway. And calling was always better. It was quicker.

"And now the weather. Low pressure centered over upper New York State is expected to sweep east and hit New

Englanders with the biggest snowstorm of the season. The National Weather Service has posted blizzard warnings, and snow may begin as early as noon today."

Blaze turned onto Route 136, then turned off it two miles up and onto the Stinkpine Road. When he passed the pond—now frozen—where he and Johnny had once watched beavers building their dam, he felt a dreamy and powerful sense of *déjà vu*. There was the abandoned farmhouse where Blaze and Johnny and an Italian-looking kid had once broken in. They had found a stack of shoeboxes in one closet. There had been dirty pictures in one of them—men and women doing everything, women and women, even one of a woman and a horse or donkey—and they had looked all afternoon, their emotions drifting from amazement to lust to disgust. Blaze couldn't remember the Italian-looking kid's real name, only that everyone had called him Toe-Jam.

Blaze turned right at the fork a mile up and onto a pitted tertiary road that had been carelessly (and narrowly) plowed, then allowed to drift back in. A quarter of a mile up, beyond a curve the boys had called Sweet Baby Turn (Blaze had known why in the long-ago, but it escaped him now), he came to a chain hung across the road. Blaze got out, went over to it, and pulled the rusted padlock free of its hasp with one gentle tug. He had been here before, and then half a dozen hard yanks had been needed to break the lock's old mechanism.

Now he laid the chain down and surveyed the road beyond. It hadn't been plowed since the last storm, but he thought the Mustang would roll okay if he backed up first and got some speed. He'd come back later and fix the chain across the road; it wouldn't be the first time. This place drew him.

And best? Snow was coming, and snow would bury his tracks.

He dropped his bulk into the bucket seat, shifted into reverse, and backed up two hundred feet. Then he dropped the drive-selector all the way down into low range and hit the gas. The Mustang went like its name. The engine was snarling and the RPM gauge the owner had installed was redlining, so Blaze knocked the gearshift up into drive with the side of his hand, figuring he could downshift again if his little stolen pony really started to labor.

He hit the snow. The Mustang tried to skid but he went with it and its pretty little nose came back around. He drove like a man in a memory that is half a dream, counting on that dream to keep him out of the hidden ditches to either side where the Mustang would mire. Snow spumed up in fans on either side of the speeding car. Crows rose from trashwood pines and lumbered into the scum-white sky.

He crested the first hill. Beyond it, the road bent left. The car tried to skid again, and Blaze once more rode it, on the very edge of control, the wheel turning itself under his hands for a moment, then coming back to his grip as the tires found some thin traction. Snow flew up and covered the windshield. Blaze started the wipers, but for a moment he was driving blind, laughing with terror and exhilaration. When the windshield cleared again, he saw the main gate dead ahead. It was closed, but it was too late to do anything about it except put a steadying hand on the sleeping baby's chest and pray. The Mustang was doing forty and running rocker panel-deep in snow. There was a bitter clang that shivered the car's frame and no doubt destroyed its alignment forever. Boards split and flew. The Mustang fishtailed . . . spun . . . stalled.

Blaze reached out a hand to re-start the engine, but it faltered and fell away.

There, in front of him, brooded Hetton House: three stories of sooty redbrick. He looked at the boarded-up windows, transfixed. It had been the same way the other times he'd come out here. Old memories stirred, took on color, started to walk. John Cheltzman doing his homework for him. The Law finding out. The discovered wallet. The long nights spent planning how they'd spend the money in the wallet, whispering bed to bed after lights-out. The smell of floor-varnish and chalk. The forbidding pictures on the walls, with eyes that seemed to follow you.

There were two signs on the door. One said NO TRES-PASSING BY ORDER OF SHERIFF, CUMBERLAND COUNTY. The other said FOR SALE OR LEASE SEE OR CALL GERALD CLUTTERBUCK REALTY, CASTLE ROCK, MAINE.

Blaze started the Mustang, shifted to low, and crept forward. The wheels kept trying to spin, and he had to keep the steering-wheel lefthauled in order to stay straight, but the little car was still willing to work and he slowly made his way down the east side of the main building. There was a little space between it and the long low storage shed next door. He drove the Mustang in there, mashing the accelerator all the way to the floorboards to keep it moving. When he turned it off, the silence was deafening. He didn't need anyone to tell him that the Mustang had finished its tour of duty, at least with him; it would be here until spring.

Blaze shivered, although it wasn't cold in the car. He felt as if he had come home.

To stay.

He forced the back door and brought Joe inside, wrapped snugly in three of his blankets. It felt colder inside than out. It felt as if cold had settled into the building's very bones.

He took the baby up to Martin Coslaw's office. The name had been scraped off the frosted glass panel, and the room beyond was a bare box. There was no feel of The Law in here now. Blaze tried to remember who had come after him and couldn't. He'd been gone by then, anyway. Gone to North Windham, where the bad boys go.

He laid Joe down on the floor and began to prowl the building. There were a few desks, some scattered hunks of wood, some crumpled paper. He scavenged an armload, carried it back to the office, and built a fire in the tiny fireplace set into the wall. When it was going to his satisfaction and he was sure the chimney was going to draw, he went back to the Mustang and began to unload.

By noon he was established. The baby was tucked into his cradle, still sleeping (although showing signs of waking up). His diapers and canned dinners were carefully arranged on the shelves. Blaze had found a chair for himself and spread two blankets in the corner for a bed. The room was a little warmer but a fundamental chill remained. It oozed from the walls and blew under the door. He would have to keep the kid bundled up good.

Blaze shrugged on his jacket and went out, first down the road to the chain. He strung it back in place and was pleased to find that the lock, although broken, would still close. You'd have to get your nose practically right down on top of it to see it wasn't right. Then he retreated to the destroyed main gate. Here he propped up the big pieces as well as he could. It looked pretty shitty, but at least when he jammed the pieces down in the snow as far as they'd go (he was sweating heavily now), they stood upright. And hell—if anyone got this close, he was in trouble, anyway. He was dumb but not *that* dumb.

When he got back, Joe was awake and screaming lustily. This no longer terrified Blaze as it had at first. He dressed the kid in his little jacket (green—and cute), then set him on the floor to paddle around. While Joe tried to crawl, Blaze opened a beef dinner. He couldn't find the damn spoon—it would probably show up eventually, most things did—and so he fed the kid off the end of his finger. He was delighted to find Joe had gotten another tooth through in the night. That made a total of three.

"Sorry it's cold," Blaze said. "We'll work somethin out, okay?"

Joe didn't care that his dinner was cold. He ate greedily. Then, after he was finished, he began to cry with the bellyache. Blaze knew that for what it was; he now knew the difference between bellyache crying, teething crying, and *I'm tired* crying. He put Joe on his shoulder and walked around the room with him, rubbing his back and crooning. Then, when he kept crying, Blaze walked up and down the cold corridor with him, still crooning. Joe began to shiver as well as to cry, so Blaze wrapped him in a blanket and flipped the corner of it over Joe's head like a hood.

He climbed to the third floor and went into Room 7, where he and Martin Coslaw had originally met in Arithmetic. There were three desks left, piled in the corner. On top of one, nearly hidden by entwinings of later graffiti (hearts, male and female sexual equipment, adjurations to suck and bend over), he saw the initials **CB**, done in his own careful block letters.

Wonderingly, he took off a glove and let his fingers trail over the ancient cuts. A boy he barely remembered had been here before him. It was incredible. And, in a strange way that made him think of birds sitting alone on telephone wires, sad. The cuts were old, the damage to the wood rubbed smooth by time. The wood had accepted them, made them part of itself.

He seemed to hear a chuckle behind him and whirled.

"George?"

No answer. The word echoed away, then bounced back. It seemed to mock him. It seemed to say there was no million, there was just this room. This room where he had been embarrassed and frightened. This room where he had failed to learn.

Joe stirred on his shoulder and sneezed. His nose was

red. He began to cry. The noise was frail in the cold and empty building. The damp brick seemed to suck it up.

"There," Blaze crooned. "It's all right, don't cry. I'm here. It's all right. You're fine. I'm fine."

The baby was shivering again and Blaze decided to take him back down to The Law's office. He would put him in his cradle by the fireplace. With an extra blanket.

"It's all right, honey. It's good. It's fine."

But Joe cried until he was exhausted, and not too long after that, it began to spit snow.

CHAPTER 18

The summer after their Boston adventure, Blaze and Johnny Cheltzman went out blueberry raking with some other boys from Hetton House. The man who hired them, Harry Bluenote, was a straight. Not in the contemptuous sense in which Blaze would later hear George use the word, but in the best Lord Baden-Powell tradition. He owned fifty acres of prime blueberry land in West Harlow, and burned it over every other spring. Each July he hired a crew of two dozen or so young misfits to rake it. There was nothing in it for him other than the thin money any small farmer gets from a cash crop. He might have hired boys from HH and girls from the Wiscassett Home for Troubled Girls and given them three cents a quart; they would have taken it and counted themselves lucky to be out in the fresh air. Instead he gave them the straight seven that local kids asked for and got. The money for bus transportation to and from the fields came out of his own pocket.

He was a tall, scrawny old Yankee with a deeply seamed face and pale eyes. If you looked into those eyes too long, you came away with the conviction that he was crazy. He was not a member of the Grange or any other farmers' association. They would not have had him, anyway. Not a man who hired criminals to pick his berries. And they *were* criminals, dammit, whether they were sixteen or sixty-one. They came into a decent little town and decent folks felt like they had to lock their doors. They had to watch out for strange teenagers walking the roads. Boys *and* girls. Put them together—criminal boys *and* criminal girls—and what you got was no better than Sodom and Gomorrah. Everyone said so. It was wrong. Especially when you were trying to raise your own young ones up right.

The season lasted from the second week of July into the third or fourth week of August. Bluenote had constructed ten cabins down by the Royal River, which ran smack through the middle of his property. There were six boys' cabins and four girls' cabins in another cluster at a little distance. Because of their relative positions on the river, the boys' quarters were called Riffle Cabins and the girls' Bend Cabins. One of Bluenote's sons—Douglas—stayed with the boys. Bluenote advertised each June for a woman to stay at Bend Cabins, someone who could double as a "camp mom" and a cook. He paid her well, and this came out of his own pocket too.

The whole scandalous affair came up at town meeting one year, when a Southwest Bend coalition tried to force a reassessment of the taxes on Bluenote's property. The idea seemed to be to cut his profit margin enough to make his pinko social welfare programs impossible.

Bluenote said nothing until the discussion's close. His boy Dougie and two or three friends from his end of town had more than held up his side. Then, just before Mr. Mod-

erator gaveled the discussion to a close, he rose and asked to
be recognized. Which he was. Reluctantly.

He said, "There's not a single one of you lost a single
thing during raking-time. There's never been a single car-
theft or home break-in or act of barn-arson. Not so much
as a stolen soup-spoon. All I want to do is show these kids
what a good life gets you. What they do about it after
they've seen it is up to them. Ain't none of you ever been
stuck in the mud and needed a push? I won't ask you how
you can be for this and still call yourselves Christians,
because one of you would have some kind of answer out
of what I call the Holy-Joe-Do-It-My-Way Bible. But,
Jeezly-Crow! How can you read the parable of the Good
Samaritan on Sunday and then say you're for a thing like
this on Monday night?"

At that, Beatrice McCafferty exploded. Heaving herself
up from her folding chair (which might have given a creak
of thanks) and without waiting for so much as a nod of rec-
ognition from Mr. Moderator, she trumpeted: "All right,
let's get to it! *Hanky-panky!* You want to stand there, Harry
Bluenote, and say there's never been none between the boys
in that one bunch of cabins and the girls in t'other?" She
looked around, grim as a shovel. "I wonder if Mr. Bluenote
was born yesterday? I wonder what he thinks goes on in the
dead of night, if it ain't robbery or barn-burning?"

Harry Bluenote did not sit during this. He stood on the
other side of the meeting hall with his thumbs hooked
into his suspenders. His face was the dusty, ruddy color of
any farmer's face. His pale, peculiar eyes might have been
tipped just the slightest bit at the corners with amusement.

Or not. When he was sure she was finished, had said her say, he spoke calmly and flatly. "I ain't never peeked, Beatrice, but it sure as hell ain't rape."

And with that the matter was "tabled for further discussion." Which, in northern New England, is the polite term for purgatory.

John Cheltzman and the other boys from Hetton House were enthusiastic about the trip from the first, but Blaze had his doubts. When it came to "working out," he remembered the Bowies too well.

Toe-Jam couldn't stop talking about finding a girl "to jazz around with." Blaze didn't believe he himself had to spend much time worrying about that. He still thought about Marjorie Thurlow, but what was the sense in thinking about the rest of them? Girls liked tough guys, fellows who could kid them along like the guys in the movies did.

Besides, girls scared him. Going into a toilet stall at HH with Toe-Jam's treasured copy of *Girl Digest* and beating off did him fine. Did him right when he was wrong. So far as he'd been able to tell from listening to the other boys, the feeling you got from beating off and the feeling you got from sticking it in stacked up about the same, and there was this to be said for beating off: you could do it four or five times a day.

At fifteen, Blaze was finally reaching full growth. He was six and a half feet tall, and the string John stretched from shoulder to shoulder one day measured out twenty-eight inches. His hair was brown, coarse, thick, and oily. His hands were blocks measuring a foot from thumb to pinky when spread. His eyes were bottle green, brilliant and arresting—not a dummy's eyes at all. He made the other boys look like pygmies, yet they teased him with easy, impudent openness. They had accepted John Cheltzman— now commonly known as JC or Jeepers Cripe—as Blaze's personal totem, and because of their Boston adventure, the two boys had become folk heroes in the closed society of Hetton House. Blaze had achieved an even more special place. Anyone who has ever seen toddlers flocking around a St. Bernard will know what it was.

When they arrived at the Bluenote place, Dougie Bluenote was waiting to take them to their cabins. He told them they would be sharing Riffle Cabins that summer with half a dozen boys from South Portland Correctional. Mouths tightened at this news. South Portland boys were known as ball-busters of the first water.

Blaze was in Cabin 3 with John and Toe-Jam. John had grown thinner since the trip to Beantown. His rheumatic fever had been diagnosed by the Hetton House doctor (a Camel-smoking old quack named Donald Hough) as nothing but a bad case of the flu. This diagnosis would kill John, but not for another year.

"Here's your cabin," Doug Bluenote said. He had his father's farmer's face, but not his father's strange pale eyes. "There's a lot of boys used it before you. If you like it, take care of it so a lot of boys can use it after you. There's a woodstove if it gets chilly at night, but it probably won't. There's four beds, so you get to choose. If we pick up another fella, he gets the one left over. There's a hot plate for snacks and coffee. Unplug it last thing you do before you leave in the mornings. Unplug it last thing before turning in at night. There's ashtrays. Your butts go there. Not on the floor. Not in the dooryard. There isn't to be any drinking or playing poker. If me or my dad catches you drinking or playing poker, you're done. No second chances. Breakfast at six, in the big house. You'll get lunch at noon, and you'll eat it in the yonder." He waved his arm in the general direction of the blueberry fields. "Supper at six, in the big house. You start in raking tomorrow at seven. Good day to you, gentlemen."

When he was gone, they poked around. It wasn't a bad place. The stove was an old Invincible with a Dutch oven. The beds were all on the floor—for the first time in years they would not be stacked up like coins in a slot. There was a fairly large common room in addition to the kitchen and the two bedrooms. Here was a bookcase made out of a Pomona orange crate. It contained the Bible, a sex manual for young people, *Ten Nights in a Barroom,* and *Gone with the Wind*. There was a faded hooked rug on the floor. The floor itself was of loose boards, very different from the tile and varnished wood of HH. These boards rumbled underfoot when you walked on them.

While the others were making their beds, Blaze went out on the porch to look for the river. The river was there. It ran through a gentle depression at this point in its course, but not too far upstream he could hear the lulling thunder of a rapids. Gnarled trees, oak and willow, leaned over the water as if to see their reflections. Dragonflies and sewing needles and skeeters flew just above the surface, sometimes stitching it. Far away, in the distance, came the rough buzz of a cicada.

Blaze felt something in him loosen.

He sat down on the top step of the porch. After awhile John came out and sat beside him.

"Where's Toe?" Blaze asked.

"Readin that sexbook. He's lookin for pictures."

"He find any?"

"Not yet."

They sat quiet for awhile.

"Blaze?"

"Yeah?"

"It's not so bad, is it?"

"No."

But he still remembered the Bowies.

They walked down to the big house at five-thirty. The path followed the river's course and soon brought them to the Bend Cabins, where half a dozen girls were clustered.

The boys from HH and the ball-busters from South Portland kept walking, as if they were around girls—girls with *breasts*—every damn day. The girls joined them, some putting on lipstick as they chatted with each other, like being around boys—boys with *beard-shadows*—was as common as swatting flies. One or two were wearing nylons; the rest were in bobby-sox. The bobby-sox were all folded at exactly the same position on the shin. Make-up had been laid over blemishes—in some cases to the thickness of cupcake frosting. One girl, much envied by the others, was sporting green eye-shadow. All of them had perfected the sort of hip-rolling walk John Cheltzman later called the Streetwalker Strut.

One of the South Portland ball-busters hawked and spat. Then he picked a piece of alfalfa grass to stick between his teeth. The other boys regarded this closely and tried to think of something—*anything*—they themselves could do in order to demonstrate their nonchalance around the fairer sex. Most settled for hawking and spitting. Some original-ists stuck their hands in their back pockets. Some did both.

The South Portland boys probably had the advantage of the Hetton boys; when it came to girls, the supply was greater in the city. The mothers of the South Portland boys might have been juicers, hypes, and ten-dollar lovers, their sisters two-buck handjob honeys, but the ball-busters in most cases at least grasped the essential *idea* of girls.

The HH boys lived in an almost exclusively male society. Their sex education consisted of guest lectures from local clergy. Most of these country preachers informed the boys that masturbation made you foolish and the risks of inter-course included a penis that turned black from disease and began to stink. They also had Toe-Jam's occasional dirty mags (*Girl Digest* the latest and best). Their ideas on how to converse with girls came from the movies. About actual intercourse they had no idea, because—as Toe once sadly observed—they only showed fucking in French movies. The only French movie they had ever seen was *The French Connection*.

And so the walk from Bend Cabins to the big house was accomplished mostly in tense (but not antagonistic) silence. Had they not been quite so involved in trying to cope with their new situation, they might have spared a glance for Dougie Bluenote, who was doing his mighty best to keep a straight face.

Harry Bluenote was leaning against the dining room door when they came in. Boys and girls alike gawked at the pictures on the walls (Currier & Ives, N.C. Wyeth), the old and mellow furniture, the long dining table with SET A SPELL carved on one bench and COME HUNGRY, LEAVE FULL carved on the other. Most of all they looked at the large oil portrait on the east wall. This was Marian Bluenote, Harry's late wife.

They might have considered themselves tough—in some ways they were—but they were still only children sporting their first sex characteristics. They instinctively formed themselves into the lines that had been their entire lives. Bluenote let them. Then he shook hands with each one as he or she filed into the room. He nodded in courtly fashion to the girls, in no way betraying that they were got up like kewpie dolls.

Blaze was last. He towered over Bluenote by half a foot, but he was shuffling his feet and looking at the floor and wishing he were back at HH. This was too hard. This was awful. His tongue was plastered to the roof of his mouth. He thrust his hand out blindly.

Bluenote shook it. "Christ, ain't you a big one. Not built for raking berries, though."

Blaze looked at him dumbly.

"You want to drive truck?"

Blaze gulped. There seemed to be something caught in

his throat that wouldn't go down. "I don't know how to drive, sir."

"I'll teach you," Bluenote said. "It ain't hard. Go on in and get y'self y'dinner."

Blaze went in. The table was mahogany. It glittered like a pool. Places were set up and down both sides. Overhead glittered a chandelier, just like in a movie. Blaze sat down, feeling hot and cold. There was a girl on his left and that made his confusion worse. Every time he glanced that way, his eye fell on the jut of her breasts. He tried to do something about this and couldn't. They were just . . . *there*. Taking up space in the world.

Bluenote and the camp mom served out. There was beef stew and a whole turkey. There was a huge wooden bowl heaped with salad and three kinds of dressing. There was a plate of wax beans, one of peas, one of sliced carrots. There was a ceramic pot filled with mashed potatoes.

When all the food was on the table and everyone was seated before their shining plates, silence dropped like a rock. The boys and girls stared at this feast as if at a hallucination. Somewhere a belly rumbled. It sounded like a truck crossing a plank bridge.

"All right," Bluenote said. He was sitting at the head of the table with the camp mom on his left. His son sat at the foot. "Let's have some grace."

They bowed their heads and awaited the sermon.

"Lord," Bluenote said, "bless these boys and girls. And bless this food to their use. Amen."

They blinked at each other surreptitiously, trying to decide if it was a joke. Or a trick. Amen meant you could eat, but if that was the case now, they had just heard the short-est goddam grace in the history of the world.

"Pass me that stew," Bluenote said.

That summer's raking crew fell to with a will.

Bluenote and his son showed up at the big house the next morning after breakfast driving two Ford two-tons. The boys and girls climbed into the backs and were driven to the first blueberry field. The girls were dressed in slacks this morning. Their faces were puffy with sleep and mostly free of make-up. They looked younger, softer.

Conversations began. They were awkward at first, but became more natural. When the trucks hit field-bumps, everyone laughed. There were no formal introductions. Sally Ann Robichaux had Winstons and shared out the pack; even Blaze, sitting on the end, got one. One of the ball-busters from South Portland began discussing girly books with Toe-Jam. It turned out that this fellow, Brian Wick, just happened to have come to the Bluenote farm equipped with a pocket-sized digest called *Fizzy*. Toe al-lowed that he had heard good things about *Fizzy*, and the two of them worked out a trade. The girls managed to ig-nore this and look indulgent at the same time.

They arrived. The low blueberry bushes were in full fruit. Harry and Douglas Bluenote dropped the truck tailgates and everyone jumped down. The field had been divided into strips with white cloth pennants fluttering from low stakes. Another truck—older, bigger—pulled up. This one had high canvas sides. It was driven by a small black man named Sonny. Blaze never heard Sonny say a single word.

The Bluenotes gave their crew short, close-tined blueberry rakes. Only Blaze did not get one. "The rake is designed to take nothin but ripe berries," Bluenote said. Behind him, Sonny got a fishing pole and creel out of the big truck. He clapped a straw hat on his head and started across the field toward a line of trees. He didn't look back.

"But," Bluenote said, raising a finger, "bein an invention of human hand, it ain't perfect. It'll get some leaves and greenies as well. Don't let that worry you, or slow you down. We pick em over back at the barn. And you'll be there, so don't worry we're shorting your wages. Got that?"

Brian and Toe-Jam, who would be inseparable pals by the end of the day, stood side by side, arms folded. They both nodded.

"Now, just so's you know," Bluenote went on. His strange pale eyes glittered. "I get twenty-six cents the quart. You get seven cents. Makes it sound like I'm makin nineteen cents a quart on the sweat of your brow, but it ain't so. After all expenses, I make ten cents the quart. Three more'n you. That three cents is called capitalism. My field, my profit, you take a share." He repeated: "Just so's you know. Any objections?"

There were no objections. They seemed hypnotized in the hot morning sunshine.

"Okay. I got me a driver; that be you, Hoss. I need a counter. You, kid. What's your name?"

"Uh, John. John Cheltzman."

"Come over here."

He helped Johnny up into the back of the truck with the canvas sides and explained what had to be done. There were

stacks of galvanized steel pails. He was to run and hand one
to anyone who called for a bucket. Each empty bucket had
a blank strip of white adhesive tape on the side. Johnny had
to print the picker's name on each full bucket. Full buckets
were tucked into a slotted frame that kept them from falling over and spilling while the truck was moving. There
was also an ancient, dusty chalkboard to keep running
totals on.

"Okay, son," Bluenote said. "Get em to line up and give
em their buckets."

John went red, cleared his throat, and whispered for
them to line up. Please. He looked as though he expected
to be ganged-up on. Instead, they lined up. Some of the
girls were putting on headscarves or tucking gum into
their mouths. John handed them buckets, printing their
names on the ID tapes in big black capital letters. The boys
and girls chose their rows, and the day's work began.

Blaze stood beside the truck and waited. There was a
great, formless excitement in his chest. To drive had been
an ambition of his for years. It was as if Bluenote had read
the secret language of his heart. *If* he meant it.

Bluenote walked over. "What do they call you, son? Besides Hoss?"

"Blaze, sometimes. Sometimes Clay."

"Okay, Blaze, c'mere." Bluenote led him to the cab of the
truck and got behind the wheel. "This is a three-speed In-
ternational Harvester. That means it's got three gears ahead
and one for reverse. This here stickin up from the floor's the
gearshift. See it?"

Blaze nodded.

"This I got my left foot on is the clutch. See that?"

Blaze nodded.

"Push it in when you want to shift. When you got the gearshift where you want it, let the clutch out again. Let it out too slow and she'll stall. Let it out too fast—pop it—and you're apt to spill all the berries and knock your friend on his fanny into the bargain. Because she'll jerk. You understand?"

Blaze nodded. The boys and girls had already worked a little distance up their first rows. Douglas Bluenote walked from one to the next, showing them the best way to handle the rake and avoid blisters. He also showed them the little wrist-twist at the end of each pull; that spilled out most of the leaves and little twigs.

The elder Bluenote hawked and spat. "Don't worry about y'gears. To start with, all you need to worry about is reverse and low range. Now watch here and I'll show you where those two are."

Blaze watched. It had taken him years to get the hang of addition and subtraction (and carrying numbers had been a mystery to him until John told him to think of it like carrying water). He picked up all the basic driving skills in the course of one morning. He stalled the truck only twice. Bluenote later told his son that he had never seen anyone learn the delicate balance between clutch and accelerator so quickly. What he said to Blaze was, "You're doin good. Keep the tires off the bushes."

Blaze did more than drive. He also picked up everyone's pails, trotted them back to the truck, handed them to John, and brought back empties to the pickers. He spent the whole day with an unvarying grin on his face. His happiness was a germ that infected everyone.

A thundersquall came up around three o'clock. The kids piled into the back of the big truck, obeying Bluenote's admonition to be damn careful where they sat.

"I'll drive back," Bluenote said, getting up on the running-board. He saw Blaze's face fall and grinned. "Give it time, Hoss—Blaze, I mean."

"Okay. Where's that man Sonny?"

"Cookin," Bluenote said briefly, punching the clutch and engaging first gear. "Fresh fish if we're lucky; more stew if we ain't. You want to run into town with me after dinner?"

Blaze nodded, too overcome to speak.

That evening he looked on silently with Douglas as Harry Bluenote haggled with the buyer from Federal Foods, Inc., and got his price. Douglas drove home behind the wheel of one of the farm's Ford pick-ups. No one talked. Watching the road unroll before the headlights, Blaze thought: I'm going somewhere. Then he thought: I *am* somewhere. The first thought made him happy. The second was so big it made him feel like crying.

Days passed, then weeks, and there was a rhythm to it all. Up early. Huge breakfast. Work until noon; huge lunch in the field (Blaze had been known to consume as many as four sandwiches, and nobody told him no). Work until the afternoon thundersqualls put an end to it or Sonny rang the big brass dinner-bell, strokes that came across the hot, fleeting day like sounds heard in a vivid dream.

Bluenote began letting Blaze drive to and from the fields

along the back roads. He drove with increasing skill, until it was something like genius. He never spilled a single container from the low wooden slat-holders. After dinner he often went to Portland with Harry and Douglas and watched Harry do his dickers with the various food companies.

July disappeared wherever used months go. Then half of August. Soon summer would be over. Thinking of that made Blaze sad. Soon, Hetton House again. Then winter. Blaze could barely stand to think of another winter at Hetton.

He had no idea how powerful Harry Bluenote's liking for him had become. The big boy was a natural peacemaker and the picking had never gone more sweetly. Only one fistfight had broken out. Usually there were half a dozen. A boy named Henry Gillette accused one of the other South Portland boys of cheating at blackjack (technically not poker). Blaze simply picked Gillette up by the scruff of the neck and hauled him off. Then he made the other boy give Gillette his money back.

Then, in the third week of August, the icing on the cake. Blaze lost his virginity.

The girl's name was Anne Bradstay. She was in Pittsfield for arson. She and her boyfriend had burned down six potato warehouses between Presque Isle and Mars Hill before getting caught. They said they did it because they couldn't think of anything else to do. It was fun to watch them burn. Anne said Curtis would call her up and say "Let's go French-fryin," and off they'd go. The judge—who had lost a son Curtis Prebble's age in Korea—had no understanding of such boredom, nor sympathy for it. He sentenced the boy to six years in Shawshank State Prison.

Anne got a year in what the girls called The Pittsfield Kotex Factory. She didn't really mind. Her stepfather had busted her cherry for her when she was thirteen and her older brother beat her when he was drunk, which was often. After that shit, Pittsfield was a vacation.

She was not a bruised girl with a heart of gold, only a bruised girl. She was not mean, but she was acquisitive, with a crow's eye for shiny things. Toe, Brian Wick, and two other boys from South Portland pooled their resources and offered Anne four dollars to lay Blaze. They had no motive save curiosity. Nobody told John Cheltzman—they were afraid he might tell Blaze, or even Doug Bluenote—but everyone else in camp knew.

Once a night, someone from the boys' cabins went down to the well on the road to the big house with two pails—one for drinking, one for washing. That particular night was Toe-Jam's turn, but he said he had the belly-gripe and offered Blaze a quarter to go in his stead.

"Naw, that's okay, I'll go for free," Blaze said, and got the buckets.

Toe smirked at the quarter saved and went to tell his friend Brian.

The night was dark and fragrant. The moon was orange, just risen. Blaze walked stolidly, thinking of nothing. The buckets clashed together. When a light hand fell on his shoulder, he didn't jump.

"Can I walk with you?" Anne asked. She held up her own buckets.

"Sure," Blaze said. Then his tongue stuck to the roof of his mouth and he began to blush.

They walked side by side to the well. Anne whistled softly through her rotting teeth.

When they got there, Blaze shifted the boards aside. The well was only twenty feet deep, but a pebble dropped into its rock-lined barrel made a mysterious, hollow splash. Timothy grass and wild roses grew luxuriously all around the concrete pad. Half a dozen old oaks stood around, as if on guard. The moon peered through one of them now, casting pale gleams.

"Can I get your water?" Blaze asked. His ears were burning.

"Yeah? Tha'd be nice."

"Sure," he said, grinning thoughtlessly. "Sure it would." He thought of Margie Thurlow, although this girl looked nothing like her.

There was a length of sunbleached rope tied to a ringbolt set in one corner of the cement. Blaze tied the free end of this rope to one of the buckets. He dropped it into the hole. There was a splash. Then they waited for it to fill up.

Anne Bradstay was no expert in the art of seduction. She put her hand on the crotch of Blaze's jeans and grasped his penis.

"Hey!" he said, surprised.

"I like you," she said. "Why don't you screw me? Want to?"

Blaze looked at her, struck dumb with amazement . . . although, within her hand, part of him was now beginning to speak its piece in the old language. The girl was wearing a long dress, but she had pulled it up to show her thighs. She was scrawny, but the moonlight was kind to her face. The shadows were even kinder.

He kissed her clumsily, wrapping his arms around her.

"Jeez, you got a real woodie, don'tcha?" she asked, gasping for breath (and grasping his cock even harder). "Now take it easy, okay?"

"Sure," Blaze said, and lifted her in his arms. He set her down in the timothy. He unbuckled his belt. "I don't know nothin bout this."

Anne smiled, not without bitterness. "It's easy," she said. She pulled her dress over her hips. She wasn't wearing underpants. He saw a thin triangle of dark hair in the moonlight and thought if he looked at it too long, it would kill him.

She pointed matter-of-factly. "Stick your pecker in here."

Blaze dropped his pants and climbed on. At a distance of about twenty feet, hunkered in some high pucky, Brian Wick looked at Toe-Jam with wide eyes. He whispered, "Get a load of that tool!"

Toe tapped the side of his head and whispered, "I guess what God took away here he put back down there. Now shut up."

They turned to watch.

The next day, Toe mentioned that he'd heard Blaze got more than water at the well. Blaze turned almost purple and showed his teeth before walking away. Toe never dared mention it again.

Blaze became Anne's cavalier. He followed her everywhere, and gave her his second blanket in case she got cold during the night. Anne enjoyed this. In her own way, she fell in love with him. She and he carried water for the girls' and boys' cabins for the rest of the picking and no one ever said anything about it. They would not have dared.

On the night before they were to go back to Hetton, Harry Bluenote asked Blaze if he would stay a bit after supper. Blaze said sure, but he began to feel uneasy. His first thought was that Mr. Bluenote had found out what he and Anne were doing down by the well and was mad. This made him feel bad, because he liked Mr. Bluenote.

When everyone else was gone, Bluenote lit a cigar and walked twice around the cleared supper-table. He coughed. He rumpled his already rumpled hair. Then he nearly barked: "Look here, you want to stay on?"

Blaze gaped, unable at first to get across the chasm between what he had believed Mr. Bluenote was going to say and what he *had* said.

"Well? Would you?"

"Yes," Blaze managed. "Yes, sure. I . . . sure."

"Good," Bluenote said, looking relieved. "Because Hetton House isn't for a boy like you. You're a good boy, but you need taking in hand. You try goddam hard, but—" He pointed at Blaze's head. "How'd that happen?"

Blaze's hand went immediately to the bashed-in dent. He blushed. "It's awful, ain't it? To look at, I mean. Lordy."

"Well, it ain't pretty, but I seen worse." Bluenote dropped into a chair. "How'd it happen?"

"My dad go an pitch me downstair. He 'us hungover or somethin. I don't remember very well. Anyway . . ." He shrugged. "That's all."

"That's all, huh? Well, I guess it was enough." He got up again, went to the cooler in the corner, drew himself a Dixie cup of water. "I went to the doctor's today—I been puttin it off because sometimes I get these little flutters— and he gave me a clean bill. I was some relieved." He drank his water, crumpled the cup, and tossed it into the wastebasket. "A man gets older, that's the thing. You don't know nothin about that, but you will. He gets older and his whole life starts to seem like a dream he had durin an afternoon nap. You know?"

"Sure," Blaze said. He hadn't heard a word of it. Live here with Mr. Bluenote! He was just beginning to grasp what that might mean.

"I just wanted to make sure I could do right by you if I went and took you on," Bluenote said. He cocked a thumb at the picture of the woman on the wall. "*She* liked boys. She give me three and died havin the last. Dougie's the middle boy. Eldest is in Washington state, buildin planes for Boeing. Youngest died in a car accident four year ago. That was a sad thing, but I like to think he's with his ma now. Could be that's a stupid idea, but we take our comfort where we can. Don't we, Blaze?"

"Yessir," Blaze said. He was thinking about Anne at the well. Anne in the moonlight. Then he saw there were tears in Mr. Bluenote's eyes. They shocked him and frightened him a little.

"Go on," Mr. Bluenote said. "And don't linger too long at the well, you hear me?"

But he did stop at the well. He told Anne what had happened, and she nodded. Then she began to cry, too.

"What's wrong, Annie?" he asked her. "What's wrong, dear?"

"Nothin," she said. "Draw my water, will you? I brought the buckets."

He drew the water. She watched him raptly.

The last day's picking was over by one o'clock, and even Blaze could see the final haul didn't amount to much. Berries was over.

He always drove now. He was in the cab of the truck, idling along in low, when Harry Bluenote called: "Okay, youse! Up in the truck! Blaze'll drive back! Change y'duds and come on down to the big house! Cake n ice cream."

They scrambled over the tailgate, yelling like a bunch of kiddies, and John had to yell back at them to watch out for the berries. Blaze was grinning. It felt like the kind of grin that might stay on all day.

Bluenote walked around to the passenger side. His face looked pale under his tan, and there was sweat on his forehead.

"Mr. Bluenote? Are you okay?"

"Sure," Harry Bluenote said. He smiled his last smile. "Just ate too much lunch, I guess. Take her in, Bla—"

He grabbed his chest. Cords popped out on both sides of his neck. He stared full at Blaze, but not as if he was seeing him.

"What's wrong?" Blaze asked.

"Ticker," Bluenote remarked, then fell forward. His forehead smacked the metal dashboard. For a moment he clutched at the old torn seatcover with both hands, as if the world had turned upside-down. Then he tilted sideways and fell out the open door onto the ground.

Dougie Bluenote had been ambling around the hood of the truck. Now he broke into a run. "*Poppa!*" he screamed.

Bluenote died in his son's arms on the wild, jouncing ride back to the big house. Blaze hardly noticed. He was hunched over the big, cracked wheel of the I-H truck, glaring at the unrolling dirt road like a madman.

Bluenote shivered once, twice, like a dog caught out in the rain, and that was it.

Mrs. Bricker—the camp mom—dropped a pitcher of lemonade on the floor when they carried him in. Icecubes sprayed every whichway on the plank pine. They took Bluenote into the parlor and put him on the couch. One arm dangled on the floor. Blaze picked it up and put it on Bluenote's chest. It fell off again. After that, Blaze just held it.

Dougie Bluenote was in the dining room, standing beside the long table, which was set for the end-of-picking ice-cream party (a small going-away present had been set beside each kid's plate), talking frantically on the phone. The other pickers clustered on the porch, looking in. All of them looked horrified except for Johnny Cheltzman, who looked relieved.

Blaze had told him everything the night before.

The doctor came and made a brief examination. When he was done, he pulled a blanket over Bluenote's face.

Mrs. Bricker, who had stopped crying, started again. "The ice cream," she said. "What will we do with all that ice cream? Oh, lands!" She put her apron over her face, then all the way over her head, like a hood.

"Have em come in and eat it," Doug Bluenote said. "You too, Blaze. Pitch in."

Blaze shook his head. He felt like he might never be hungry again.

"Never mind, then," Doug said. He ran his hands through his hair. "I'll have to call Hetton . . . and South Portland . . . Pittsfield . . . Jesus, Jesus, Jesus." He put his face to the wall and began to cry himself. Blaze just sat and looked at the covered shape on the couch.

The station wagon from HH came first. Blaze sat in the back, looking out the dusty rear window. The big house dwindled and dwindled until it was finally lost to view.

The others began to talk a little, but Blaze kept his silence. It was beginning to sink in. He tried to work it out in his mind and couldn't. It made no sense, but it was sinking in anyway.

His face began to work. First his mouth twitched, then his eyes. His cheeks began to tremble. He couldn't control these things. They were beyond him. Finally he began to cry. He put his forehead against the rear window of the station wagon and wept great monotonous sobs that sounded like a horse neighing.

The man driving was Martin Coslaw's brother-in-law. He said, "Somebody shut the moose up, how about it?"

But nobody dared touch him.

Anne Bradstay's baby was born eight and a half months later. It was a whopping boy—ten pounds, nine ounces. He was put up for adoption and taken almost immediately by a childless couple from Saco named Wyatt. Boy Bradstay became Rufus Wyatt. He was named All-State Tackle from his high school team when he was seventeen; All–New England a year later. He went to Boston University with the intention of majoring in literature. He particularly enjoyed Shelley, Keats, and the American poet James Dickey.

CHAPTER 19

Dark came early, wrapped in snow. By five o'clock, the only light in the headmaster's office was the flickering fire on the hearth. Joe was sleeping soundly, but Blaze was worried about him. His breathing seemed fast, his nose was running, and his chest sounded rattly. Bright red blotches of color glowed in each cheek.

The baby book said fever often accompanied teething, and sometimes a cold, or cold symptoms. *Cold* was good enough for Blaze (he didn't know what *symptoms* were). The book said just keep em warm. Easy for the book-writing guy to say; what was Blaze supposed to do when Joe woke up and wanted to crawl around?

He had to call the Gerards now, tonight. They couldn't drop the money from a plane in this snowstorm, but the snow would probably stop by tomorrow night. He would get the money, and keep Joe, too. Fuck those rich Republicans. He and Joe were for each other now. They would get away. Somehow.

He stared into the fire and fell into a daydream. He saw himself lighting the road-flares in a clearing. Running lights of a small plane appearing overhead. Wasp-buzz of the engine. Plane banks toward the signal, which is burning like a birthday cake. Something white in the air—a parachute with a little suitcase attached to it!

Then he's back here. He opens the suitcase. It's stacked with dough. Each bundle is neatly banded. Blaze counts it. It's all there.

Next he's on the small island of Acapulco (which he believed was in the Bahamas, although he supposed he could be wrong about that). He's bought himself a cabin on a high spur of land that overlooks the breakers. There are two bedrooms, one large, one small. There are two hammocks out back, one large, one small.

Time passes. Maybe five years. And here comes a kid pounding up the beach—a beach that shines like a wet muscle in the sunlight. He's tanned. He's got long black hair, like an Indian brave's. He's waving. Blaze waves back.

Again Blaze seemed to hear the sound of fugitive laughter. He turned around sharply. No one was there.

But the daydream was broken. He got up and poked his arms into his coat. He sat down and pulled on his boots. He was going to make this happen. His feet and his head were set, and when he got that way, he always did what he said he was going to do. It was his pride. The only one he had.

He checked the baby again, then went out. He closed the office door behind him and clattered down the stairs. George's gun was tucked in the waistband of his pants, and this time it was loaded.

The wind coming across the old play-yard was howling hard enough to push him into a stagger before he got used to it. Snow belted his face, needling his cheeks and forehead. The tops of the trees leaned this way and that. New drifts were forming on the crusted layers of old snow, already three feet deep in places. He didn't need to worry about the tracks he'd made coming in anymore.

He waded to the Cyclone fence, wishing he had snow-shoes, and climbed awkwardly over it. He landed in snow up to his thighs and began to flounder north, setting off cross-country toward Cumberland Center.

It was three miles, and he was out of breath before he was halfway there. His face was numb. So were his hands and feet, despite heavy socks and gloves. Yet he kept on, making no attempt to go around drifts but plowing straight through. Twice he stumbled over fences buried in the snow, one of them barbed wire that ripped his jeans and tore into his leg. He merely picked himself up and went on, not wasting breath on a curse.

An hour after setting out, he entered a tree farm. Here perfectly pruned little blue spruces marched away in rows, each one growing six feet from its fellows. Blaze was able to walk down a long, sheltered corridor where the snow was only three inches deep . . . and in some places, there was no snow at all. This was the Cumberland County Reserve, and it bordered the main road.

When he reached the western border of the toy forest, he sat on top of the embankment and then slid down to Route 289. Up the road, almost lost in the blowing snow, was a blinker-light he remembered well—red on two sides, yellow on the other two. Beyond it, a few streetlights glimmered like ghosts.

Blaze crossed the road, which was snow-coated and empty of traffic, and walked up to the Exxon on the corner. A small pool of light on the side of the cinderblock building highlighted a pay phone. Looking like an ambulatory snowman, Blaze stepped to it—hulked over it. He had a panicky moment when it seemed he had no change, but he found two quarters in his pants and another in his coat pocket. Then—bool!—his money came back in the coin return. Directory Assistance was free.

"I want to call Joseph Gerard," he said. "Ocoma."

There was a blank pause, and then the operator gave him the number. Blaze wrote it on the fogged glass that shielded the phone from the worst of the snow, unaware that he had asked for an unlisted number and the operator had given it to him per FBI instructions. This of course opened the floodgates to well-wishers and cranks, but if the kidnappers didn't call, the traceback equipment couldn't be used.

Blaze dialed 0 and gave the lady the Gerard phone number. He asked if that was a toll-call. It was. He asked if he could talk three minutes for seventy-five cents. The operator said no; a three-minute call to Ocoma would cost him a dollar-ninety. Did he have a telephone credit card?

Blaze didn't. Blaze had no credit cards of any kind.

The operator told him he could charge the call to his home phone, and there *was* a phone at the shack (although it hadn't rung a single time since George died), but Blaze was too clever for that.

Collect, then? the operator suggested.

"Collect, yeah!" Blaze said.

"Your name, sir?"

"Clayton Blaisdell, Junior," he said at once. In his relief at finding he hadn't made this long slog just to come up empty for lack of phone-change, Blaze would not realize this tactical error for almost two hours.

"Thank you, sir."

"Thank *you*," Blaze said, feeling clever. Feeling cool as a fool.

The phone rang only once on the other end before being picked up. "Yes?" The voice sounded wary and weary.

"I've got your son," Blaze said.

"Mister, I've had ten calls today saying the same thing. Prove it."

Blaze was flummoxed. He hadn't expected this. "Well, he's not with me, you know. My partner's got him."

"Yeah?" Nothing else. Just *Yeah?*

"I seen your wife when I come in," Blaze said. It was the only thing he could think of. "She's real pretty. She 'us in a white nightie. You guys had a pitcher on the dresser—well, three pitchers all put together."

The voice on the other end said, "Tell me something else." But he didn't sound tired anymore.

Blaze racked his brain. There was nothing else, nothing that would convince the stubborn man on the other end. Then there was. "The ole lady had a cat. That's why she came downstairs. She thought I was the cat . . . that I was . . ." He racked his brain some more. "*Mikey!*" he shouted. "I'm sorry I hit her so hard. I sure didn't mean to, but I was scared."

The man on the other end of the line began to cry. It was

sudden and shocking. "Is he all right? For God's sake, is Joey okay?"

There was a confused babble in the background. A woman seemed to be speaking. Another was yelling and crying. The one yelling and crying was probably the mother. Narmenians were probably specially emotional. Frenchies were the same way.

"Don't hang up!" Joseph Gerard (it just about had to be Gerard) said. He sounded panicky. "Is he okay?"

"Yeah, he's good," Blaze said. "Got another tooth through. That makes three. Di'per rash is clearing up good. I—I mean *we*—keep 'is bottom greased up real good. What's the matter with your wife? Is she too good to grease his bottom?"

Gerard was panting like a dog. "We'll do anything, mister. It's all your play."

Blaze started a little at that. He had almost forgotten why he called.

"Okay," he said. "Here's what I want you to do."

In Portland, an AT&T operator was speaking to SAC Albert Sterling. "Cumberland Center," she said. "Gas station pay phone."

"Got it," he said, and pumped his fist in the air.

"Get in a light plane tomorrow night at eight," Blaze said. He was beginning to feel uneasy, beginning to feel he'd been on the phone too long. "Start flying south along Route 1 toward the New Hampshire border. Fly low. Got it?"

"Wait . . . I'm not sure . . ."

"You *better* be sure," Blaze said. He tried to sound like George would. "Don't try to stall me, unless you want your kid back in a bag."

"Okay," Gerard said. "Okay, I hear you. I'm just writing it down."

Sterling handed a scrap of paper to Bruce Granger and made dialing motions. Granger called the State Police.

"The pilot'll see a signal light," Blaze said. "Have the money in a suitcase attached to a parachute. Drop it like you wanted it to land right on top of the fla—of the light. The signal. You can have the kid back the next day. I'll even send some of the stuff I—we, I mean—use on his bottom." A witticism occurred to him. "No extra charge."

Then he looked at his free hand and saw he had crossed his fingers when he said they could have Joe back. Just like a little kid telling his first lie.

"Don't hang up!" Gerard said. "I don't think I quite understand—"

"You're a smart guy," Blaze said. "I think you do."

He hung up and left the Exxon station at a dead run, not sure why he was running, only knowing that it seemed like the right thing to do. The only thing. He ran under the blinker-light, angled across the road, and scaled the embankment in giant leaps. Then he disappeared into the spruce-lined rows of the County Reserve.

Behind him, a giant monster with glaring white eyes came snarling over the hill. It plunged through the teeming air, nine-foot sidewings sending up sprays of snow.

The plow obliterated Blaze's tracks where they angled across the road. When two State Police cars converged on the Exxon station nine minutes later, Blaze's footprints up the embankment to the Reserve were no more than blurry indentations. Even as the Troopers stood around the pay phone with their flashlights pointed, the wind did its work behind them.

Sterling's phone rang five minutes later. "He was here," the State cop on the other end said. Sterling could hear wind blowing in the background. No, shrieking. "He was here but he's gone."

"Gone how?" Sterling asked. "Car or on foot?"

"Who knows? Plow went through just before we got here. But if I had to guess, I'd say he drove."

"Nobody's asking you to guess. Gas station? Anybody see him?"

"They're closed because of the storm. Even if they'd been open . . . the phone's on a wall around to the side."

"Lucky sonofabitch," Sterling said. "*Blind*-lucky sonofabitch. We surround that crappy little cabin in Apex and arrest four girly magazines and a jar of strained peas. Tracks? Or did the wind take em?"

"There were still tracks around the phone," the Trooper said. "Wind blurred the treads, but it was him."

"Guessing again?"

"No. They were big."

"Okay. Roadblocks, right?"

"Every road big and small," the Trooper said. "It's happening as we speak."

"Logging roads, too."

"Logging roads, too," the Trooper said. He sounded insulted.

Sterling didn't care. "So he's bottled up? Can we say that, Trooper?"

"Yes."

"Good. We're going in there with three hundred guys soon as the weather lifts tomorrow. This has gone on too long."

"Yes, sir."

"Snow plow," Sterling said. "My sister's rosy *chinchina*." He hung up.

By the time Blaze got back to HH, he was exhausted. He climbed the Cyclone fence and fell face-first into the snow on the other side. His nose was bloody. He had made his way back in just thirty-five minutes. He picked himself up, staggered around the building, and went inside.

Joe's furious, agonized howls met him.

"Christ!"

He ran up the stairs two at a time and burst into Coslaw's office. The fire was out. The cradle was tipped over. Joe was lying on the floor. His head was covered with blood. His face was purple, his eyes were squeezed shut, his small hands powdered white with dust.

"Joe!" Blaze cried. "Joe! Joe!"

He swept the baby into his arms and ran into the corner where the diapers were stacked. He grabbed one and swabbed the gash on Joe's forehead. The blood seemed to be pouring out in freshets. There was a splinter sticking out of the wound. Blaze plucked it out and threw it on the floor.

The baby struggled in his arms and screamed more loudly still. Blaze wiped away more blood, holding Joe firmly, and bent in for a closer look. The cut was jagged, but with the big splinter removed, it didn't look so bad. Thank Christ it hadn't been his eye. It could have been his eye.

He found a bottle and gave it to Joe cold. Joe grabbed it with both hands and began to suck greedily. Panting, Blaze got a blanket and wrapped the baby in it. Then he lay down on his own blankets with the wrapped baby on his chest. Blaze closed his eyes and was immediately seized by horrible vertigo. Everything in the world seemed to be slipping away: Joe, George, Johnny, Harry Bluenote, Anne Bradstay, birds on wires, and nights on the road.

Then he was all right again.

"From now on, it's us, Joey," he said. "You got me and I got you. It'll be all right. Okay?"

Snow struck the windows in hard, rattling bursts. Joe turned his face from the rubber nipple and coughed thickly, his tongue popping out with the effort of his chest to clear itself. Then he took the nipple again. Beneath his hand, Blaze could feel the small heart hammering.

"It's how we roll," Blaze said, and kissed the baby's bloody forehead.

They fell asleep together.

CHAPTER 20

Hetton House included a large parcel of land in back of the main buildings, and here was planted what generations of boys had come to call the Victory Garden. The headmistress before Coslaw went slack on it, telling people she had a brown thumb rather than a green one, but Martin "The Law" Coslaw saw at least two shining potentialities in the Victory Garden. The first was to make a substantial saving in HH's food-budget by having the boys grow their own vegetables. The second was to acquaint the boys with good hard work, which was the foundation of the world. "Work and mathematics built the pyramids," Coslaw liked to say. And so the boys planted in the spring, weeded in the summer (unless they were "working out" on one of the neighboring farms), and harvested in the fall.

About fourteen months after the end of what Toe-Jam called "the fabulous blueberry summer," John Cheltzman was among the pumpkin-picking crew at the north end of the VG. He took a cold, sickened, and died. It happened just that fast. He was packed off to Portland City Hospital on Halloween, while the rest of the boys were at their classes or "away schools." He died in City Hospital's charity ward, and he did it alone.

His bed at HH was stripped, then re-made. Blaze spent most of one afternoon sitting on his own bed and looking at John's. The long sleeping room—which they called "the ram"—was empty. The others had gone to Johnny's funeral. For most it was their first funeral, and they were quite excited about it.

Johnny's bed frightened and fascinated Blaze. The jar of Shedd's Peanut Butter that had always been stuffed down between the head of the bed and the wall was gone; he'd looked. So were the Ritz Crackers. (After lights-out, Johnny often said, "Everything tastes better when it shits on a Ritz," which never failed to crack Blaze up.) The bed itself was made up in stark Army fashion, the top blanket pulled taut. The sheets were perfectly white and clean, even though Johnny had been an enthusiastic lights-out masturbator. Many nights Blaze lay in his own bed, looking up into the dark and listening to the soft creak of the springs as JC flogged his doggy. There were always stiff yellow places on his sheets. Christ, those stiff yellow places were on the sheets of all the bigger boys. They were on his own, right now, beneath him as he sat on his bed, looking at Johnny's bed. It came to him like a revelation that if he died, his bed would be stripped and his come-stained sheets would be replaced with sheets like the ones that were on Johnny's now—sheets that were perfectly white and clean. Sheets without a single mark on them to say someone lay there, dreamed there, was lively enough to squirt off there. Blaze began to cry silently.

It was a cloudless afternoon in early November, and the ram was flooded with impartial light. Squares of sun and the shadow-crosses of muntings lay on JC's cot. After awhile Blaze got up and tore the blanket from the bed where his pal had slept. He threw the pillow the length of the ram. Then he stripped off the sheets and pushed the mattress on the floor. It still wasn't enough. He turned the bed over on the mattress with its stupid little legs sticking up. It still wasn't enough, so he kicked one of the jutting bed-legs and succeeded in nothing more than hurting his foot. After that he lay on his bed with his hands over his eyes and his chest heaving.

When the funeral was over, the other boys mostly left Blaze alone. No one asked him about the overturned bed, but Toe did a funny thing: he took one of Blaze's hands and kissed it. That was a funny thing, all right. Blaze thought about it for years. Not all the time, but every now and then.

Five o'clock came. It was free time for the boys, and most of them were out in the yard, goofing around and working up an appetite for supper. Blaze went to Martin Coslaw's office. The Law was sitting behind his desk. He had changed into his slippers and was rocked back in his chair, reading the *Evening Express*. He looked up and said, "What?"

"Here, you sonofabitch," Blaze said, and beat him unconscious.

He set off walking for the New Hampshire border because he thought he would be picked up inside of four hours driving a hot car. Instead, he was collared in two hours. He was always forgetting how large he was, but Martin Coslaw didn't forget, and it didn't take the Maine State Police long to locate a six-foot-seven male Caucasian youth with a bashed-in forehead.

There was a short trial in Cumberland County District Court. Martin Coslaw appeared with one arm in a sling and a huge white head-bandage that dipped to cover one eye. He walked to the stand on crutches.

The prosecutor asked him how tall he was. Coslaw responded that he was five feet and six inches. The prosecutor asked how much he weighed. Coslaw said that he weighed one hundred and sixty pounds. The prosecutor asked Coslaw if he had done anything to provoke, tease, or unjustly punish the defendant, Clayton Blaisdell, Junior. Coslaw said he had not. The prosecutor then yielded the witness to Blaze's attorney, a cool drink of lemonade fresh out of law school. The cool drink of lemonade asked a number of furious, obscure questions which Coslaw answered calmly while his cast, crutches, and head-bandage continued their own testimony. When the cool drink of lemonade said he had no further questions, the State rested its case.

Blaze's court-appointed called him to the stand and asked why he had beaten up the headmaster of Hetton House. Blaze stammered out his story. A good friend of his had died. He thought Coslaw was to blame. Johnny shouldn't have been sent out to pick pumpkins, specially not when it was cold. Johnny had a weak heart. It wasn't fair, and Mr. Coslaw knew it wasn't fair. He had it coming.

At that, the young lawyer sat down with a look of despair in his eyes.

The prosecutor rose and approached. He asked how tall Blaze was. Six-foot-six or maybe -seven, Blaze said. The prosecutor asked how much he weighed. Blaze said he didn't know, exactly, but not three hunnert. This caused some laughter among the press. Blaze stared out at them with puzzled eyes. Then he smiled a little, too, wanting them to know he could take a joke as well as the next one. The prosecutor had no more questions. He sat down.

Blaze's court-appointed made a furious, obscure summary, then rested his case. The judge looked out a window with his chin propped on one hand. The prosecutor then rose. He called Blaze a young thug. He said it was the State of Maine's responsibility to "snub him up fast and hard." Blaze had no idea what that meant, but he knew it wasn't good.

The judge asked Blaze if he had anything to say.

"Yessir," Blaze said, "but I don't know how."

The judge nodded and sentenced him to two years in South Portland Correctional.

It wasn't as bad for him as it was for some, but bad enough so he never wanted to go back again. He was big enough to avoid the beatings and the buggery, and he walked outside all the underground cliques with their tinpot leaders, but being locked up for long periods of time in a tiny barred cell was very hard. Very sad. Twice in the first six months he "went stir," howling to be let out and banging on the bars of his cell until the guards came running. The first time, four guards responded, then had to call in first another four and then a full half-dozen to subdue him. The second time they gave him a hypo that knocked him out for sixteen hours.

Solitary was worse still. Blaze paced the tiny cell end-lessly (six steps each way) while time faltered and then stopped. When the door was finally opened and he was let back into the society of the other boys—free to walk the exercise yard or pitch bundles off the trucks that came into the loading dock—he was nearly mad with relief and grati-tude. He hugged the jailer who let him out on the second occasion and gained this note in his jacket: *Shows homosexual tendencies.*

But solitary wasn't the worst thing. He was forgetful, but the memory of the worst thing never left him. That was how they got you. They took you to a little white room and gathered around you in a circle. Then they began asking questions. And before you had time to think what the first question meant—what it *said*—they were on to the next, and the next, and the next. They backtracked, sidetracked, went uptrack and down. It was like being caught in a spi-derweb. In the end, you would admit anything they asked you to admit, just to shut them up. Then they brought you a paper and told you to sign your name to it and brother, you signed.

The man in charge of Blaze's interrogation had been an assistant district attorney named Holloway. Holloway didn't come into the little room until the others had been going at him for at least an hour and a half. Blaze had his sleeves rolled up and the bottom of his shirt had come untucked. He was covered with sweat and needed to go Number Two Bathroom, *bad*. It was like being in the Bow-ies' dogpen again, with the Collies snapping all around him. Holloway was cool and natty in a blue pinstriped suit. He had on black shoes with galaxies of tiny holes in the fronts. Blaze never forgot the holes in the fronts of Mr. Holloway's shoes.

Mr. Holloway sat on the table in the middle of the room, his ass half on and half off, one of his legs swinging back and forth, one of those elegant black shoes moving like the pendulum in a clock. He gave Blaze a friendly grin and said, "Want to talk, son?"

Blaze began to stammer. Yes, he did want to talk. If someone really wanted to listen, and be a little bit friendly, he did.

Holloway told the others to get out.

Blaze asked if he could go to the bathroom.

Holloway pointed across the room to a door Blaze hadn't even noticed and said, "What are you waiting for?" He was wearing that same friendly grin when he said it.

When Blaze came out, there was a pitcher of icewater and an empty glass on the table. Blaze looked at Holloway, and Holloway nodded. Blaze drank three glasses in a row, then sat back with what felt like an icepick planted in the center of his forehead.

"Good?" Holloway asked.

Blaze nodded.

"Yeah. Answering questions is thirsty work. Cigarette?"

"Don't use em."

"Good kid, that'll never get you in trouble," Holloway said, and lit one for himself. "Who are you to your pals, son? What do they call you?"

"Blaze."

"Okay, Blaze, I'm Frank Holloway." He stuck out his

hand, then winced and clamped the end of his cigarette with his teeth as Blaze wrung it. "Now tell me exactly what you did to wind up here."

Blaze began to pour out his story, beginning with The Law's arrival at Hetton and Blaze's problems with Arithmetic.

Holloway held up his hand. "Mind if I get a stenographer in on this, Blaze? That's a kind of secretary. Save you repeating all this."

No. He didn't mind.

Later, at the end, the others came back in. When they did, Blaze noticed that Holloway's eyes had lost their friendly glint. He slipped off the table, dusted his ass with two brisk whacks, and said, "Type it up and have the dummy sign it." He left without looking back.

He left prison not quite two years after entering it—he got four months off for good behavior. They gave him two pairs of prison jeans, a prison denim jacket, and a holdall to carry them in. He also had his prison savings: a check for $43.84.

It was October. The air was flushed sweet with wind. The gate-guard waved one hand back and forth like a windshield wiper and told him to stay clean. Blaze walked past without looking or speaking, and when he heard the heavy green gate thud shut behind him, he shivered.

He walked until the sidewalks ended and the town disappeared. He looked at everything. Cars whipped past, looking strangely updated. One slowed, and he thought maybe he would be offered a ride. Then someone shouted, "*Heyyy, JAILBIRD,*" and the car scooted away.

At last he sat down on the rock wall surrounding a little country graveyard and just looked down the road. It came to him that he was free. He had no one to boss him, but he was bad at bossing himself and had no friends. He was out of solitary, but had no job. He didn't even know how to turn the piece of stiff paper they'd given him into money.

Still, a wonderful soothing gratitude stole over him. He closed his eyes and turned his face up to the sun, filling his head with red light. He smelled the grass and fresh asphalt where some road-crew had recently fixed a pothole. He smelled exhaust from cars that went wherever their drivers wanted to go. He clutched himself with relief.

He slept in a barn that night and the next day got a job picking taters for a dime a basket. That winter he worked in a New Hampshire woolen mill, strictly non-union. In the spring he took a bus to Boston and got a job in the laundry of the Brigham and Women's Hospital. He had been working there six months when a familiar face from South Portland turned up—Billy St. Pierre. They went out and bought each other many beers. Billy confided to Blaze that he and a friend were going to hold up a liquor store in Southie. The place was a tit. He said there was room for one more.

Blaze was up for it. His cut was seventeen dollars. He went on working at the laundry. Four months later, he and Billy and Billy's brother-in-law Dom knocked over a combination gas station and grocery store in Danvers. A month after that, Blaze and Billy, plus another South Portland alum named Calvin Surks, knocked over a loan agency with a betting room in the back. They took over a thousand dollars.

"We're hitting the big time now," Billy said as the three of them split the swag in a Duxbury motel room. "This is just the start."

Blaze nodded, but went on working in the hospital laundry.

For awhile life rolled like that. Blaze had no real friends in Boston. His only acquaintances were Billy St. Pierre and the loosely orbiting crew of small-timers of which Billy was a member. Blaze took to hanging out with them during his off-hours in a Lynn candy-store called Moochie's. They played pinball and horsed around. Blaze had no girl, steady or otherwise. He was painfully shy and self-conscious about what Billy called his busted head. After they did a successful job, he sometimes bought a whore.

About a year after Blaze fell in with Billy, a fast-talking part-time musician introduced him to heroin—a skin-pop. It made Blaze violently sick, either from some additive or a natural allergy. He never tried it again. He would sometimes take a few tokes on a reef or fry-daddy just to be sociable, but he had no use for harder drugs.

Not long after the heroin experiment, Billy and Calvin (whose proudest possession was a tattoo reading LIFE SURKS, THEN YA DIE) were busted trying to heist a supermarket. There were others willing to take Blaze on their current gags, however. Eager, even. Someone nicknamed him The Boogeyman, and it stuck. Even with a mask to hide his disfigured forehead, his immense size made any clerk or storekeeper think twice about grabbing the piece he might have under the counter.

In the two years after Billy fell, Blaze just missed going

down himself half a dozen times, some of those by the narrowest of margins. On one occasion, two brothers with whom he had heisted a clothing store in Saugus were grabbed just around the corner from where Blaze said thanks and got out of their car. The brothers would have been glad to give Blaze up in order to earn a break, but they only knew him as The Big Boogie, thus giving the police the idea that the third member of the gang had been African-American.

In June, Blaze was laid off at the laundry. He didn't even bother looking for another straight job. He simply drifted through the days until he met George Rackley, and when he met George, his future was set.

CHAPTER 21

Albert Sterling was dozing in one of the overstuffed chairs in the Gerard study when the first hints of dawn crept into the sky. It was February first.

There was a knock on the side of the door. Sterling's eyes opened. Granger was standing there. "We might have something," Granger said.

"Tell me."

"Blaisdell grew up in an orphanage—well, state home, same difference—called Hetton House. It's in the area his call came from."

Sterling got up. "Is it still operating?"

"Nope. Closed fifteen years ago."

"Who lives there now?"

"Nobody. The town sold it to some people who tried to run a day-school out of it. Place went broke and the town took it back. It's been vacant ever since."

"I bet that's where he is," Sterling said. It was just intuition, but it felt true. They were going to nail the bastard this morning, and anyone who was running with him. "Call the State Police. I want twenty Troopers, twenty at least, plus you and me." He thought. "And Frankland. Get Frankland out of the office."

"He'll be in bed, actually—"

"Get him out. And tell Norman to get his ass over here. He can mind the phone."

"You're sure that's how you want to—"

"Yes. Blaisdell's a crook, he's an idiot, and he's lazy." That crooks were lazy was an article of faith in Albert Sterling's private church of beliefs. "Where else would he go?" He looked at his watch. It was 5:45. "I just hope the kid's still alive. But I'm not betting on it."

Blaze woke up at 6:15. He turned on his side to look at Joe, who had slept the night with him. The extra body-warmth seemed to have done the little guy some good. His skin was cool, and the bronchial sound of his breathing had diminished. Those hectic red spots were still on his cheeks, though. Blaze put a finger in the baby's mouth (Joe began to suck at once), and felt a new swelling in the left gum. When he pressed down, Joe moaned in his sleep and pulled his face away.

"Damn teeth," Blaze whispered. He looked at Joe's forehead. The wound had clotted, and he didn't think it would leave a scar. That was good. Your forehead led the charge through life. It was a lousy place to have a scar.

His inspection was finished, but still he looked into the baby's sleeping face, fascinated. Except for the jagged, healing scratch, Joe's skin was perfect. White, but with glowing olive undertones. Blaze thought he would never burn in the sun but tan to the color of nice old wood. He'll get so dark some people will take him for a black guy, maybe, Blaze thought. He won't get all lobster red like me.

Joe's lids were a faint but discernible blue. That same blue made a pair of tiny arcs beneath his closed eyes. The lips were rosy and slightly pursed.

Blaze picked up one of the hands and held it. The fingers curled instantly over his pinky. Blaze thought they were going to be big hands. They might someday hold a carpenter's hammer or a mechanic's wrench. Even an artist's brush.

The dawning of the child's possibilities made him shiver. He felt an urge to snatch the baby up. And why? So he could watch Joe's eyes open and look at him. Who knew what those eyes might see in the years ahead? Yet now they were closed. *Joe* was closed. He was like a wonderful, terrible book where a story had been written in invisible ink. Blaze realized he didn't care about the money anymore, not really. What he cared about was seeing what words would appear on all those pages. What pictures.

He kissed the clean skin just above the scrape, then threw back his blankets and went to the window. It was still snowing; air and earth were white on white. He figured there must have been eight inches come down in the night. And it wasn't done yet.

They've almost got you, Blaze.

He whirled around. "George?" he called softly. "That you, George?"

It wasn't. That had come from his own head. And why in the name of God would he have a thought like that?

He looked out the window again. His mutilated brow drew down in thought. They knew who he was. He had been stupid and given that operator his real name, right down to the Junior on the end. He had thought he was being smart, but he was being stupid. Again. Stupid was a prison they never let you out of, no time off for good behavior, you were in for life.

George would have given him the old horselaugh for sure. George would have said, *I bet they went right to work diggin up your records. Clayton Blaisdell's Greatest Hits.* It was true. They'd read about the religious con, his stay in South Portland, his time at HH—

And then, like a meteor streaking across his troubled consciousness: *This was HH!*

Blaze looked around wildly, as if to verify this.

They've almost got you, Blaze.

He began to feel hunted again, trapped in a narrowing circle. He thought of the white interrogation room, of having to go to the bathroom, of having questions thrown at you that they didn't even give you time to answer. And this time it wouldn't be a little trial in a half-empty courtroom. This time it would be a circus, with every seat full. Then prison forever. And solitary confinement if he went stir.

These thoughts filled him with terror, but they were far from the worst. The worst was thinking of them bursting in with their guns drawn and taking the baby back. Kidnapping him again. His Joe.

Sweat sprang up on his face and arms in spite of the room's chill.

You poor sucker. He'll grow up hating your guts. They'll see to that.

That wasn't George, either. That was his thought, and it was true.

He began to rack his brains furiously, trying to make a plan. There ought to be a place to go. There *had* to be.

Joe began to stir awake, but Blaze didn't even hear him. A place to go. A safe place. Someplace close by. A secret place where they couldn't find him. A place that even George wouldn't know about, a place—

Inspiration burst upon him.

He whirled to the bed. Joe's eyes were open. When he saw Blaze, he gave him a grin and stuck his thumb in his mouth—a gesture that was almost jaunty.

"Gotta eat, Joe. Quick. We're on the run, but I got an idea."

He fed Joe strained beef and cheese. Joe had been woofing down a full jar of this stuff at a go, but this time he started turning his head aside after the fifth spoonful. And when Blaze tried to force the issue, he began to cry. Blaze switched to one of the bottles and Joe sucked at it greedily. Trouble was, there were only three left.

While Joe lay on the blanket with the bottle clasped in his starfish hands, Blaze raced around the room picking up and packing up. He broke open a package of Pampers and stuffed his shirt with them until he puffed out like the circus fatman.

Then he knelt and began to dress Joe as warmly as he could: two shirts, two pairs of pants, a sweater, his tiny knitted hat. Joe screamed indignantly all through this tribulation. Blaze took no notice. When the baby was dressed, he folded his two blankets into a small, thick pouch and slipped Joe inside.

The baby's face was now purple with rage. His screams

echoed up and down the decaying hallway when Blaze carried him from the headmaster's office to the stairs. At the foot of the stairs, he put his own cap on Joe's head, taking care to cock it to the left. It covered him down to the shoulders. Then he stepped out into the driving snow.

Blaze crossed the back yard and clambered awkwardly over the cement wall at its far end. The land on the other side had once been the Victory Garden. There was nothing here now but scrub bushes (only rounded humps beneath the snow) and scraggly young pines that were growing with no rhyme or reason. He jogged with the baby pulled tightly to his chest. Joe wasn't crying now, but Blaze could feel his short, quick gasps for breath as he struggled with the ten-degree air.

At the far end of the Victory Garden was another wall, this one of piled rock. Many of the stones had fallen out of it, leaving big gaps. Blaze crossed at one of these and descended the steep grade on the other side in a series of skidding leaps. His heels drove up clouds of powdery snow. At the bottom, woods took over again, but a fire had burned through here thirty-five or forty years before, a bad one. The trees and underbrush had grown back helter-skelter, fighting each other for space and light. There were blowdowns everywhere. Many were concealed by the snow, and Blaze had to slow down in spite of his need to hurry. The wind howled in the treetops; he could hear the trunks groaning and protesting.

Joe began to whimper. It was a guttural, out-of-breath sound.

"It's all right," Blaze said. "We're gettin there."

He wasn't sure the old bobwire fence would still be there, but it was. It was drifted in right to the top, though, and he almost stumbled over it, plunging both himself and the baby into the snow. He stepped over instead—carefully— and walked down a deepening cleft of ground. The soil parted here and the land's skeleton showed. The snow was thinner. The wind was now howling over their heads.

"Here," Blaze said. "Here someplace."

He began to hunt back and forth about halfway to where the ground leveled off again, peering at jumbles of rocks, half-exposed roots, snow pockets, and caches of old pine needles. He couldn't find it. Panic began to rise in his throat. The cold would be seeping through the blankets now, and through Joe's layers of clothes.

Farther down, maybe.

He began to descend again, then slipped and fell on his rump, still clutching the baby to his chest. There was a sharp flare of pain in his right ankle, as if someone had struck sparks inside his flesh. And he found himself staring at a triangular patch of shadow between two rounded rocks that bulged toward each other like breasts. He crawled toward it, still holding Joe against him. Yes, that was it. Yes and yes and yes. He ducked his head and crawled inside.

The cave was dark and moist and surprisingly warm. The floor was covered with soft, ancient pine-boughs. Blaze was swept with *déjà vu*. He and John Cheltzman had dragged the boughs in after stumbling on this place by accident on a forbidden afternoon away from HH.

Blaze set the baby down on a bed of boughs, fumbled in

his jacket pocket for the kitchen matches he always kept in there, and lit one. By its wavering light he could see Johnny's neatly made printing on the wall.

Johnny C and Clay Blaisdell. August 15th. Third year of Hell.

It was written in candlesmoke.

Blaze shivered—not from the cold, not in here—and shook out the match.

Joe was staring up at him in the gloom. He was gasping. His eyes were full of dismay. Then he stopped gasping.

"Christ, what's wrong with you?" Blaze cried. The rock walls knocked his voice back into his own ears. "What's wrong? What's—"

Then he knew. The blankets were too tight. He had pulled them around Joe when he put him down, and he'd pulled too hard. Kid couldn't breathe. He loosened them with trembling fingers. Joe whooped in a huge lungful of damp cave air and began to cry. It was a weak, trembling sound.

Blaze shook the Pampers out of his shirt, then got one of the bottles. He tried to give Joe the nipple, but Joe turned his head away.

"Wait then," Blaze said. "Just wait."

He took his cap, put it on, gave it a tug to the left, and went out.

He got some good deadwood from a tangle at the end of the gulch, and several handfuls of duff from beneath it. These he stuffed in his pockets. When he got back to the cave, he made a little fire and lit it. There was a small fissure like a cleft palate above the main opening, enough to create a draft and pull most of the smoke outside. He didn't have to worry about anyone seeing this little bit of smoke, at least not until the wind died and the snow stopped.

He fed the fire stick by stick, until it was crackling briskly. Then he put Joe on his lap before it and warmed him. The little guy was breathing more naturally now, but that bronchial rattle was still there.

"Gonna take you to a doctor," Blaze told him. "Soon as we get outta this. He'll fix you up. You'll be as cool as a fool."

Joe grinned at him abruptly, showing off his new tooth. Blaze grinned back, relieved. The kid couldn't be too bad off if he was still grinning, right? He offered Joe a finger. Joe wrapped his hand around it.

"Shake, pard," Blaze said, and laughed. Then he took the cold bottle out of his jacket pocket, brushed off the clinging bits of duff, and set it next to the fire to get warm. Outside, the wind howled and shrieked, but in here it was warming up nicely. He wished he had remembered the cave first. It would have been better than HH. It had been wrong to bring Joe to an orphanage. It was what George would have called bad mojo.

"Well," Blaze said, "you won't remember. Willya?"

When the bottle felt warm to the touch, he gave it to Joe. This time the baby latched on eagerly, and took the whole thing. While putting away the last two ounces, his eyes took on the glassy, faraway look Blaze had come to know well. He put Joe on his shoulder and rocked him back and forth. The baby burped twice and talked his little nonsense words for maybe five minutes. Then he ceased.

His eyes were closed again. Blaze was getting used to his schedule. Joe would sleep now for forty-five minutes—maybe an hour—and then want to be active the rest of the morning.

Blaze dreaded leaving him, especially after the accident of the night before, but it was vital. His instincts told him so. He laid Joe down on one of the blankets, put the other over him, and anchored the top blanket with big rocks. He thought—hoped—that if Joe awoke while he was gone, he could turn over but not crawl out. It would have to be good enough.

Blaze backed out of the cave, then started back the way he'd come, following his tracks. They were already starting to drift in. He hurried, and when the ground opened out, he began to run. It was quarter past seven in the morning.

While Blaze prepared to feed the baby, Sterling was in the arrest-and-recovery operation's command vehicle, a 4X4. He sat in the shotgun seat. A State Trooper was driving. With his big flat hat off, the Statie looked like a Marine recruit after his first haircut. To Sterling, most Staties looked like Marine recruits. And most FBI agents looked like lawyers or accountants, which was perfectly fitting, since—

He caught his flying thoughts and pulled them back down to ground level. "Can't you push this thing a little faster?"

"Sure," the Statie said. "Then we can spend the rest of the morning picking our teeth out of a snowbank."

"There's no need to take that tone, is there?"

"This weather makes me nervous," the Statie said. "This is a shitstorm. Slippery as hell underneath."

"All right." Sterling looked at his watch. "How far to Cumberland?"

"Fifteen miles."

"How long?"

The Trooper shrugged. "Twenty-five minutes?"

Sterling grunted. This was a "cooperative venture" between the Bureau and the Maine State Police, and the only thing he hated more than "cooperative ventures" were root canals. The possibility of clusterfucks grew when you brought in state law enforcement. Of course it jumped to a *probability* when the Bureau was forced into the dreaded "cooperative venture" with local law enforcement, but this was bad enough: running point with a fake Marine who was afraid to push it past fifty.

He shifted in the seat and the butt of his pistol dug into the small of his back. But it was where he always wore it. Sterling trusted his gun, his Bureau, and his nose. He had a nose like a good bird dog. A good bird dog could do more than smell a partridge or a turkey in the bushes; a good bird dog could smell its fear, and which way its fear would cause it to break, and when. It knew when the bird's need to fly was going to overmaster its need to stay still, in its hide.

Blaisdell was in a hide, probably this defunct orphan home. That was all very well, but Blaisdell was going to break. Sterling's nose told him so. And although the asshole had no wings, he had legs and he could run.

Sterling was also becoming sure that Blaisdell was in it alone. If there was someone else—the brains of the opera-

tion Sterling and Granger had taken for granted at first—
they would have heard from him by now, if for no other
reason than that Blaisdell was dumb as a stump. No, he was
probably in it alone, and probably hunkered down in that
old orphanage (like a half-assed homing pigeon, Sterling
thought), certain no one would look for him there. No
reason to believe they wouldn't find him squatting like a
scared quail behind a bush.

Except Blaisdell had his wind up. Sterling knew it.

He looked at his watch. It was just past 6:30.

The net would drop over a triangular area: along Route 9
to the west, a secondary road called Loon Cut on the north,
and an old logging road to the southeast. When everyone
was in position the net would begin to close, collapsing on
Hetton House. The snow was a pain in the ass now, but it
would give them cover when they moved in.

It sounded good, but—

"Can't you roll this thing a little faster?" Sterling asked.
He knew it was wrong to ask, wrong to push the guy, but
he couldn't help it.

The Trooper looked at the man sitting beside him.
At Sterling's small, pinched face and hot eyes. And he
thought: This Type A fuck means to kill him, I think.

"Fasten your seatbelt, Agent Sterling," he said.

"It is," Sterling said. He thumbed it out like a vest.

The Statie sighed and stepped down a little harder on
the gas.

Sterling gave the order at seven AM, and the assembled
forces moved in. The snow was very deep—four feet in

places—but the men floundered and came on, staying in radio contact with each other. No one complained. A child's life was at stake. The falling snow gave everything a heightened, surreal urgency. They looked like figures in an old silent movie, a sepia melodrama where there was no doubt about who the villain was.

Sterling ran the operation like a good quarterback, staying on top of things by walkie-talkie. The men coming from the east had the easiest going, so he slowed them down to keep them in sync with those coming in from SR 9 and down Loon Hill from Loon Cut. Sterling wanted Hetton House surrounded, but he wanted more. He wanted every bush and grove of trees beaten for his bird on the way in.

"Sterling, this is Tanner. You copy?"

"Got you, Tanner. Come back."

"We're at the head of the road leading to the orphanage. Chain's still across the road, but the lock's been busted. He's up there, all right. Over."

"That's a ten-four," Sterling said. Excitement raced along his nerves in all directions. In spite of the cold, he felt sweat break in his crotch and armpits. "Do you see fresh tire tracks, come back?"

"No, sir. Over."

"Carry on. Over and out."

They had him. Sterling's big fear had been that Blaisdell had beaten them again—driven out with the baby and beaten them again—but no.

He spoke softly into the walkie and the men moved faster, panting their way through the snow like dogs.

•   •   •

Blaze clambered over the wall between the Victory Garden and HH's back yard. He ran to the door. His mind was in a frightful clamor. His nerves felt like bare feet on broken glass. George's words echoed in his brain, coming at him over and over: *They've almost got you, Blaze.*

He ran up the stairs in mad leaps, skidded into the office, and began to load everything—clothes, food, bottles—into the cradle. Then he thundered back down the stairs and sprinted outside.

It was 7:30.

7:30.

"Hold it," Sterling said quietly into his walkie-talkie. "Everybody just hold it for a minute. Granger? Bruce? Copy?"

The voice that came back sounded apologetic. "This is Corliss."

"Corliss? I don't want you, Corliss. I want Bruce. Over."

"Agent Granger's down, sir. Think he broke his leg. Over?"

"*What?*"

"These woods are lousy with deadfalls, sir. He, ah, stumbled into one and it gave way. What should we do? Over."

Time, slipping away. Vision in his mind of a great big hourglass filled with snow and Blaisdell slipping through the waist. On a fucking sled.

"Splint it and wrap him up warm and leave him your walkie. Over."

"Yessir. Do you want to talk to him? Over?"

"No. I want to move. Over."

"Yessir, I'm clear."

"Fine," Sterling said. "All you group leaders, let's hump. Out."

Blaze ran across the Victory Garden, gasping. He reached the ruined rock wall at the far end, climbed over, and skidded willy-nilly down the slope into the woods, clutching the cradle to his chest.

He got up, started to step forward, then stopped. He set the cradle down and pulled George's gun out of his belt. He had seen nothing and heard nothing, but he *knew*.

He moved behind the trunk of a big old pine. Snow whipped against his left cheek, numbing it. He waited without moving. Inside, his mind was a fury. The need to get back to Joe was an ache, but the need to stand here and wait and be quiet was just as strong.

What if Joe got out of the blankets and crawled into the fire?

He won't, Blaze told himself. Even babies are ascairt of fire.

What if he crawled out of the cave into the snow? What if he was freezing to death right now, as Blaze stood here like a lump?

He won't. He's asleep.

Yes, and no guarantee how long he'll stay that way, in a strange place. Or what if the wind shifts around and the cave fills up with smoke? While you stand here, the only living person in two miles, maybe five—

He *wasn't* the only one. Someone was around. *Someone.*

But the woods were silent except for the wind, the creaking trees, and the faint hiss of falling snow.

Time to go.

Only it wasn't. It was time to wait.

You should have killed the kid when I told you, Blaze.

George. In his *head* now. Christ!

I wasn't ever nowhere else. Now go!

He decided he would. Then he decided he would count to ten first. He had gotten up to six when something detached itself from the gray-green belt of trees farther down the slope. It was a State Policeman, but Blaze felt no fear. Something had burned it away and he was deadly calm. Only Joe mattered now, taking care of Joe. He thought the Trooper would miss him, but the Trooper wouldn't miss the tracks, and that was just as bad.

Blaze saw that the Trooper would pass his position on the right, so he slipped around the trunk of the big pine tree to the left. He thought of how many times he and John and Toe and the others had played in these woods; cowboys and Indians, cops and robbers. Bang with a crooked piece of stick and you're dead.

One shot would end it. It didn't have to kill or even wound either of them. The sound would be enough. Blaze felt a pulse thudding in his neck.

The Trooper paused. He'd seen the tracks. Must have. Or a piece of Blaze's coat peeking around the tree. Blaze flicked the safety off George's pistol. If there was going to be a shot, he wanted it to be his.

Then the Trooper moved on again. He glanced down at

the snow from time to time, but he directed most of his attention into the thickets. Fifty yards away now. No—less.

Off to the left, Blaze heard someone else crash through a deadfall or some low branches and utter a curse. His heart sank even deeper in his chest. The woods were full of them, then. But maybe . . . maybe if they were all going in the same direction . . .

Hetton! They were surrounding Hetton House! Sure! And if he could get back to the cave, he'd be on the other side of them. Then, farther into the woods, maybe three miles, there was a logging road—

The Trooper had closed to twenty-five yards. Blaze sidled a little farther around the tree. If someone popped out of the brush on his open side now, he was dead-dog fucked.

The Trooper was passing the tree. Blaze could hear the crunch of his boots in the snow. He could even hear something jingling in the Trooper's pockets—change, maybe keys. And the creak of his belt. That, too.

Blaze moved even farther around the tree, taking little sidle-steps. Then he waited. When he looked out again, the Trooper had his back to Blaze. He hadn't seen the tracks yet, but he would. He was walking on top of them.

Blaze stepped out and walked toward the Trooper in large, soundless steps. He reversed George's pistol so he was gripping it by the barrel.

The Trooper looked down and saw the tracks. He stiffened, then grabbed for the walkie-talkie on his belt. Blaze raised the gun up high and brought it down hard. The Trooper grunted and staggered, but his big hat absorbed much of the blow's force. Blaze swung again, sidehand, and hit the Trooper in the left temple. There was a soft thud. The Trooper's hat slewed around to the side and hung on his right cheek. Blaze saw he was young, hardly more than a kid. Then the Trooper's knees unlocked and he went down, puffing up snow all around him.

"Fucks," Blaze said. He was crying. "Why can't you just leave a fella alone?"

He gripped the Trooper under the armpits and dragged him to the big pine. He propped the guy up and set his hat back on his head. There wasn't much blood, but Blaze wasn't fooled by that. He knew how hard he could hit. No one knew better. There was a pulse in the Trooper's neck, but it wasn't much. If his buddies didn't find him soon, he would die. Well, who had asked him to come? Who had asked him to stick his goddam oar in?

He picked up the cradle and began to move on. It was quarter to eight when he got back to the cave. Joe was still sleeping, and that made Blaze cry again, this time from relief. But the cave was cold. Snow had blown in and put the little fire out.

Blaze began to build it up again.

Special Agent Bruce Granger watched Blaze come down the ravine and crawl into the slit mouth of the cave. Granger had been lying there stolidly, waiting for the hunt to end one way or another so someone could carry him out. His leg hurt like hell and he'd felt like a fool.

Now he felt like someone who'd won the lottery. He reached for the walkie Corliss had left him and picked it up. "Granger to Sterling," he said quietly. "Come back."

Static. Peculiar blank static.

"Albert, this is Bruce, and it's urgent. Come on back?"

Nothing.

Granger closed his eyes for a moment. "Son of a bitch," he said. Then he opened his eyes and began to crawl.

8:10.

Albert Sterling and two State Troopers stood in Martin Coslaw's old office with their guns drawn. There was a blanket squashed up in one corner. Sterling saw two empty plastic nursing bottles, and three empty cans of Carnation Evaporated Milk that looked like they had been opened with a jackknife blade. And two empty boxes of Pampers.

"Shit," he said. "Shit, shit, *shit*."

"He can't be far," Franklin said. "He's on foot. With the kid."

"It's ten degrees out there," someone in the hall remarked.

Sterling thought: One of you guys tell me something I don't fucking know.

Franklin was looking around. "Where's Corliss? Brad, did you see Corliss?"

"I think he might still be downstairs," Bradley said.

"We're going back into the woods," Sterling said. "The moke's got to be in the woods."

There was a gunshot. It was faint, muffled by the snow, but unmistakable.

They looked at each other. There were five seconds of perfect, shocked silence. Maybe seven. Then they broke for the door.

•   •   •

Joe was still asleep when the bullet came into the cave. It ricocheted twice, sounding like an angry bee, chipping away splinters of granite and sending them flying. Blaze had been laying out diapers; he wanted to give Joe a change, make sure he was dry before they set out.

Now Joe started awake and began to cry. His small hands were waving in the air. One of the granite chips had cut his face.

Blaze didn't think. He saw the blood and thought ceased. What replaced it was black and murderous. He burst from the cave and charged toward the sound of the shot, screaming.

CHAPTER 22

Blaze was sitting at the counter in Moochie's, eating a doughnut and reading a Spider-Man funnybook, when George walked into his life. It was September. Blaze hadn't worked for two months, and money was tight. Several of the candy-store wiseguys had been pinched. Blaze himself had been taken in for questioning about a loan-office holdup in Saugus, but he hadn't been in on that job and had come across so honestly bewildered that the cops let him go. Blaze was thinking about trying to get back his old job at the hospital laundry.

"That's him," someone said. "That's The Boogeyman."

Blaze turned and saw Hankie Melcher. Standing with him was a little guy in a sharp suit. The little guy had sallow skin and eyes that seemed to burn like coals.

"Hi, Hank," Blaze said. "Ain't seenya."

"Ah, little state vacation," Hank said. "They let me out cause they can't count right up there. Ain't that so, George?"

The little guy said nothing, only smiled thinly and went on looking at Blaze. Those hot eyes made Blaze uncomfortable.

Moochie walked down, wiping his hands on his apron. "Yo, Hankie."

"Chocolate egg cream for me," Hank said. "Want one, George?"

"Just coffee. Black."

Moochie went away. Hank said, "Blaze, like you to meet my brother-in-law. George Rackley, Clay Blaisdell."

"Hi," Blaze said. This smelled like work.

"Yo." George shook his head. "You're one big mother, know it?"

Blaze laughed as if no one had ever observed he was one big mother before.

"George is a card," Hank said, grinning. "He's a regular Bill Crosby. Only white."

"Sure," Blaze said, still smiling.

Moochie came back with Hankie's egg cream and George's coffee. George took a sip, grimaced. He looked at Moochie. "Do you always shit in your coffee cups, or do you sometimes use the pot, Sunshine?"

Hank said to Moochie: "George don't mean nothin by it."

George was nodding. "That's right. I'm just a card, that's all. Get lost a little while, Hankie. Go in the back and play pinball."

Hankie was still grinning. "Yeah, okay. Rightie-O."

When he was gone and Moochie was back down at the far end of the counter, George turned to Blaze again. "That retard says you might be lookin for work."

"That's about right," Blaze said.

Hankie dropped coins into the pinball machine, then raised his hands and began to vocalize what might have been the theme from *Rocky*.

George jerked his head at him. "Now that he's out again, Hankie's got big plans. A gas station in Malden."

"That so?" Blaze asked.

"Yeah. Crime of the fuckin century. You want to make a hundred bucks this afternoon?"

"Sure." Blaze answered without hesitation.

"Will you do exactly what I tell you?"

"Sure. What's the gag, Mr. Rackley?"

"George. Call me George."

"What's the gag, George?" Then he reconsidered the hot, urgent eyes and said, "I don't hurt nobody."

"Me either. Bang-bang's for mokes. Now listen."

That afternoon George and Blaze walked into Hardy's, a thriving department store in Lynn. All the clerks in Hardy's wore pink shirts with white arms. They also wore badges that said HI! I'M DAVE! Or JOHN! Or whoever. George was wearing one of those shirts under his outside shirt. His badge said HI! I'M FRANK! When Blaze saw that, he nodded and said, "That's like an alias, right?"

George smiled—not the one he'd used around Hankie Melcher—and said: "Yes, Blaze. Like an alias."

Something in that smile made Blaze relax. There was no hurt or mean in it. And since it was just the two of them on this gag, there was no one to nudge George in the ribs when Blaze said something dumb, and make him the outsider. Blaze wasn't sure George would've grinned even if there *had* been someone else. He might have said something like *Keep your fuckin elbows to yourself, shitmonkey.* Blaze found himself liking someone for the first time since John Cheltzman died.

George had hoed his own tough row through life. He had been born in the charity ward of a Providence Catholic hospital called St. Joseph's: mother unwed, father unknown. She resisted the nuns' suggestions that she give the boy up for adoption and used him as a club to beat her family with instead. George grew up on the patched-pants side of town and pulled his first con at the age of four. His mother was about to give him a whacking for spilling a bowl of Maypo. George told her a man had brought her a letter and left it in the hall. While she was looking for it, he locked her out of the apartment and booked it down the fire escape. His whacking later was double, but he never forgot the exhilaration of knowing he had won, at least for a little while; he would chase that *I gotcha* feeling the rest of his life. It was ephemeral but always sweet.

He was a bright and bitter boy. Experience taught him things that losers like Hankie Melcher would never learn. George and three older acquaintances (he did not have pals) stole a car when George was eleven, took a joyride from Providence to Central Falls, got pinched. The fifteen-year-old who had been behind the wheel went to the reformatory. George and the other boys got probation. George also got a monster whacking from the gray-faced pimp his mother was by then living with. This was Aidan O'Kellaher, who had notoriously bad kidneys—hence his street-name, Pisser Kelly. Pisser beat on him until George's half-sister screamed for him to stop.

"You want some?" Pisser asked, and when Tansy shook her head he said, "Then shut your fucking airscoop."

George never stole another car without a reason. Once was enough to teach him there was no percentage in joyriding. It was a joyless world.

At thirteen, he and a friend got caught boosting in Woolworth's. Probation again. And another whacking. George didn't stop boosting, but improved his technique, and wasn't caught again.

When George was seventeen, Pisser got him a job running numbers. At this time, Providence was enjoying the sort of half-assed revival that passed for prosperity in the economically exhausted New England states. Numbers were going good. So was George. He bought nice clothes. He also began to jiggle his book. Pisser thought George a fine, enterprising boy; he was bringing in six hundred and fifty dollars every Wednesday. Unknown to his stepfather, George was socking away another two hundred.

Then the Mob came north from Atlantic City. They took over the numbers. Some of the mid-level locals got pink-slipped. Pisser Kelly was pink-slipped to an automobile graveyard, where he was discovered with his throat cut and his balls in the glove compartment of a Chevrolet Biscayne.

With his living taken away, George set off for Boston. He took his twelve-year-old sister with him. Tansy's father was also unknown, but George had his suspicions; Pisser had had the same weak chin.

During the next seven years, George refined any number of short cons. He also invented a few. His mother listlessly signed a paper making him Tansy Rackley's legal guardian, and George kept the little whore in school. Came a day when he discovered she was skin-popping heroin. She was also, happy days, knocked up. Hankie Melcher was eager to marry her. George was surprised at first, then wasn't. The world was full of fools falling all over themselves to show you how smart they were.

George took to Blaze because Blaze was a fool with no pretensions. He wasn't a sharpie, a dude, or a backroom Clyde. He didn't shoot pool, let alone H. Blaze was a rube. He was a tool, and in their years together, George used him that way. But never badly. Like a good carpenter, George loved good tools—ones that worked like they were supposed to every time. He could turn his back on Blaze. He could go to sleep in a room where Blaze was awake, and know that when he woke up himself, the swag would still be under the bed.

Blaze also calmed George's starved and angry insides. That was no small thing. There came a day when George understood that if he said, "Blazer, you have to step off the top of this building, because it's how we roll," . . . well, Blaze would do it. In a way, Blaze was the Cadillac George would never have—he had big springs when the road was rough.

When they entered Hardy's, Blaze went directly to menswear, as instructed. He wasn't carrying his own wallet; he was carrying a cheap plastic job which contained fifteen dollars cash and ID tabbing him as David Billings, of Reading.

As he entered the department, he stuck his hand in his

back pocket—as if to check his wallet was still there—and pulled it three-quarters of the way out. When he bent over to check out some shirts on a low shelf, the wallet fell on the floor.

This was the most delicate part of the operation. Blaze half-turned, keeping an eye on the wallet without seeming to keep an eye on it. To the casual observer, he would have seemed entirely engrossed in his inspection of the Van Heusen short-sleeves. George had laid it out for him carefully. If an honest man noticed the wallet, then all bets were off and they would move on to Kmart. Sometimes it took as many as half a dozen stops before the gag paid off.

"Gee," Blaze said. "I didn't know so many people were honest."

"They're not," George said with a wintry smile. "But plenty are scared. And keep your eye on that fuckin wallet. If someone dips it on you, you're out fifteen bucks and I'm out ID worth a lot more."

That day in Hardy's they had beginner's luck. A man wearing a shirt with an alligator on the tit strolled up the aisle, spied the wallet, then looked both ways down the aisle to see if anyone was coming. No one was. Blaze exchanged one shirt for another and then held it up in front of him in the mirror. His heart was pumping like a sweetmother.

Wait until he pockets it, George said. *Then raise holy hell.*

The man in the alligator shirt hooked the wallet against the rack of sweaters he was looking at. Then he reached into his pocket, took out his car-keys, and dropped them on the floor. Oops. He bent down to get them and gleeped the wallet at the same time. He shoved them both into his front pants pocket, then started to stroll off.

Blaze let out a bull bellow. "Thief! *Thief! Yeah, YOU!*"

Shoppers turned and craned their necks. Clerks looked around. The floorwalker spotted the source of the trouble and began to hurry toward them, pausing at a cash register location to push a button labeled *Special*.

The man with the alligator on his tit went pale . . . looked around . . . bolted. He got four steps before Blaze collared him.

Rough him up but don't hurt him, George had said. *Keep hollering. And whatever you do, don't let him ditch that wallet. If he looks like he's tryin to get rid of it, knee him in the jukebox.*

Blaze grabbed the man by the shoulders and began shaking him up and down like a man with a bottle of medicine. The man in the alligator shirt, maybe a Walt Whitman fan, voiced his barbaric yawp. Change flew from his pockets. He stuck a hand in the pocket with the wallet in it, just as George had said he might, and Blaze popped him one in the nuts—not too hard. The man in the alligator shirt screamed.

"I'll teachya to steal my wallet!" Blaze screamed at the guy's face. He was getting into it now. "I'll *killya!*"

"Somebody get him off me!" the guy screamed. "Get him *off!*"

One of the menswear clerks poked his nose in. "Hey, that's enough!"

George, who had been examining casual wear, unbuttoned his outer shirt, took it off with absolutely no effort at concealment, and stashed it under a stack of Beefy Tees. No one was looking at him, anyway. They were looking at

Blaze, who gave a mighty tug and tore the shirt with the alligator on the tit right down the middle.

"Break it up!" the clerk was shouting. "Cool it!"

"Sonofabitch has got my wallet!" Blaze cried.

A large crowd of rubberneckers began to gather. They wanted to see if Blaze would kill the guy he had hold of before the floorwalker or store detective or some other person in authority arrived.

George punched NO SALE on one of the two Menswear Department cash registers and began scooping out the currency. His pants were too large, and a pouch—sort of like a hidden fanny-pack—was sewn in the front. He stuffed the bills in there, taking his time. Tens and twenties first—there were even some fifties, beginner's luck indeed—then fives and ones.

"Break it up!" the floorwalker was yelling as he cut through the crowd. Hardy's did have a store detective, and he followed on the floorwalker's heels. "That's enough! Hold it!"

The store detective shoved himself between Blaze and the man in the torn alligator shirt.

Stop fighting when the store dick comes, George had said, *but keep making like you want to kill the guy.*

"Check his pocket!" Blaze yelled. "Sonofabitch dipped me!"

"I picked a wallet up off the floor," the alligator-man admitted, "and was just glancing around for the possible owner when this . . . this *thug*—"

Blaze lunged at him. The alligator-man cringed away. The store dick pushed Blaze back. Blaze didn't mind. He was having fun.

"Easy, big fella. Down, boy."

The floorwalker, meanwhile, asked the alligator-man for his name.

"Peter Hogan."

"Dump out your pockets, Mr. Hogan."

"I certainly will not!"

The store dick said, "Dump em out or I'll call the cops."

George strolled toward the escalator, looking as alert and lively as the best Hardy's employee who ever punched a time-clock.

Peter Hogan considered whether or not to stand on his rights, then dumped out his pockets. When the crowd saw the cheap brown wallet, it went ahhhh.

"That's it," Blaze said. "That's mine. He must've took it out of my back pocket while I was lookin at shirts."

"ID in it?" the store dick asked, flipping open the wallet.

For a horrible moment Blaze went blank. Then it seemed like George was standing right there beside him. *David Billings, Blaze.*

"Sure, Dave Billings," Blaze said. "Me."

"How much cash in it?"

"Not much. Fifteen bucks or so."

The store dick looked at the floorwalker and nodded. The crowd ahhh-ed again. The store dick handed the wallet to Blaze, who pocketed it.

"You come with me," the store dick said. He grabbed Hogan's arm.

The floorwalker said, "Break it up, folks, this is all over. Hardy's is full of bargains this week, and I urge you to shop them." Blaze thought he sounded as good as a

radio announcer; it was no wonder he had such a respon-
sible job.

To Blaze, the floorwalker said: "Will you come with
me, sir?"

"Yeah." Blaze glared at Hogan. "Just let me get the shirt
I wanted."

"I think you'll find that your shirt is a gift from Hardy's
today. But we *would* like to see you briefly on the third
floor, ask for Mr. Flaherty. Room 7."

Blaze nodded and turned to the shirts again. The floorwalker left. Not far away, one of the clerks was getting
ready to punch NO SALE on the register George had
robbed.

"Hey, you!" Blaze said to him, then beckoned.

The clerk came over . . . but not too close. "May I help
you, sir?"

"This joint got a lunch counter?"

The clerk looked relieved. "First floor."

"You the man," Blaze said. He made a gun of his right
thumb and forefinger, tipped the clerk a wink, and strolled
off toward the escalator. The clerk watched him go. By the
time he got back to his register, where all the bill compart-
ments in the tray were now empty, Blaze was out on the
street. George was waiting in a rusty old Ford. And off
they drove.

They scored three hundred and forty dollars. George split it
right down the middle. Blaze was ecstatic. It was the easiest job he had ever done. George was a mastermind. They
would pull the gag all over town.

George took all this with the modesty of a third-rate magician who has just run the jacks at a children's birthday party. He didn't tell Blaze the gimmick went back to his grammar school days, when two buckies would start a fight by the meat-counter and a third would scoop the till while the owner was breaking it up. Nor did he tell Blaze they would be collared the third time they tried it, if not the second. He simply nodded and shrugged and enjoyed the big guy's amazement. Amazement? Blaze was fucking awestruck.

They drove into Boston, stopped at a liquor store, and picked up two fifths of Old Granddad. Then they went to a double feature at the Constitution on Washington Street and watched car-chases and men with automatic weapons. When they left at ten o'clock that evening, they were both blotto. All four hubcaps had been stolen off the Ford. George was mad, even though the hubcaps had been as shitty as the rest of the car. Then he saw someone had also keyed off his VOTE DEMOCRAT bumper-sticker and started to laugh. He sat down on the curb, laughing until tears rolled down his sallow cheeks.

"Taken off by a Reagan-lover," he said. "My fuckin word."

"Maybe the guy who spoiled your fumper-licker wasn't the same guy was took your wheelcaps," Blaze said, sitting down beside George. His head was whirling, but it was a good whirl. A nice whirl.

"*Fumper-licker!*" George cried. He bent over as if he had a stomach cramp, but he was screaming with laughter. He tromped his feet up and down. "*I always knew there was a word for Barry Goldwater! Fuckin fumper-licker!*" Then he stopped laughing. He looked at Blaze with swimming, solemn eyes and said, "Blazer, I just pissed myself."

Blaze began to laugh. He laughed until he fell back on the sidewalk. He had never laughed so hard, not even with John Cheltzman.

Two years later, George was busted for passing bad checks. Blaze's luck was in again. He was getting over the flu, and George was alone when the cops grabbed him outside of a Danvers bar. He got three years—a stiff sentence for first-time forgery—but George was a known bunco and the judge was a known hardass. Perhaps even a fumper-licker. It was twenty months, with time served and time off for good behavior.

Before the sentencing, George took Blaze aside. "I'm going to Walpole, big boy. A year at least. Probably longer."

"But your lawyer—"

"The fuckhead couldn't defend the Pope on a rape charge. Listen: you stay away from Moochie's."

"But Hank said if I came around, he could—"

"And stay away from Hankie, too. Get a straight job until I come out, that's how you roll. Don't go trying to pull any cons on your own. You're too goddam dumb. You know that, don't you?"

"Yeah," Blaze said, and grinned. But he felt like crying.

George saw it and punched Blaze on the arm. "You'll be fine," he said.

Then, as Blaze left, George called to him. Blaze turned. George made an impatient gesture at his forehead. Blaze nodded and swerved the bill of his cap around to the good-luck side. He grinned. But inside he still felt like crying.

He tried his old job, but it was too square after life with George. He quit and looked for something better. For awhile he was a bouncer at a place in the Combat Zone, but he was no good at it. His heart was too soft.

He went back to Maine, got a job cutting pulp, and waited for George to get out. He liked pulping, and he liked driving Christmas trees south. He liked the fresh air and horizons that were unbroken by tall buildings. The city was okay sometimes, but the woods were quiet. There were birds, and sometimes you saw deer wading in ponds and your heart went out to them. He sure didn't miss the subways, or the pushing crowds. But when George dropped him a short note—*Getting out on Friday, hope to see you*—Blaze put in his time and went south to Boston again.

George had picked up an assortment of new cons in Walpole. They tried them out like old ladies test-driving new cars. The most successful was the queer-con. That bastard ran like a railroad for three years, until Blaze was busted on what George called "the Jesus-gag."

George picked something else up in prison: the idea of one big score and out. Because, he told Blaze, he couldn't see spending the best years of his life hustling homos in bars where everybody was dressed up like *The Rocky Horror Picture Show*. Or peddling fake encyclopedias. Or running a Murphy. No, one big score and out. It became his mantra.

A high school teacher named John Burgess, in for manslaughter, had suggested kidnapping.

"You're trippin!" George said, horrified. They were in the yard on ten o'clock exercise, eating bananas and watching some mokes with big muscles throw a football around.

"It's got a bad name because it's the crime of choice for idiots," Burgess said. He was a slight balding man. "Kidnap a baby, that's the ticket."

"Yeah, like Hauptmann," George said, and jittered back and forth like he was getting electrocuted.

"Hauptmann was an idiot. Hell, Rasp, a well-handled baby snatch could hardly miss. What's the kid going to say when they ask him who did it? Goo-goo ga-ga?" He laughed.

"Yeah, but the heat," George said.

"Sure, sure, the heat." Burgess smiled and tugged his ear. He was a great old ear-tugger. "There *would* be heat. Baby snatches and cop-killings, always a lot of heat. You know what Harry Truman said about that?"

"No."

"He said if you can't stand the heat, get out of the kitchen."

"You can't collect the ransom," George said. "Even if you did, the money would be marked. Goes without saying."

Burgess raised one finger like a professor. Then he did that dopey ear-tugging thing, which kind of spoiled it. "You're assuming the cops would be called in. If you scared the family bad enough, they'd deal privately." He paused. "And even if the money was hot . . . you saying you don't know some guys?"

"Maybe. Maybe not."

"There are guys who buy hot money. It's just another investment to them, like gold or government bonds."

"But collecting the swag—what about that?"

Burgess shrugged. He pulled on his ear. "Easy. Have the marks drop it from a plane." Then he got up and walked away.

Blaze was sentenced to four years on the Jesus-gag. George told him it would be a tit if he kept his nose clean. Two at most, he said, and two was what it turned out to be. Those years inside weren't much different than the jail-time he'd put in after beating up The Law; only the inmates had grown older. He didn't spend any time in solitary. When he got the heebie-jeebies on long evenings, or during one interminable lockdown when there were no exercise privileges, he wrote George. His spelling was awful, the letters long. George didn't answer very often, but in time the very act of composition, laborious as it was, became soothing. He imagined that when he wrote, George was standing behind him, reading over his shoulder.

"Prisin laundre," George would say. "My fuckin word."

"That wrong, George?"

"*P-r-i-s-o-n,* prison. *L-a-u-n-d-r-y,* laundry. Prison laundry."

"Oh yeah. Right."

His spelling and even his punctuation improved, even though he never used a dictionary. Another time:

"Blaze, you're not using your cigarette ration." This was during the golden time when some of the tobacco companies gave out little trial packs.

"I don't hardly smoke, George. You know that. They'd just pile up."

"Listen to me, Blazer. You pick em up on Friday, then sell em the next Thursday, when everybody's hurtin for a smoke. That's how you roll."

Blaze began to do this. He was surprised how much people would pay for smoke that didn't even get you stoned.

Another time:

"You don't sound good, George," Blaze said.

"Course not. I just had four fuckin teeth out. Hurts like hell."

Blaze called him the next time he had phone privileges, not reversing the charges but feeding the phone with dough he'd made selling ciggies on the black market. He asked George how his teeth were.

"What teeth?" George said grumpily. "Fuckin dentist is probably wearin em around his neck like a Ubangi." He paused. "How'd you know I had em out? Someone tell you?"

Blaze suddenly felt he was on the verge of being caught in something shameful, like beating off in chapel. "Yeah," he said. "Someone told me."

They drifted south to New York City when Blaze got out, but neither of them liked it. George had his pocket picked, which he took as a personal affront. They took a trip to Florida and spent a miserable month in Tampa, broke and unable to score. They went north again, not to Boston but to Portland. George said he wanted to summer in Maine and pretend he was a rich Republican fuckstick.

Not long after they arrived, George read a newspaper story about the Gerards: how rich they were, how the youngest Gerard had just gotten married to some good-looking spic chick. Burgess's kidnap idea resurfaced in his mind—that one big score. But there was no baby, not then, so they went back to Boston.

The Boston-in-the-winter, Portland-in-the-summer thing became a routine over the next two years. They'd roll north in some old beater in early June, with whatever remained of the winter's proceeds stashed in the spare tire: seven hundred one year, two thousand the next. In Portland, they pulled a gag if a gag presented itself. Otherwise, Blaze fished and sometimes laid a trap or two in the woods. They were happy summers for him. George lay out in the sun and tried to get a tan (hopeless; he only burned), read the papers, swatted blackflies, and rooted for Ronald Reagan (who he called Old White Elvis Daddy) to drop dead.

Then, on July 4th of their second summer in Maine, he noticed that Joe Gerard III and his Narmenian wife had become parents.

Blaze was playing solitaire on the porch of the shack and listening to the radio. George turned it off. "Listen, Blazer," he said, "I got an idea."

He was dead three months later.

They had been attending the crap-game regularly, and there had never been any trouble. It was a straight game. Blaze didn't play, but he often faded George. George was very lucky.

On this night in October, George made six straight passes. The man kneeling across from him on the other side of the blanket bet against him every time. He had lost forty dollars. The game was in a warehouse near the docks, and it was full of smells: old fish, fermented grain, salt, gasoline. When the place was quiet, you could hear the *tack-tack-tack* of seagulls walking around on the roof. The man who had lost forty dollars was named Ryder. He claimed to be half Penobscot Indian, and he looked it.

When George picked up the dice a seventh time instead of passing them, Ryder threw twenty dollars down on the crap-out line.

"Come, dice," George said—crooned. His thin face was bright. His cap was yanked around to the left. "Come big dice, come come come *now*!" The dice exploded across the blanket and came up eleven.

"Seven in a row!" George crowed. "Pick up that swag, Blazerino, daddy's goin for number eight. Big eighter from Decatur!"

"You cheated," Ryder said. His voice was mild, observational.

George froze in the act of picking up the dice. "Say what?"

"You switched them dice."

"Come on, Ride," someone said. "He didn't—"

"I'll have my money back," Ryder said. He stretched his hand out across the blanket.

"You'll have a broken arm if you don't cut the shit," George said. "That's what you'll have, Sunshine."

"I'll have my money back," Ryder said. His hand still out.

It was one of those quiet times now, and Blaze could hear the gulls on the roof: *tack-tack-tack*.

"Go fuck yourself," George said, and spat on the outstretched hand.

So then it happened quickly, as those things do. The quickness is what makes the mind reel and refuse. Ryder reached his spit-shiny hand into the pocket of his jeans, and when it came out, it was holding a spring-knife. Ryder thumbed the chrome button in the imitation ivory handle, and the men around the blanket scattered back.

George shouted: "*Blaze!*"

Blaze lunged across the blanket at Ryder, who rocked forward on his knees and put the blade in George's stomach. George screamed. Blaze grabbed Ryder and slammed his head against the floor. It made a cracking sound like a breaking branch.

George stood up. He looked at the knife-handle sticking out of his shirt. He grabbed it, started to pull, then grimaced. "Fuck," he said. "Oh fuck." He sat down hard.

Blaze heard a door slam. He heard running feet on hollow boards.

"Get me outta here," George said. His yellow shirt was turning red around the knife-handle. "Get the swag, too— *oh Jesus this hurts!*"

Blaze gathered up the scattered bills. He stuffed them into his pockets with fingers that had no feeling in them. George was panting. He sounded like a dog on a hot day.

"George, let me pull it out—"

"No, you crazy? It's holding my guts in. Carry me, Blaze. *Oh my fuckin Jesus!*"

Blaze picked George up in his arms and George screamed again. Blood dripped onto the blanket and onto Ryder's shiny black hair. Under the shirt, George's belly felt as hard as a board. Blaze carried him across the warehouse and then outside.

"No," George said. "You forgot the bread. You never got any goddam bread." Blaze thought maybe George was talking about the swag and he started to say he had it, when George said: "And the salami." He was beginning to breathe very rapidly. "I got that book, you know."

"George!"

"That book with the picture of—" But then George began to choke on his own blood. Blaze turned him over and whammed him on the back. It was all he could think of to do. But when he turned George over again, George was dead.

Blaze laid him on the boards outside the warehouse. He backed away. Then he crept forward again and closed George's eyes. He backed away a second time, then crept forward again and knelt. "George?"

No answer.

"You dead, George?"

No answer.

Blaze ran all the way to the car and got in and threw himself behind the wheel. He screamed away, peeling rubber for twenty feet.

"Slow down," George said from the back seat.

"George?"

"Slow *down,* goddammit!"

Blaze slowed down. "George! Come on up front! Climb over! Wait, I'll pull over."

"No," George said. "I like it back here."

"George?"

"What?"

"What are we going to do now?"

"Snatch the kid," George said. "Just like we planned."

CHAPTER 23

When Blaze blundered out of the little cave and got his feet under him, he had no idea how many men were out there. Dozens, he supposed. It didn't matter. George's pistol fell out of the waistband of his pants and that didn't matter, either. He trod it deep into the snow as he charged the first guy he saw. The guy was lying in the snow a little distance away, resting on his elbows and holding a gun in both hands.

"Hands up, Blaisdell! Stay still!" Granger shouted.

Blaze leaped at him.

Granger had time to fire twice. The first shot creased Blaze's forearm. The second plugged nothing but snow-storm. Then Blaze crashed all two hundred and seventy pounds into the guy who had hurt Joe, and Granger's weapon went flying. Granger screamed as the bones of his broken leg grated together.

"You hit the kid!" Blaze yelled into Granger's terrified face. His fingers found Granger's throat. "You hit the kid, you stupid sonofabitch, you hit the kid, you hit the kid, you hit the kid!"

Granger's head was flopping and nodding now, as if to say he understood, he was getting the message. His face had gone purple. His eyes bulged from their sockets.

They're coming.

Blaze stopped choking the guy and looked around. No one in sight. The woods were silent except for the wind and the faint hissing noise the snow made as it fell.

No, there *was* another sound. There was Joe.

Blaze ran back up the embankment to the cave. Joe was rolling around, wailing and clutching at the air. The flying chip of rock had done more damage than the fall from the cradle; his cheek was covered in blood.

"God *damn* it!" Blaze cried.

He picked Joe up, wiped his cheek, slipped him into the envelope of blankets again, and stuck his cap back over the baby's head. Joe whooped and screamed.

"We gotta run now, George," Blaze said. "Full-out run. Right?"

No answer.

Blaze backed out of the cave holding the baby to his chest, turned into the wind, and fled toward the logging road.

"Where did Corliss leave him?" Sterling panted at Franklin. The men had paused at the edge of the woods, breathing hard.

Franklin pointed. "Down there. I can find it."

Sterling turned to Bradley. "Call your people. And the Cumberland County Sheriff. I wanted that logging road plugged at both ends. What's past it if he slips through?"

Bradley barked a laugh. "Nothing but the Royal River. Like to see him ford that."

"Is it iced over?"

"Sure, but not enough to walk on."

"All right. Let us press on. Franklin, take point. *Short* point. This guy is very dangerous."

They moved down the first slope. Fifty yards into the woods, Sterling made out a blue-gray figure slumped against a tree.

Franklin got there first. "Corliss," he said.

"Dead?" Sterling asked, joining him.

"Oh yeah." Franklin pointed to tracks that were now little more than vague dips.

"Let's go," Sterling said. This time he took point.

They found Granger five minutes later. The marks on his throat were at least an inch deep.

"Guy must be a brute," someone said.

Sterling pointed into the snow. "That's a cave up there. I'm almost positive. Maybe he left the kid."

Two State Troopers scrambled up toward the triangular patch of shadow. One of them paused, bent, picked something out of the snow. He held it up. "A gun!" he yelled.

As if the rest of us are blind, Sterling thought. "Never mind the frigging *gun,* see about the kid! And be careful!"

One of them knelt, used his flashlight, then crawled after the beam. The other bent forward, hands on knees, listened, then turned back to Sterling and Franklin. "Not here!"

They spotted tracks leading from the cave toward the logging road even before the Trooper who had gone into the cave was out again. They were little more than vague humps in the fast-falling snow.

"He can't have more than ten minutes on us," Sterling

said to Franklin. Then he raised his voice. "Spread out! We're going to sweep him out onto that road!"

They headed out fast, Sterling tromping in Blaze's tracks.

Blaze ran.

He went in stumbling leaps, crashing straight through tangles of brush rather than trying to find a way around, bending over Joe to try and shield him from stabbing branches. Breath tore in and out of his lungs. He heard faint yelling behind him. The sound of those voices filled Blaze with panic.

Joe was whooping and struggling and coughing, but Blaze held him fast. Just a little more, a little farther, and they would come out on the road. There would be cars there. Police cars, but he didn't care about that. As long as there were keys left in them. He would drive as far and fast as he could, then dump the police cruiser and switch to something else. A truck would be good. These thoughts came and went in his head like big colored cartoons.

He blundered through a marshy place where the thin ice surrounding the snow-covered hummocks gave way and plunged him into frigid water up to his ankles. He kept going and came to a head-high wall of brambles. He went straight through, only turned around backwards to protect Joe. One of them got under the cap Joe was wearing, though, and slingshotted it back toward the marsh. No time to get it.

Joe stared around, his eyes wide with terror. Without the enveloping hat to warm the air in front of his face, he began to gasp harder. Now his cries sounded thin. Behind them, the faint blue voice of the law was yelling something else. It didn't matter. Nothing did except getting to the road.

The land began to slope upward. The going became a little easier. Blaze lengthened his stride, running for his life. And Joe's.

Sterling was also going full out, and he had drawn thirty yards ahead of the others. He was gaining. Why not? The big bastard was breaking trail for him. The walkie on his belt crackled. Sterling pulled it but didn't waste his breath, only double-keyed it.

"This is Bradley, come back?"

"Yeah." That was all. Sterling needed the rest of his breath to run with. The most coherent thought in his mind, overlaying the others like a bright red film, was the knowledge that the homicidal fuck had killed Granger. Had killed an Agent.

"County Sheriff has placed units on that logging road, boss. State Police will reinforce ASAP. Over?"

"Good. Over and out."

He ran on. Five minutes later he came upon a red cap lying in the snow. Sterling stuck it in his coat pocket and kept running.

Blaze struggled the last fifty uphill yards to the logging road, almost winded. Joe wasn't crying anymore; he no longer had breath to waste on crying. Snow had clotted on his eyelids and in his lashes, weighting them down.

Blaze went to his knees twice, each time holding his

arms against his sides to cushion the baby. At last he reached the top. And bingo. There were at least five empty State Police cruisers parked up and down the road.

Below him, Albert Sterling broke from the woods and looked up the incline Blaze had already climbed. And damn, there he was. There the big bastard finally was.

"Stop, Blaisdell, FBI! Stop and put your hands up!"

Blaze looked over his shoulder. The cop looked tiny from up here. Blaze turned back and ran out into the road. He stopped at the first cruiser and looked in. Once again, bingo. Keys dangling from the ignition. He was about to put Joe on the seat beside the officer's citation book when he heard an engine revving. He turned and saw a white cruiser slewing up the road toward him. He turned the other way and saw another one.

"George!" he screamed. "Oh, George!"

He clutched Joe against him. The baby's respiration was very fast and shallow now, the way George's had been after Ryder stabbed him. Blaze slammed the State Police car's door and ran around the hood.

A Cumberland County Sheriff's deputy leaned from the car that was coming from the north. He had a battery-powered bullhorn in one gloved hand. *"Stop, Blaisdell! It's over! Stay where you are!"*

Blaze ran across the road and someone fired at him. Snow puffed up on his left. Joe began to let out a series of gasping whimpers.

Blaze plunged down the other side of the road, taking gigantic leaps. Another bullet droned past his head, snapping splinters and bark from the side of a birch tree. At the bottom he stumbled over a log hidden beneath the fresh snow. He went down into a drift, the baby beneath him. He struggled to his feet and brushed Joe's face off. It was powdered with snow. "Joe! You all right?"

Joe was breathing in hoarse, convulsive gasps. Each one seemed to come an age apart.

Blaze ran.

Sterling got to the road and ran across it. One of the County Sheriff's cars had come to a skidding, veering stop on the far side. The deputies were out and standing there, looking down, guns pointing.

Sterling's cheeks were stretched and his gums were cold, so he supposed he was grinning. "We *got* the bastard."

They ran down the embankment.

Blaze dodged through a skeletal stand of poplar and ash. On the other side, everything opened up. The trees and underbrush were gone. There was a flat white stillness in front of him, and that was the river. On the far side, gray-green masses of spruce and pine marched toward a snow-choked horizon.

Blaze began to walk out onto the ice. He got nine steps before the ice broke, plunging him in frigid water up to his thighs. Struggling for breath, he lurched back to the bank and climbed it.

Sterling and the two deputies burst through the last clump of trees. "FBI," Sterling said. "Lay the baby down on the snow and step back."

Blaze turned to the right and began to run. His breath

was hot and hard going down his throat now. He looked for a bird, any bird over the river, and saw none. What he saw was George. George was standing eighty yards or so ahead. He was mostly obscured by blowing snow, but Blaze could see his cap, slewed around to the left—the good-luck side.

"Come on, Blaze! Come on, you fucking slowpoke! Show em your heels! Show em how we roll, goddammit!"

Blaze ran faster. The first bullet took him in the right calf. They were firing low to protect the baby. It didn't slow him down; he didn't even feel it. The second hit the back of his knee and blew his kneecap out in a spray of blood and bone fragments. Blaze didn't feel it. He kept running. Sterling would say later he never would have thought it possible, but the bastard just kept running. Like a gutshot moose.

"Help me, George! I'm in trouble!"

George was gone, but Blaze could hear his hoarse, raspy voice—it came to him on the wind. "Yeah, but you're almost out of it. Shag, baby."

Blaze let out the last notch. He was gaining on them. He was getting his second wind. He and Joe were going to get away after all. It had been a close shave, but it was all going to turn out okay. He looked at the river, straining his eyes, trying to see George. Or a bird. Just one bird.

The third bullet struck him in the right buttock, angled up, shattered his hip. The slug also shattered. The largest piece hung a left and tore open his large intestine. Blaze staggered, almost fell, then took off running again.

Sterling was down on one knee with his gun in both hands. He sighted quickly, almost off-handedly. The trick was not to let yourself think too much. You had to trust your hand-eye coordination and let it do its work. "Jesus, work Your will," he said.

The fourth bullet—Sterling's first—struck Blaze in the lower back, severing his spinal cord. It felt like being punched by a big hand in a boxing glove, just above the kidneys. He went down, and Joe flew from his arms.

"Joe!" he cried, and began to haul himself forward on his elbows. Joe's eyes were open; he was looking at him.

"He's going for the kid!" one of the deputies yelled.

Blaze reached for Joe with one large hand. Joe's own hand, searching for anything, met it. The tiny fingers wrapped around Blaze's thumb.

Sterling stood behind Blaze, panting. He spoke low, so the deputies couldn't hear him. "This is for Bruce, sweetheart."

"George?" Blaze said, and then Sterling pulled the trigger.

CHAPTER 24

Excerpt from a news conference held February 10th:

Q: How's Joe, Mr. Gerard?

Gerard: The doctors say he's going to be fine, thank God. It was touch and go there for awhile, but the pneumonia's gone now. He's a fighter, no doubt about that.

Q: Any comments about the way the FBI handled the case?

Gerard: You bet. They did a fine job.

Q: What are you and your wife going to do now?

Gerard: We're going to Disneyland!

[Laughter]

Q: Seriously.

Gerard: I almost was being serious! Once the doctors give Joey a clean bill, we're going on vacation. Somewhere warm, with beaches. Then, when we're home, we're going to work at forgetting this nightmare.

Blaze was buried in South Cumberland, less than ten miles from Hetton House and about the same distance from where his father threw him down a flight of apartment house stairs. Like most paupers in Maine, he was buried on the town. There was no sun that day, and no mourners.

Except for the birds. Crows, mostly. Near cemeteries in the country, there are always crows. They came, they sat in the branches, and then flew away to wherever birds go.

Joe Gerard IV lay behind plate glass, in a hospital crib. He was well again. His mother and father would be back this very day to take him home, but he didn't know it.

He had a new tooth, and knew that; it hurt. He lay on his back and looked at the birds over his crib. They were on wires, and flew whenever a breath of air stirred them into motion. They weren't moving now, and Joe began to cry.

A face bent over him and a voice began cooing. It was the wrong face, and he began to cry louder.

The face pursed its mouth and blew on the birds. The birds began to fly. Joe stopped crying. He watched the birds. The birds made him laugh. He forgot about wrong faces, and he forgot the pain of his new tooth. He watched the birds fly.

(1973)